Books by Susan Quilty

Novels
The Insistence of Memory
To the Left of Death

The Psychic Traveler Society Series (Young Adult)
Healers and Thieves
Family and Foes

Short Fiction
Audrey and Esther Geekify Greenville
Freely Written Vol.1

THE PSYCHIC TRAVELER SOCIETY
BOOK 1

HEALERS
AND
THIEVES

SUSAN QUILTY

First printing, 2019

Cover Design: Susan Quilty
Publisher: Bitter Lily Books, LLC

Second edition, 2022

ISBN: 978-1-7379702-4-8
ISBN: 978-1-7379702-5-5

Bitter Lily Books, LLC
Ashburn, Virginia

SusanQuilty.com

To all the
daydreamers:

Keep reaching
for your dreams

CHAPTER 1
A NIGHT IN THE ATTIC

Amanda Jones loved to read on her own but listening to Mr. Hewlett drone on about symbolism and significance sapped all joy from the experience. As far as Amanda was concerned, if an author had something to say, they should simply say it. Besides, Amanda reasoned, Mr. Hewlett's search for a book's hidden secrets probably just added meaning the author never even intended.

Mr. Hewlett's English class bothered Amanda for another reason, too. His love of reciting lengthy passages, followed by long-winded explanations, gave Amanda's mind too much space to wander away. When that happened, her mind always wandered to the same place.

The Victorian house in Amanda's head was shadowed but warm, ostentatious but inviting. The lower floors were filled with antique furniture, textured wallpapers, and heavy draperies. The attic, which she had only recently begun to explore, was cooler in both tone and temperature than the rest of the house. It had a shabby, unkempt atmosphere. Its floorboards were silvered with age. Its walls gleamed a bluish gray that was nearly indistinguishable from the wooden doors facing Amanda now.

Six doors. Two doors on each of the three walls.

Amanda could not see the space behind her, yet she knew she was standing in a small attic alcove in a home that was more familiar than her own apartment. She also knew that this home, as real as it felt, did not exist in the world outside of her dreams.

The doors in front of Amanda were identical. They were paneled and worn. Their dull pewter knobs showed a patina of age that matched the dry, dusty floors. There was one that spoke to her more than the rest. The second door on the left. It seemed to be nestled a hair closer to its corner, almost as if cowering from Amanda's touch. It also tempted her, beckoning her to take a look inside.

As Amanda puzzled over her conflicted reaction to the door, a slight rattle drew her eyes toward its strangely oval knob. She squinted, waiting, holding her breath. And there, again, a tiny rattle. It was more vibration than movement. As if someone was standing behind the door and holding on to the knob while a tremor passed from their shaky hand into the aged metal.

Amanda inched forward, listening for sounds of movement. The silence was complete, except for her own breath. And then, again, the rattle. Peering into the dim light, she focused all of her attention on the doorknob, beginning to discern its faint, yet definite quiver.

"Hey!"

Amanda pivoted toward the sharp voice, banging her knee on the underside of her desk.

"Hellooo?" The voice sang with a laugh. "You in there?"

Through rapid blinks, Amanda identified Trina's round face and thick, curling hair.

The classroom lights were overly bright. The sounds of shuffling feet and rustling papers were deafening. Amanda blinked against both. She turned back toward the six doors, confirming they had been replaced by a classroom wall bearing a long stretch of whiteboards.

"Come on," Trina nodded her head toward the students straggling out the door. "The bell rang. We're outta here."

After all their years of friendship, Trina was still amused by Amanda's moony lapses. Amanda was not. With a flutter of embarrassment, she gathered her things and tried not to look toward Mr. Hewlett's desk. There was a dull pressure growing in the front of her head and an ache of tension stiffening her neck. They were familiar feelings.

The noise around Amanda and Trina only increased when they stepped into the school hallway. Lockers slammed, kids chatted, and teachers chided. For a dizzying moment, Amanda wondered if she had one more class today or two, whether it was time to eat lunch or time to go home. Yet with each step, the fog cleared a bit more. Gradually, the world came back into focus. The books in her arms became solid, heavy, and her feet navigated their way quite naturally to Geometry, her last class of the day.

"Tell you the rest later," Trina called as their paths split. Amanda flashed a smile, completely unaware of whatever story Trina had been telling.

Stepping into her math class, Amanda felt a sense of calm drape over her shoulders. In the chaos of messy emotions and confusing social interactions, math was a constant. The rules didn't change, the formulas stayed the same. The puzzles in math could reliably be solved, unlike the shadowy rooms that were always whispering for her attention.

Students were still wandering in as Amanda arranged her books in a neat stack and opened her notebook to their most recent homework assignment. The numbers swam and faded before her eyes. The paper's blue lines brightened, then wobbled into a hazy blur. With her eyes closed, Amanda curled her fingers around the edges of her desk and focused on feeling the smooth, slick wood under her palms. She tried to deny it, but the aftereffects of her house visits were getting stronger and lasting longer.

I am here, Amanda silently repeated to herself. *I am here. I am here. I am here.*

When she opened her eyes, the numbers on her paper were back in focus. Crisp and clear. The lines were solid and unwavering. Amanda looked up, saw Ms. Randall watching her curiously and knew it wasn't the first time she had come in with odd behavior. Her face flushed as their gaze held, and then the class bell rang, startling them both.

Ms. Randall stood, wiped her hands together and announced, "Right triangles and the Pythagorean Theorem. Who wants to come up and show us how to solve our first problem from last night's homework?"

Feet shuffled and papers rustled around the room, but Amanda smiled in quiet relief. It was exactly what she needed. The smell of the markers and the sound of their subtle squeak on the glossy white surface. Something real to distract her from her imaginary world. Yet even as she carried her notebook to the front of the room, a small part of Amanda's mind stayed fixed on the image of that oval doorknob. Fixed on the sound of its gentle rattle. Fixed on the question of what could possibly exist behind that wooden door.

§

Dinner was grilled cheese sandwiches and tomato soup. It was Amanda's specialty, but tonight she burned the bread. She'd been absorbed in her history assignment, reading about the European Renaissance, until the smell of smoke caught her attention. Her mom, listening to headphones and typing away on their old computer in the adjacent living room, glanced up when Amanda jumped to switch on the stove's exhaust fan.

"Oh, is it time to eat?"

Her finger hovered over the pause button on her audio player, and her eyes strayed back to the screen. She bit her lip as she checked her watch.

"You need to finish?" Amanda was already nodding, anticipating the reply.

"Five more minutes," her mom promised. "I'm almost done. Or you can start without me."

"It's okay. I have more reading to do anyway."

Amanda's stomach grumbled. She knew *five minutes* would be ten or more. Patty Jones had many good qualities but keeping track of time wasn't one of them.

"Chad should be home any minute," Patty added before resuming her work. She didn't see the smile fade from Amanda's face. Amanda had made a grilled cheese for Chad but was hoping he'd work late again and only show up after she'd gone to her room for the night.

In the kitchen, Amanda pulled out some tin foil to keep the plate of sandwiches warm. She had finished reading and begun to answer her homework questions by the time her mom joined her in the kitchen. Setting aside the book, Amanda peeled away the foil to reveal a pile of grilled cheese sandwiches that were now both burnt and cold.

"We can always stick them in the microwave," Patty shrugged. The apartment door banged open, and Chad walked in with a bucket of fried chicken.

"*Ugh!*" He laughed, wrinkling his nose at the plate. "Looks like I got here just in time!"

"Oh, chicken!" Patty beamed as if he'd brought home a bag of gold. "Amanda, you like chicken!"

But Amanda didn't like fried chicken. She liked the baked chicken her mom used to make—before she was laid off from the bank and before Chad had moved in with them.

"I'll have grilled cheese," Amanda frowned, adding, "I like it cold anyway."

Which wasn't exactly true.

"More for us!" Chad laughed and kissed her mom hello.

Amanda quickly turned back to the stove and reached for a soup ladle.

"We can have both," Patty offered weakly, but Chad said that he wasn't eating burnt bread and congealed cheese when he'd spent good money on fried chicken.

Amanda put her soup and sandwich on a tray.

"Can I eat in my room?"

"Sure," Chad grinned, responding before her mom could give a different answer.

Safe in the quiet of her bedroom, Amanda frowned over her dinner. There hadn't been time to reheat the soup and the sandwich really had become a mess of burnt bread and congealed cheese. She'd also forgotten to grab a spoon and had left her history book on the kitchen counter. Amanda sighed dramatically, performing for an invisible audience, then began dunking her grilled cheese into the tomato soup. She'd rather drink straight from the bowl than face Chad and his bucket of chicken.

Without her history book, Amanda couldn't finish her homework. She didn't have a computer in her room and her cell phone was just a phone. It had no games to play or internet to surf. There was another text waiting from her Aunt Judy, but she didn't feel like responding.

Having nothing else to do, Amanda pulled out the blue notebook where she liked to sketch rooms from her imaginary house. The attic alcove with its six doors was the most recent place she had visited, but there were many more rooms. Some were small, like cozy dens or libraries, others were larger with connecting double doors that could perhaps be left open during a fancy party. There were no bathrooms or closets that Amanda had seen, but she assumed they must exist behind the numerous doors scattered around each room.

Amanda had first begun to visit the house a few years ago when she was eleven or twelve. She would close her eyes in a quiet place and find herself in a big, old house with the kind of fancy furniture she had seen when touring Victorian homes with her mom and Aunt Judy. The house she imagined was always the same. It had spacious rooms with high ceilings and a tight clutter of furniture. There were upholstered couches with strangely sloping backs and carved, wooden frames. There were marble-topped coffee tables and iron plant stands. There were ornate desks and crystal lamps, as well as chairs that looked like miniature thrones.

Amanda was looking over her sketches of the second floor when there was a knock on her bedroom door. She quickly closed the book.

"Thought you might need these."

Patty held up Amanda's history book and notebook. There was an awkward pause as she handed them over.

"Did you get enough to eat?" She asked at last, reaching for the tray. "I had one of your sandwiches and some soup. It was good. There's still chicken left. If you want...?"

Amanda gave a half shrug and small head shake. She appreciated the effort her mom was making but didn't know how to show that while avoiding the subject of Chad and his fried chicken.

"How was school today? Anything interesting happen?"

The image of a wooden door sprang to Amanda's mind. She could hear its faint rattle as her bedroom began to gently blur and fade away. A faint smell of dust and furniture polish, old carpets, and older wood began to creep in.

"Amanda?"

The sharp tone pulled her back. Abruptly.

"What?" Amanda snapped with more annoyance than she'd intended, but her mom only pressed her lips together and took a deep breath.

"Do you want to talk about what happened? About dinner?"

"No." Amanda shook her head. She wasn't thinking about dinner.

"Amanda, if you're upset—"

"No," Amanda repeated, feeling off balance and slightly nauseated. "It's not that, I just… I have a headache."

And there *was* an ache in her head. It was the ache that often came after resisting an urge to visit the house, but her mom would never understand that.

§

Amanda was finishing her homework when she saw a light turn on in a certain apartment at the opposite end of her L-shaped building. She hadn't been watching for the light, not exactly, but it was hard to miss from her seat by the window. A smile tugged at the corner of her mouth when a text alert rang on her phone a moment later.

"Homework? Still?"

"Done now," she texted back. "How was practice?"

Amanda and Drew had lived in the same apartment building since they were seven. They'd chased and climbed on the playground and taken turns riding Drew's bike, following the path that circled the parking lot and snaked into the neighboring park. They'd become inseparable during Amanda's first few weeks in the apartment building, while she was still getting used to life without her dad. Yet, after a few years, they outgrew the playground and the small park. They went to middle school and met new friends. Their time together dwindled to treks to and from the bus stop, until even those walks became strained, and they fell out of step. Eventually, their paces had drifted so much that they spent each school day walking several feet apart on the same lonely path.

It was only in the past several weeks, now that they were navigating their first year of high school, that they'd started talking again as they made their way to and from the bus. At first, they talked about their schedules and teachers. Soon they were discussing their friends and activities, swapping jokes and stories as if no time had passed. The walks were short, and their conversations had begun to spill into nightly texting.

Amanda leaned back in her secondhand desk chair and tried to ignore the sound of her mom and Chad laughing in the next room. She didn't want to hear them being happy.

"You were quiet today."

Amanda read Drew's message and wasn't surprised. It was the kind of thing they were more likely to text than say in person. On their walks, the conversations were light, usually about other people and things happening at school. Over text, they could share more about themselves and their feelings.

Amanda started to type an answer, then deleted the half-formed thought. She was still holding her fingers over the tiny keypad, not sure where to begin, when a new text popped up on the screen.

"Everything ok?"

"Yes," she typed back. Then took a deep breath. "Thinking about stuff, I guess."

She hit send, then bit her lip. Her stomach flipped and twitched.

"Real stuff or dream stuff?"

Amanda had told Drew about her imaginary house, a little bit, describing it as a recurring dream that was kind of weird, but not a big deal. Her fingers trembled as she typed a one-word response.

"Dream."

She looked out the window toward Drew's room. His light was on and his curtains were open, but he was sitting out of sight. She imagined him moving around the room, doing other things between texts. Maybe getting ready for bed.

"In the attic?"

"Yes," Amanda wrote back cautiously. There was a fluttery feeling in her chest. She'd told him about the attic and about the six doors, saying she'd dreamed about them a few times and sometimes daydreamed about them during class. "But today, one of the doors..."

Once she started typing, Amanda couldn't stop. She sent seven rapid texts, telling Drew about the rattle of the door handle and how it had seemed to draw her in, but also scare her away. She told him there were times when it was hard to not drift into daydreams about the house. She typed that sometimes the attic, the house, seemed more real than the actual world around her.

And then she stared at the screen, wanting all of those texts back.

Time slowed as she waited for a response that refused to show up. Her eyes flicked from the phone to the window, but there was still no sign of Drew. Maybe he'd left his room. Maybe he hadn't read them yet. Or, worse, he had read them and had nothing to say.

After two full minutes with no answer, Amanda shut her blinds and turned off her ceiling light. She changed into her pajamas by the light of the small lamp on her nightstand, sneaking quick glances toward her stubbornly silent phone.

By the time she came back into the room from brushing her teeth, there was a single text message waiting for her response.

"You know there's an obvious answer, right?"

Amanda blinked and read the text again. An obvious answer to why she would imagine a house in her head? To why she'd been drawn back inside her own crazy imagination day after day? Did he think she was crazy? Her heart raced. Was he going to say she should tell a teacher, or her mother, or some other adult?

Amanda texted back a single question mark.

Drew's answering text came so fast she knew he had already typed it and had been waiting to press send.

"You need to open the door."

§

Later that night, as she settled into bed, Amanda thought about Drew's advice. *Open the door.* It was simple. It was obvious. Yet the idea made her stomach clench and her mouth go dry. *Open the door.* Maybe it was *too* simple.

Amanda wondered if she actually *could* open the door. She couldn't remember opening a single door in any part of her dream house before. She'd always wandered through whatever doorways were already open and only looked at the doors that were closed. She was an observer, not someone who took action.

Amanda wondered why the thought of opening the attic door was so frightening. What could possibly be behind an imaginary door? Anything, she supposed, but nothing that could *actually* hurt her. The more she thought about it, the more irritated Amanda became with her own fear. *What am I afraid of?*

It would bother her if the space behind the door was empty, she decided. If it were a vast and endless darkness. It would upset her if it was just a blank wall with nowhere to go and nothing to see. But that couldn't be true. There had to be *something* behind the door, behind all the doors, she decided, because it wouldn't make sense to have a door with nothing behind it.

Besides, she thought angrily, *it's my door and I can open my own door if I want to.*

With that in mind, Amanda propped herself up in bed. She scooted her back against the headboard, sat up tall, and let her eyes go slowly out of focus. It was easy to drift back into the waiting attic and find her usual spot in front of the six doors. The same door drew her attention, but Amanda forced herself to look around more carefully.

She studied each of the doors, noticing the variations in their wood grain and shading. She turned around to see a much larger space than she had expected. It wasn't an endless void, but it was a large attic scattered with boxes, trunks, and covered pieces of furniture. Squinting her eyes, Amanda was fairly certain she could see more doors clustered in groups around the otherwise empty walls.

Screwing up her courage, Amanda turned her eyes back toward the second door from the left.

There was a pounding tightness in her chest now. Her palms felt damp and itchy as her fingers slowly flexed and clenched. Just as her foot lifted to step forward, a quite definite rattle froze her in place. Her throat went dry and her eyes widened as Amanda watched the doorknob slowly turn. The door cracked open, then paused. Amanda could hear voices filtering in from the other side of the door.

With a quick scurry, Amanda crouched behind an armchair covered by a dingy white sheet. Her heart pounded in her ears. There had never been other voices in the house before. She'd always been there alone. Alone with her own thoughts. The idea of someone else, of *anyone* else, being there felt like a violation. It felt like her house—*like her mind*—was being invaded by voices that were clearly not her own.

In a moment, the muffled conversation stopped. Amanda heard heavy footsteps, followed by the closing of a door. The closing of *her* door. The attic threatened to fade away then, but this time Amanda fought to stay. Her need to see who was here was stronger than her fear.

Very carefully, Amanda peeked around the back of the covered chair. The attic walls and doors were becoming blurry, but the man who stood in front of them was clear and steady, as real as any person she had ever seen.

He wasn't just a man. He was a *knight*. He was an actual knight, wearing lightweight chainmail under a pale blue tunic. Amanda gripped the chair to steady herself. As she did, the sheet slipped under her fingers, pulling halfway off the chair and sending up a thick cloud of dust.

The knight turned toward the sound of her coughing and gasping. For a moment, their eyes locked, and then Amanda pulled back sharply, so sharply that she pulled out of the attic completely and found herself sitting upright in her dark bedroom. Her knees were clasped to her chest and her breath was choked. She coughed until tears stung her eyes.

Hurrying footsteps fueled Amanda's panic, but when her bedroom door opened it was only her mom who rushed in to sit by her side and rub her shuddering back.

"Are you okay? Amanda? Amanda?" With a jerky movement, Amanda managed to nod that she was fine. The coughing stopped.

Patty moved closer, putting her arms around her daughter.

"It's okay," she murmured. "Just breathe. You're okay."

Amanda let herself be rocked, fighting against the pain in her head. When she lifted her gaze, she saw Chad leaning in the doorframe.

"She okay?"

"Yes," Patty answered quickly. "I think so." Her hand rested briefly on Amanda's forehead, then on each cheek. "No fever."

"Great," Chad answered with a touch of irritation. "So, uh, I've got the movie all queued up."

"In a minute," Patty snapped, adding, "You could get her some water, you know."

Amanda saw Chad look up from his phone with indignant surprise.

"No," Amanda swallowed harshly, cutting off whatever he was about to say. "Thanks, but I'm, uh, I'm fine. It was just a, uh, a tickle in my throat."

But later, when she was alone, Amanda found she couldn't close her eyes without feeling the shock of seeing a man *(a knight?)*, someone who clearly did not belong, simply walking into her mind.

It felt wrong. It felt unsafe.

It felt like she might be going insane.

Amanda stayed upright, leaning against the headboard and clutching her knees to her chest. She fought to stay awake and ignore the lingering smell of dust. She struggled not to think at all until she eventually fell into a mercifully dreamless sleep.

Chapter 2
The Tuntum Trees

Amanda did not visit the house again for the rest of the week. She thought about the attic, and the knight, frequently, but her mind stayed firmly in the present. There was no fading into that hazy world. No draw to explore the house and no rattle of doorknobs. The knight had effectively scared her away, leaving Amanda to wonder if that was the point.

She hadn't told Trina about the attic or the knight. After years of teasing about her constant daydreaming, Amanda was a little surprised when Trina didn't notice it had stopped. She hadn't meant to tell Drew about the knight either, but the morning after it happened, Amanda found the whole story spilling out during their walk to the bus.

"Was he wearing a helmet?" Drew asked as they rounded a corner. His eyebrows lowered thoughtfully when Amanda answered no. "You saw what he looked like then. Did you recognize him?"

"No," Amanda shook her head again. "He was a total stranger."

"He didn't look like anyone?" Drew pressed. "He didn't even *resemble* anyone?"

"Like who? You?" Amanda laughed, trying to joke, but Drew stopped walking and faced her with serious eyes.

"Like your dad."

"My dad?" Amanda puzzled over the suggestion, picturing the tall, blond knight and her own dark-haired, bearded father. "No, not even close. Not even a little."

"Okay," Drew started walking again, slowly until Amanda caught up.

They were almost to the bus stop when Amanda finally asked, "Why my dad?"

Drew stopped walking again, keeping their distance from the crowd of kids waiting at the intersection ahead. He took a deep breath and shifted his backpack more firmly over his shoulder.

"Well, if the house is a metaphor for your mind, then maybe the doors in it are the places where you keep different memories. And if there's something you kind of want to remember, but you're also kind of afraid to remember, maybe it's something about your dad. And a knight showing up could be your brain's way of keeping you safe. Or something. And I thought maybe the knight would look like your dad, since he's someone who would protect you if…"

Drew stopped talking.

"I mean, it was just an idea." He looked back at the other kids and then down the street for the bus. He was looking at everything except Amanda.

"Oh, I, uh…" Amanda blinked at her feet, taking time to process Drew's theory and realizing he might be onto something. She hadn't considered it being about her dad, but if it was something she was hesitant to think about…

"It was just a stupid thought." Drew turned as if he were about to start walking again, but Amanda stopped him with a quick touch on his arm.

"No, it makes a lot of sense, except… Well, it *all* makes sense, except the knight didn't look like my dad."

Drew nodded thoughtfully. "What did he look like?"

Amanda looked up, opened her mouth to answer, but stopped as she noticed how much older, and bigger, Drew looked this year. She choked back the words *tall* and *broad shoulders*, feeling her face getting hot.

"Damn." Drew looked over her head. "There's the bus."

Amanda felt a shaky sense of relief as they hurried the rest of the way down the street.

§

A few days later, Amanda and Trina were lazily passing notes during English class while Mr. Hewlett read aloud from the collection of short stories they had been studying all week. Having already read the story, Amanda let her mind wander, wondering where it would end up now that she could daydream about something other than a musty old house.

Her eyes drifted toward the window, where thick clouds were stretching their way across the gray-blue sky. As she idly watched, Amanda noticed that the cloud-streaked sky looked like the swirled marble that framed the fireplace in an upstairs bedroom of her secret house. It was an errant thought, passing by without drawing her out of the class-room. Amanda was still there. She was not drifting away. The sensation felt both pleasant and a little sad.

Still musing over the feeling, Amanda startled when Trina slid a folded note under her slack hand. Mr. Hewlett looked their way just in time to see Amanda flatten her hand protectively over the folded paper. With his eyes locked on Amanda, he finished his final sentence, closed the book, and crossed the room. Amanda's heart hammered against her ribs. Her eyes slid toward Trina, who stared straight at the front wall. She felt embarrassed tears gathering and willed them not to fall.

Mr. Hewlett stopped next to Amanda's desk and took a long look at her trembling hand before slowly meeting her watery eyes.

"Do you like to write, Amanda?" Her lips parted, but no sound came past the lump in her throat. "Short stories, that is."

Amanda hesitated, not daring to look back at Trina or at anyone else in the room. Her mouth went dry. She shook her head, with a slight shrug of her shoulders.

"No?" Mr. Hewlett didn't sound angry, but Amanda felt pinned to her chair by his steady gaze.

"I don't know," she managed at last, wondering if it would be a mistake to try casually sliding the covered note into her lap.

"You don't know?" Mr. Hewlett persisted, using a genial tone that gave Amanda the distinct impression of walking into a trap.

"My dad wrote stories." The words tumbled out, without thought. "I mean, he would tell me stories, when I was little. Stories he made up." Amanda rushed on, trying to sound natural despite the eyes of every student boring into her soul. "And they were good, like really good, but I've never been able to... Or, well, I haven't really tried to write myself, much. Stories, I mean."

With her gaze firmly planted on her desk, Amanda could not see Mr. Hewlett's expression. She did hear his soft sigh.

"Well," he said, after a pause that lasted an eternity. "You'll have a chance to try now."

He walked back toward the front of the room, without mentioning the hidden note, then mercifully drew everyone's attention by announcing they were going to start writing their own short stories.

A groan went through the room, but Mr. Hewlett's friendly laugh gave Amanda the courage to look up from her desk. He looked directly at her and smiled with a kindness that steadied her heart. Mouthing the word, "*sorry*," she let him see her slide the unopened note into the bag beside her desk. He nodded in acknowledgment.

"Now," Mr. Hewlett continued smoothly past their silent exchange, "we're going to try a little exercise to get the creative juices flowing. Clear your desks. Everything away. Books, pencils, notebooks. Everything."

Under the cover of movement, Amanda chanced a look at Trina, who only shrugged and rolled her eyes. Mr. Hewlett moved to the panel of switches by the door and shut off every other row of overhead lights. It dimmed the room but gave it an oddly striped appearance. The class quieted, waiting, and Amanda felt relieved to be sitting in a section of shadow.

"Okay." Mr. Hewlett moved back to the front of the room and lightly cleared his throat. "We're going to use our imaginations now as we go on a little, guided journey. Close your eyes. Come on, close your eyes."

Amanda let her eyes mostly shut, catching tiny glimpses of her lap through the blur of her lowered lashes. An airy melody played, and Amanda heard a few stifled giggles from the back of the room.

"Begin to notice your breath." Mr. Hewlett spoke slowly, in a voice that was steadier and deeper than his usual classroom pitch. Deeper even than the tone he used when reading poetry. "Feel the sensations throughout your body as your breath begins to slow just a bit, becoming smoother and more even."

His words continued to pour gently through the room, describing their steady breath, the softness in the air around them, and how safe and secure they were in their comfortable, grounded seats. As he spoke, Amanda's eyes shut for long, slow moments before an urge to resist would bring back a tiny crack of light. She wanted to stop the familiar sensation of floating away, of sinking deeper into her own mind, but the rhythmic cadence of his words had lulled her into a half-aware state that felt almost, but not quite, like falling asleep.

"You are in a storage room." His voice broke softly through the flowing music, and Amanda realized that he had been silent for some time. "You see a closed box in front of you. Picture the box. Is it large or small? Wooden or metal? What color is it?"

But Amanda did not see a box. Amanda saw a door. A silvery-gray door with an old-fashioned, oval doorknob. She was in the attic. Her attic. Amanda's eyes never strayed from the door, but she knew she was alone. The doorknob did not rattle. There were no voices or footsteps from the other side. She felt safe and calm.

As she studied the door, Amanda could hear an echo of Mr. Hewlett's voice, as if it were traveling to her over a great distance. He was talking about the box, urging them to step forward, open the lid, and see what was inside. Without conscious decision, Amanda reached out and grasped the doorknob. It was cold and rough under her hand. She noticed that the metal was embossed with a subtle, raised pattern. Her hand formed a gentle grip and turned the knob with ease. She could feel the click as the latch released and the door moved softly toward her.

"Take a deep breath in," Mr. Hewlett intoned from his faraway classroom, and Amanda felt a flurry of panic as his voice started to pull her back. She gripped the door frame, peering into the golden light that streamed from beyond the door.

"And breathe out," his voice continued in a slightly louder, stronger tenor.

Amanda squinted into the light. There was an expanse beyond the door, a large stretch of meadow that led toward a thicket of trees. Yet the meadow and trees were like none she had ever seen. The grass in the meadow was long and flowing. And deeply purple.

The trees had a pale purple hue as well. While they were too far away to make out details, Amanda had the distinct impression the trees were slowly rising toward the hazy sky, getting taller before her eyes.

"Bring awareness back into your body."

Amanda fought the instruction, but the door was slipping from her grasp. The attic was fading away.

"Begin to blink your eyes open."

Amanda heard Mr. Hewlett's words, close and real. It was dark behind her eyes and there were sounds of shifting from the students around her. She pressed her eyes closed, willing herself to go back to the attic, to step through the door. But the attic was gone.

§

When class was over, Amanda didn't tell Trina what she had seen during their guided meditation, and she didn't tell Drew about it on the way home from school. There was something about this visit that felt different, special. It felt like something she should keep to herself. For now.

At home, Patty was in the kitchen, chopping carrots while onions simmered in the pot beside her.

"Beef stew tonight," she greeted with a smile. "Your favorite."

"Mmmmm." Amanda stepped to the stove and looked down at the onions that were beginning to brown. Potatoes and celery crowded the countertop, beside a peeler and a second paring knife.

"Give me a hand?" Her mom asked casually. Amanda was happy to help, when Chad wasn't there to get in the way.

"Aunt Judy is going to visit," Patty said, after several minutes of chopping and chatting about her day, "for your birthday."

"Oh?" Aunt Judy's visit wasn't much of a surprise, since she came to celebrate Amanda's birthday every year, but Amanda couldn't think of any other response. Her mind had wandered back to the purple meadow and to the nagging feeling that there was something strangely familiar about those distant trees.

"We're writing short stories in English," Amanda shared abruptly, feeling her chest tighten as the words came out.

Her mom's "Oh?" held much more surprise than Amanda's had. It also carried a noticeable touch of concern. The sound of that single syllable made them both wary, careful, though Amanda didn't know why.

"Yeah, we're supposed to *tap into our imaginations,*" Amanda slipped into a fair imitation of Mr. Hewlett's smooth voice, then laughed nervously. Patty didn't crack a smile.

The rhythmic drum of her knife on the cutting board filled the space between them.

"What are you going to write about?"

"I don't know," Amanda answered with a frown. She wanted to mention the purple meadow and strange trees, but something held her back.

"You could write about that hike we went on last month. Remember when we saw the deer through the trees? And crossing that rope bridge? That was fun."

"Uh, yeah."

What Amanda remembered was lagging behind so she wouldn't have to listen to Chad drone on about every plant and tree they passed, as if he hadn't just read the information from the same sign they'd read, too. She also remembered the way Chad's loud talking had scared away the deer before Amanda could take their picture. And then she remembered the long drive to the state park—and back home again—while she sat alone in the backseat unable to hear any conversation over Chad's thumping, earsplitting music.

It wasn't exactly short story material, at least not for a story that her mom would like to read.

"Actually," Amanda kept her eyes on the cutting board as she spoke. "I think we're supposed to come up with something more creative than that. Like, Mr. Hewlett made a big deal about letting our imaginations run wild. And walking through the woods isn't exactly, um, exciting. On paper."

"It could be," Patty said. "If you made it descriptive."

The clipped response brought back all the times Amanda's mom had told her to get her head out of the clouds, stop daydreaming, and pay attention to the real world.

"I guess. Maybe."

There was a different feeling in the kitchen now. The air between them felt strained. Cold. Amanda didn't understand why her mom was so set against fantasy and daydreams but knowing she was made Amanda wish she'd never mentioned the short story assignment.

"I'm not good at coming up with imaginary things anyway," Amanda added weakly. "I think I've outgrown it actually."

It was an attempt to diffuse the situation, but Patty seemed lost in another thought herself. She was frowning, the knife still in her hand, but no longer cutting.

"I should work on that though." Amanda set down her own knife. "I mean, because it is homework, so…"

"What?" Patty turned back with a quick shake of her head. "Oh, yes, sure. If you need to get started, I can manage here."

Amanda paused, gently biting on her lower lip. She hadn't meant that she would go work on it right this minute, but her mom was smiling now, in an encouraging way, and it felt strange to correct her. Besides, thoughts of the door, and its meadow beyond, were softly calling Amanda back to explore.

"Amanda," Patty called just as she was about to leave the room. "I don't mean to—"

Amanda waited, taking in her mom's uncertain smile and the puzzled wrinkle of her forehead.

"There's nothing wrong with imagination," she continued haltingly. "I just, well, I just want you to know the difference between imagination and reality. Okay? I want you to know where one ends and the other begins. And if you're ever not sure... Well. Just talk to me. Okay?"

§

In the privacy of her bedroom, Amanda flopped onto her bed and felt the weight of the day settling over her body. She'd been happy that morning. She'd felt normal. Now here she was, back in her room, brooding over a fantasy world that somehow felt more important, more urgent, than her actual reality. Again.

What was it about that house that drew her back, over and over?

What was it about those trees? That purple grass?

And then, with a jolt of remembrance, Amanda heard it. *Tuntum. Tuntum.* It had been more than the look of the trees that had drawn her attention. It had been the sound pulsating within her when she'd caught sight of them. *Tuntum. Tuntum.*

Dragging her desk chair across the room, Amanda fished a dusty box from her closet's top shelf. Sifting through the papers, pictures, and small mementos, she eventually pulled out a crayon drawing on lined notepaper. The picture was thick with shades of waxy purple. It showed long violet grass beside squat trees with twisting fuchsia trunks and a heavy scribble of royal purple leaves. One word was blodly printed across the center of the page in clumsy magenta letters: *Terra-V.*

Staring at her own childish art brought a flood of memories. There was her dad, tucking her into bed with fantastic stories of exotic, faraway places. Terra-V had been the setting of her favorite adventures. It was a place where plants grew purple, instead of green, and where the people used sound and touch to heal wounds and illnesses.

Terra-V.

The name washed over Amanda with a loving warmth, as if being back in her father's arms. It whispered through her mind as she pictured the violet meadow and the far off, pulsing trees. They were the tuntum trees that had once mesmerized her and filled her earliest childhood dreams. That was what she was remembering. The attic door had opened on Terra-V, one of the imaginary worlds her dad had created just for her.

Amanda's heart swelled at the realization, but also throbbed with the pain of loss and, deeper still, an undercurrent of shame. How could she have forgotten her beloved Terra-V until this very moment? How had she not recognized what she was seeing the instant the attic door had opened?

Brushing away her tears, Amanda set those nostalgic thoughts aside. She remembered her special world now, and that was all that mattered.

Terra-V had appeared a little differently to her now than in her childhood drawing—the trees were a paler purple, more lavender than violet, and the sun had shone more softly lemon than she used to imagine—but the memory of Terra-V still clearly lived in her mind. It had simply hidden away for a while. Maybe because it had been too hard to daydream about that world without feeling the pain of missing her dad.

Amanda thought of Drew, remembering his theory about the house being a symbol for her mind and the memories locked within. He was right. It all made perfect sense.

The phone was in her hand, ready to text him, before Amanda had a better idea. She could write a story about Terra-V and share that with him first. In a story, she could describe the soft purple meadow. She could explain the twin trunks of the spiraling tuntum trees and the rhythmic pulse they sounded.

Opening a notebook, Amanda wrote a title across the top of a blank page: *In the Sheltering Arms of the Tuntum Trees.* It was a phrase she could now remember her father whispering as he carried her to bed, saying, *"It's time to sleep in the sheltering arms of the tuntum trees."*

She didn't know where her story should begin. She couldn't clearly remember the stories her dad had told her about the people who lived in that world. Were they friendly? Were they kind? She seemed to remember kindness, paired with a magical song, but that felt vague, distant, without any detail. What she did remember, clearly, were the tuntum trees. Closing her eyes, Amanda listened for her dad's voice, trying to combine his stories with what she had imagined behind the attic door.

The tuntum trees were not like trees here on Earth, he had said. Tuntum trees had silvery purple bark and lavender leaves that were wide and soft, like large, silky feathers. They stood tall in the daytime, with two slender trunks nestled side-by-side and branches that reached up and out toward the pale sun. If you stepped close to those trees, he had told her, you would hear a gentle rhythm. *Tuntum. Tuntum.* If you put your hand against their bark, you would feel something warm pulsing in time. It was the sap that ran thick and steady beneath the rough, almost sandy bark. But the real magic happened at night. As the sun passed by, the tuntum trees' twin trunks would slowly spiral down toward the ground, bringing their canopy of leaves closer and closer until the lowest branches would droop enough to nearly touch the purple grass below.

Amanda could see them behind her eyes now, remembering his description of blossoms dotted throughout the leaves. Night-blooming flowers that would begin to glow with an iridescent shimmer after the sun went down. At night, those who lived in the forest could take shelter under the silky curtains of those shimmering, feathery leaves.

Picturing the trees, Amanda longed to remember more. His stories were somewhere in her memory, but just out of reach. The tuntum trees. The purple meadow. Amanda could take those memories and add her own heroine, her own story, into the world her dad had created.

Putting her pen to the paper, Amanda hesitated. She saw her dad's colorful world in her mind's eye but also heard her mom's cryptic message. There was a line between reality and imagination, but did that line really have to hold firm in a short story? Weren't there ways to blend reality with fiction? Couldn't she do the same thing with her own imaginary world?

Amanda thought carefully and then wrote:

Kara was an ordinary girl, on an ordinary hike through some ordinary woods. She had spent the day walking on the well-marked trail and reading scattered signposts along the way. The sky was blue. The grass was green. The trees were a mix of gray and brown trunks topped by a leafy green canopy. Small evergreens, dark and thick, were mixed throughout.

It was a day like any other. Nothing special. Nothing interesting. Until Kara had a sudden urge to wander off the well-marked path.

The urge came out of nowhere, but once she noticed it, Kara felt powerless against its call. There was something inside her that longed to see something more. Anything more. There was something inside her that suddenly knew, without a doubt, that there was more out there. Somewhere.

Seeing no one else around, Kara peered into the tangle of trees. She wondered what might exist in the depth of the woods. She wondered what she might find if she were brave enough to leave the path, thread her way through the darkest center of the forest, and come out on the other side. Was that where it was? The something new? Was this well-tended path meant to keep her from it? Or was the path there only because that's as far as anyone had explored?

With shaking breath and an excited heart, Kara braced herself and took her first step off the path...

CHAPTER 3

THE STORIES WE TELL

Earth Science was the only class Amanda and Drew shared, and they never sat together. Drew sat near the windows with a group of boys from his basketball team. Amanda sat closer to the door, near the shelves that held various rocks and minerals. They rarely spoke in class. Today though, Drew kept flashing encouraging smiles her way. He knew Amanda was nervous about getting her graded story back next period. Though she insisted she wasn't.

Drew had read Amanda's short story the morning after she wrote it, before walking to the bus. They'd met early and sat on the apartment steps where he'd read with a look of intense concentration on his face. Amanda had occasionally read over his shoulder, skimming a few words at a time before looking away to chew on her bottom lip.

"Wow." Drew handed the notebook back with a wide smile. "That's really, really good."

"You think?"

They started walking then, partly to avoid being late and partly because walking made it easier for Amanda to listen to his glowing review. Despite Drew's reassurance, Amanda had her doubts.

"There's not much that happens," she pointed out. "I mean, it's just the one person walking around."

"And finding an awesome new world," Drew added.

"Well, yes," Amanda frowned. "But shouldn't there be some other people there or something? Someone to talk to? Something that, I don't know, actually happens?"

They walked quietly for a moment, giving Drew time to think it over. His next response sounded hesitant, as if he were still figuring out his own idea.

"Her *thoughts* happen," he began simply. "And sometimes the thoughts and feelings in a story are a lot, you know? Even when not much else happens, I mean, like physically happens. Like car chases and stuff."

Not sure how to respond, Amanda listened to the sound of their feet on the pavement and considered what he had said. There was a strange sensation bubbling up from her stomach. She didn't know how to put that feeling into words. She didn't even know if it was a good or bad feeling. It was that vulnerable queasiness that came with trying something new.

After a few more steps, Drew continued, sounding more confident in his opinion.

"You know, that might be my favorite thing about it. I liked that it was just Kara. Just her noticing the path she was on and deciding to take a chance on something else. You know? The story is really about her taking a risk and discovering something else out there. It doesn't even matter so much what she found. Just that there was something there to find. Something more than what other people had already discovered."

"I guess," Amanda wasn't so sure. It seemed to her that it *did* matter what was out there, even if the *out there* was only in her own imagination. But she was glad Drew liked the story.

Now, sitting in class and waiting to see what Mr. Hewlett would say, the butterflies were back in Amanda's stomach. Writing had always been a struggle for her. Whatever she wrote on paper never seemed quite as good as she imagined it would be in her head. Besides, writing assignments weren't something anyone could definitely get right. They weren't like solving math problems. There wasn't one solution, one correct answer, and that bothered Amanda. How could she know whether she'd done well if there wasn't a specific answer to find? If Mr. Hewlett didn't like her story, but she liked it—and Drew liked it—did that mean it was a good story or a bad story? Or somewhere in between?

When the bell finally let them out of class, Amanda was so distracted she didn't hear Drew call her name until he was right beside her.

"Hey." He nudged her arm, matching her stride.

"Hey." She glanced up, surprised. He'd never walked with her in the school hallway before.

"He's gonna love it." Drew winked, then darted off to catch up with his friends, nearly running down Trina in the process.

"Whoops, sorry!"

"No problem," Trina laughed, before turning her smile toward Amanda.

"So, Drew?" She hinted with a raised eyebrow that Amanda tried to ignore.

Down the hall, they could hear Drew's group of friends laughing about something. Amanda watched them shove each other playfully, carelessly jostling other students passing by. Trey grabbed something from Drew's hand—his phone maybe—and started tossing it around the group. When Drew grabbed it back, he shoved Trey hard enough to send him stumbling into a locker. There was a stunned pause, then they both laughed and turned the corner at the far end of the hall.

"Boys," Amanda smirked with an exasperated laugh.

"Uh huh." Trina flashed an amused grin.

"We're friends, Trina." Amanda rolled her eyes. "Just friends."

"Fine, fine." Trina twirled a tress of hair and waited a beat. "Speaking of friends… Like Drew and his basketball friends. We need to meet up with them at the next home game. Think you can make that happen?"

"It's football season."

"Exactly!" Trina agreed. "And they'll be there, in the stands, where we can actually sit with them. So much better than when they're the ones playing!"

"Yeah," Amanda shrugged. Mr. Hewlett's door was now in sight. "I guess."

"Oh, come on," Trina half-laughed but her eyes were sharp. "Drew goes to the home games, right? And Trey? Trey's usually with him?"

"I guess," Amanda repeated with more annoyance as they entered the room. Mr. Hewlett sat at his desk with his head bent over some papers. There were two stacks of notebooks next to him. Their graded short stories.

"You'll set it up then?" Trina pressed. "You'll talk to Drew? Make sure he'll be there? And Trey, too?"

"Whatever." Amanda arranged her books on her desk, ignoring the stacked notebooks and trying to remember what Trina had been saying. Something about Trey again. She was always finding a way to talk about Trey. And Drew. Losing track of the conversation had left Amanda flustered and searching for a better response.

"Whatever?" Trina laughed. Then added sarcastically, "Yeah, you're just friends."

"I…" Amanda's face grew hot, but the bell to start class cut off her chance to explain that she hadn't been listening and wasn't sure what Trina had asked. Something about a football game? And then she pieced it together. *Had she agreed to set up a meeting with Drew and Trey at a football game? What did that even mean?*

She and Drew were kind of friends. They were friends when they were walking to and from the bus stop or texting at night. And he had just talked to her in the hall… But were they friends who met up at football games? Wouldn't it be weird to ask Drew if he and Trey were going to the next home game? And even weirder to ask if they wanted to sit together? Did people plan that kind of thing or just run into each other once they got there? Anyway, Amanda thought angrily, if Trina wanted to set this up so badly, why couldn't she just take care of it herself?

"All right." Mr. Hewlett stood at the front of the room, hands clasped in front of his chest, and tipped his fingers toward the notebooks piled on the small table next to his desk. Amanda pushed boys, and football, and Trina, out of her mind. She thought her notebook might be on top of one stack, but it was hard to tell from across the room.

"You all made a great start with your short stories," he told them. "A lot of imagination in this room. Some more than others," he added, with a mimed look of horror toward Ryan and Ben, which made everyone laugh. "But, overall, a great start. A really great start."

The class shifted, realizing his choice of words.

"That's right." Mr. Hewlett's smile widened. "What's a work of fiction without revision?"

A groan rippled across the room.

"Writing fiction is like sculpting with words." He spoke expansively, his hands gesturing freely. "You've created the clay with your first drafts, now we get to shape, and mold, and sculpt that clay into works of art!"

The class was not as excited by this prospect.

"Okay." He clapped his hands again, beaming around the room. "We're going to pair up, read each other's stories, and give some constructive feedback. Emphasis on *constructive*—that means helpful comments, right? Then we'll find new partners and do it again. Won't that be fun?"

The class grumbled.

"Well, I'm excited!" Mr. Hewlett assured them before walking toward his desk.

"Let's see," he continued. "Trina? Amanda? Safe to assume you'll be paired up? Okay, come on up here and help me pass back these notebooks. Everyone else, find your partners."

Trina and Amanda headed to the front of the room as the class broke into a dozen conversations. They each took a stack of notebooks, but Mr. Hewlett held Amanda back, telling Trina to start without her. There was one notebook sitting separately on his desk and Amanda recognized it as her own.

Dropping from his front-of-the-room teacher voice into a softer tone, Mr. Hewlett picked up her notebook and told Amanda, "I was impressed by your story."

His words brought a warm glow beneath her ribs, along with a tremble of embarrassment that shook her voice when she thanked him. She hoped no one at the front of the room could hear him, even as she hoped they could.

"Was this inspired by one of your father's stories?"

"Oh." Amanda froze, unsure. "Yes, a bit. I mean, is that okay? I made up most of it."

"Of course." Mr. Hewlett waved away her worry. "I only ask because it felt like a very personal story. Like something written with love."

"Oh," Amanda stammered, her cheeks burning. *Written with love* sounded so personal, especially when her mind flashed on an image of Drew, reading her story on their front stoop.

"*The Sheltering Arms of the Tuntum Trees*," Mr. Hewlett recited her story's title with a whispery rhythm. "There may be a touch of the poet in you."

"That was something my dad would say." Amanda watched the toe of her shoe twist on the polished floor. "The title, I mean, not the poet part. The tuntum trees were his idea, and he'd say that about them. Um, sometimes."

"You described them beautifully." Mr. Hewlett cleared his throat, tapping the front cover of Amanda's notebook. "I think your story may be worth submitting to a county-wide fiction contest that runs every December. It would need to be longer to qualify, nearly twice the length. Do you think you could expand on this?"

"I… I guess so."

"I think you can," Mr. Hewlett nodded firmly. "And I'm here to help. Okay?"

Amanda nodded, and he added her notebook to the pile already in her arms, dismissing her to hand them out. When she got back to her seat, Amanda tried for a casual air as she flipped to the first page of her story. Then she felt a genuine smile spread across her face. There was an *A* written in blue pen at the top of the paper.

§

"Babe, what are you so upset about? She got an A."
Amanda flattened herself against the hallway wall, trying to silence her breath. She'd been on her way to the bathroom when she'd heard her mom and Chad talking in the living room. She knew she shouldn't eavesdrop, but it was hard not to listen in when they were clearly talking about her.

"It's not the grade." Patty sounded agitated. "It's the story. Did you even read it?"

"You watched me read it," Chad reminded, showing his own irritation.

Amanda longed to peer around the corner, but one of them was sure to be facing the hall. She forced herself to stay out of sight, listening for any warning they might have gotten up from the couch.

"But I don't get the problem," Chad went on. "It's just some story about a girl wandering around in the woods. Those purple trees were pretty cool though."

"The purple trees." Patty sounded sarcastic now, or maybe just exasperated. "The purple trees were not cool. They were… They were the *purple* trees!"

"Ah, yeah? It's just a story. I mean, she knows there aren't *really* purple trees."

"Does she?" Amanda flinched at the harshness of her mom's voice.

"Babe…" Chad sounded as confused as Amanda felt.

"No, I mean, yes," Patty interrupted, then let out a loud sigh. "I know that she knows that. It's not even about the trees being purple—not really—it's about… It's about *those* purple trees, those trees specifically. Amanda didn't make up those trees. They're the trees Gabe made up, in the stories he was always telling Amanda."

"Oh." Chad didn't sound any less confused. "Okay. She wrote about some trees her dad made up, for a homework assignment. What's wrong with that? I mean, who didn't cheat a bit in high school? If that's even cheating?"

That would be his reaction, Amanda thought with annoyance. *Chad probably had to cheat his way through school just to graduate. And it wasn't cheating!*

"That's not it." Patty sighed again, after a long pause. "It's just that Gabe was… Well, to him, they weren't just…"

41

She stopped again, regrouping. "You don't know what it was like. Gabe was always off in his head, tuning us out. He'd be here one minute and gone the next. He couldn't help it, and I tried to understand and not worry, but… You don't know how hard it was. No one knows how hard it was."

Amanda's heart hurt. Her mom often said her dad always had his head in the clouds, and she'd complained about his traveling for work a lot, but this sounded like something else. It sounded like something darker and more frightening. And then Chad asked a question that shook Amanda to her core.

"It was part of the sickness, huh?"

Sickness? Amanda's palms tingled as they pressed into the wall behind her.

"Yes, no, I don't know." It sounded like her mom might be crying now, pausing to blow her nose. "He said it was under control. His doctors said it was under control, but… I don't know."

Doctors? Amanda suddenly wished to be back in her own room, even as she knew it was too late to pull herself away. *Had her dad been sick? What kind of sick? Had he been mentally ill?*

"And it wasn't just his crazy stories." Patty's voice became angry. "It was that stupid job. He was always dashing off for some emergency. Traveling who knows where at a moment's notice. Never being able to tell me where he'd been or what he'd been doing. He never should have had a job like that, not with his condition."

Amanda closed her eyes, taking in what she'd heard and trying to conjure up a picture of her dad. She only had a few clear memories of him, and they were all happy. He'd held her, loved her, and told her stories. She'd always thought she only had a few memories of him because he'd died when she was six years old. Were there other reasons?

"He was some kind of diplomat, right?"

For the second time, Chad had asked a question that showed he knew more about Amanda's dad than she did. It made her angry, and it justified her eavesdropping. If her mom wasn't going to tell Amanda the truth about her dad, this was her only option.

"Yes," Patty spoke slowly, "but I can't say more. I mean, I *really* can't tell you more, because I don't *know* anything more. We were still in college when it all started. When he started getting... sick. There were doctors, then specialists. The next thing I knew, they said he was better, and he started training for some secret government program. He'd leave for days or weeks at a time, and he would never say what he was doing.

"I wasn't sure it was even real, at first." Her voice was barely a whisper, making Amanda strain to hear more. "Until I met some of the people he worked with. And his doctors said it was a good environment for him. They insisted he was okay, and it was... under control.

"I guess maybe it seemed exciting, too. Back then, when we were young, but after a few years... After we were married and had Amanda... But then he wouldn't get a new job. He said there were too many people who needed him. But he couldn't tell me who."

There was a sharp intake of breath before Amanda heard the distinct sound of sobbing.

"Hey, hey, babe," Chad soothed.

Amanda pressed her fists against her mouth.

"We needed him, too," Patty gasped between sobs. "We needed him here. With us." Her words became stronger, her crying softer. "But Gabe would just leave, for days or weeks at a time. Then he'd come back, winking and smiling. Joking about these crazy places he'd been. He'd never tell me the truth. He'd never just live here, in our real world, with his real family."

"Babe, babe," Chad kept crooning, grating Amanda's strained nerves.

"He wasn't even here with us when he died."

Amanda couldn't listen anymore. She hurried into the dark bathroom, leaned against the closed door and felt tears running down her own cheeks. There was so much she still didn't know. There was so much she'd been too young to remember—or understand. Had there really been something wrong with her dad? Or had he been off doing something he shouldn't have been doing?

Sometimes she could get her mom to talk about her dad. Patty would tell stories of how they first met or when Amanda was a baby. They were happy stories, and Amanda thought the edge of sadness in her mom's voice only showed how much she missed him.

As her eyes slowly adjusted to the dark, Amanda saw the shadowy figure of her own reflection in the bathroom mirror. The vague shape frightened her into snapping on the light, but as she squinted and blinked at her familiar face, she still felt unsettled and alone.

CHAPTER 4

A VISIT TO TERRA-V

"I can't get back there," Amanda admitted a few days later. She and Drew were sitting on a bench in the small park by their apartment building. The air was cool and crisp. Dry leaves scuttled in the wind and there was no one else in sight. They rarely stopped like this, on their way home from school, but Amanda's mom was working a temp job today and wouldn't be home for at least another hour.

"You can't get to the attic or can't open the door?" Drew asked.

"Either," Amanda sighed. Then corrected herself, "I mean, I can get to the attic, briefly. I show up there, see the door and then... I don't know. It all disappears."

She hadn't told Drew the whole conversation she'd overheard. She had told him her mom was upset by the reminder of her dad's stories, and she'd told him her mom had complained to Chad about her dad being away a lot. For work.

"It makes sense," Drew began. "You don't want to upset your mom. But that shouldn't keep you away from your own memories. If you want to explore them."

Amanda nodded slowly. She didn't want to tell Drew about her dad's mysterious sickness, but she did want to see what she could remember herself. Even if it risked bringing up upsetting memories.

Drew lightly touched Amanda's arm.

"Maybe you need some help," he suggested tentatively.

"Help?" Amanda noticed how deep his eyes appeared in the soft light of the wooded park.

"Well, it helped when Mr. Hewlett did that meditation thing in class, right?" He glanced down and swallowed hard. "I searched online for how to do that. Like some guided meditation stuff. Maybe we could try something like that? Try to relax you into the memories?"

"Oh." Amanda's heart raced, feeling anything but relaxed. Still, there was something she liked about the idea, too. Maybe Drew was right. It had worked in class. It could work again.

"What do we do?"

"Okay," Drew smiled, and his shoulders visibly dropped with relief. "Uh, well, you just sit here, and, uh, close your eyes. And I'll say some stuff. About breathing and relaxing."

"Now?"

"Yeah," Drew nodded. "I mean, if you want? It shouldn't take too long."

Amanda sat back on the bench, fixing Drew with a sidelong glance before closing her eyes. As soon as her eyes were shut, she became intensely aware of Drew watching her.

"Slow and deep breaths, okay?" Drew's voice became soft and shaky. "Breathe in and breathe out."

Amanda's eyes opened, catching Drew by surprise.

"You have to close your eyes," he laughed nervously.

"I can't," Amanda laughed back. "Not with you looking at me."

"Why not?"

"It just…" Amanda made a face, "It feels really weird."

"Okay," Drew sighed. "What if I don't look at you? What if we just sit here, side by side, on the bench, with both of our eyes closed, and I just talk?"

"You won't look?" Amanda squinted her eyes at him.

"I swear," he promised, crossing a finger over his heart. "Eyes closed the whole time."

"Well…" Amanda sat back on the bench, waiting for Drew to do the same. He closed his own eyes first, letting his hands rest gently in his lap.

"Ready?" He asked, with his eyes tightly shut.

"Ready," Amanda agreed, settling into the darkness behind her eyelids.

"Okay. Now, slowly. Breathe in. Breathe out. Breathe in. Breathe out."

Amanda listened to his words, noticing how much steadier his voice sounded now that their eyes were both closed. She listened to the dry leaves blow past in a chilling breeze. She pictured the sun shining weakly through the tree branches.

"Breathe in," Drew intoned. "Breathe out."

Without trying to find the attic, Amanda focused on the feelings inside her own body. She told herself Drew was there, sitting beside her. His voice made it easier to relax into the bench and quiet her mind. She could hear his breath, matching her own.

"You're safe," Drew said softly, as if reading her thoughts. "You're safe in this park. Safe to let your mind wander. Safe to go wherever your thoughts take you."

His words faded as Amanda felt a familiar tug draw her gradually into the world within her own mind. She was in the attic… She was opening the door…

§

Amanda blinked, slow and hard, trying to clear the nausea spreading through her stomach and the buzzing vibrating behind her eyes. The sky was growing dark. The purple grass beneath her feet glistened in the fading light and the air held a damp chill. In the distance, a line of tuntum trees faintly creaked with a hum that rolled across the meadow in deep, even waves. *Tuntum. Tuntum.*

She was alone.

Looking around, her breath short and her heartbeat fast, Amanda tried to make sense of the sensations on and in her body. She tried to recall stepping through the door from the attic, but there was only the vague memory of a bright flash and sizzle. It felt like hours had passed since she had stood in the attic. Or maybe only seconds.

Standing here, in this meadow, felt nothing like the softened daydream of the house in her head. Everything here felt more solid. More real. The house was a vividlly immersive dream, but this… The air around her and the ground beneath her felt exactly as real as in the park back home. As real as the park bench where she'd sat next to Drew and felt his arm brush her own. But that was impossible.

"I fell asleep," Amanda muttered under her breath. "I fell asleep and I'm dreaming."

The thought settled her fear a bit, though her heart still pounded, fast and tight. She traced one shoe through the grasping threads of long purple grass. *Only a dream. Only a dream.* She repeated the phrase like a mantra while looking up at the stars that had begun to shine in the darkening sky. The phrase stuttered to a stop as she lowered her gaze across the meadow and paused to watch the gradual sinking of the tuntum trees. *Tuntum. Tuntum.*

Is it a dream?

Turning around, Amanda was surprised to see the attic door she knew so well now standing alone in the middle of the meadow. There was no wall. There was no attic. There was only a closed door that looked hazy and nearly transparent, like a mirage.

Her head throbbed as the buzzing behind her eyes grew louder.

Amanda reached toward the door, not close enough to touch it. The door seemed to fade and sharpen before her eyes, bringing along the phantom scent of the dusty attic. Amanda knew it was the same wooden door she had been studying for months. Though she was seeing it now from the wrong side.

Inching forward, her fingertips swiped its wispy surface as the door faded entirely away.

It's only a dream. Amanda reassured herself. *It's only a dream.*

With the door no longer there, Amanda faced the lavender forest again. The tuntum trees were noticeably lower now but still descending with an eerie, rhythmic hum. *Tuntum. Tuntum.* Across the meadow, she could see a break in the ring of trees where a path wound deeper into the forest.

Amanda trekked toward the path, feeling the weight of each step vibrating through her aching head. She noticed the tug of the damp grass as it dragged across her jeans and the continued whisper of the breeze against her skin.

Amanda didn't get far before a sound startled her into a low crouch.

"Hello?" The voice was gentle and clear, yet it seemed to be carried across a great distance.

Scanning the tree line, Amanda saw someone had emerged from the forest path and was now crossing the meadow at a quick pace. There was a sort of loping grace in the movement, fast enough to close the distance between them in what felt like seconds. Though time still felt fluid in the shock of her strange circumstances. It was all Amanda could do to hold her ground, frozen, feeling the pain of her headache now intensified by the thundering rush of blood through her terrified body.

"Drew?" Amanda whispered, half expecting him to take her hand and gently shake her awake. He was supposed to be beside her, keeping her safe. "Drew?"

Nothing happened.

Amanda stood up, alone and exposed, in the darkening meadow.

"Hello?" The figure stopped just a few feet away.

She was a girl. Or something like a girl. She had the shape of a human, and about the same build as Amanda, but those similarities were quickly overshadowed by her differences.

Even in the dim twilight, the creature's skin appeared a glittering white with shimmering patches of pale green and blue, like the surface of an opal. Her hair was a deep cobalt blue and her eyes were vivid purple. Her body was thick and compact, like a gymnast, though she stood in front of Amanda with a friendly smile and relaxed stance.

"What are you doing here?" Her eyes blinked twice in rapid succession.

"I…" Amanda's mind went blank as she noticed the long, purple-hued staff in the girl's hand.

"I've never seen one as young as you," the girl continued smoothly before frowning thoughfully. "And you haven't been presented yet."

"Presented?" Amanda managed to repeat her, though she was having trouble hearing and speaking over the resounding buzz in her head. Something in this creature's manner—or maybe a look in her eyes—told Amanda she was not a girl, but a woman. A much older woman.

"You're English," the woman clarified. It wasn't a question.

"American, actually," Amanda responded instinctively, pressing her fingers into her aching temples, but the answer only brought a deeper frown to the woman's face.

"A-mer-i-can?" She sounded the word out, cocking her head to one side. Then shook her head knowingly. "But you're English."

"I'm dreaming actually." Amanda tried a small laugh, despite the pain. She closed her eyes for a moment and was surprised to open them on a look of amazement spreading over the woman's shining white and pastel face.

"You dream while you're awake?" Her voice was hollow now, reverent.

"Oh, no," Amanda began distractedly before rethinking her answer. "Well, yes, actually. I'm kind of known for it. But I'm clearly not awake now."

"Not awake?" The woman lifted one hand and swiftly poked Amanda's shoulder, using enough force to make her stumble off balance.

"Hey!" Amanda struggled to steady herself, feeling increasingly sick and dizzy. A thought broke through her confusion: That poke had felt awfully strong and awfully real for this to be a dream.

Her vision dimmed then. The buzzing overpowering her as her stomach continued to churn. This couldn't be real, she told herself. It had to be a dream. It *had* to be. Amanda pictured herself asleep on the park bench. Her eyes closed. Maybe leaning her head on Drew's shoulder.

Wake me up! She thought urgently, feeling her gasps growing shallow. *Wake me up!*

"American?" The woman shook Amanda's arm, peering with worry into her ashen face. "Can you hear me, American?"

"What?"

The meadow felt far away, as if Amanda were fading into nothing, just like the attic door. She fought to stay another minute, narrowing in on the purple of the woman's kind, concerned eyes. There were flecks of deep blue and pale gold within the purple swirls.

"American?"

The woman curled her hand gently around Amanda's upper arm and a subtle vibration pulled the world gradually back into focus. Amanda's stomach relaxed. The buzzing in her head quieted enough for Amanda to hear a new, melodic murmur overriding the sound of the distant trees. It was a low, steady chant. A single tone that seemed to pull her entire essence back into alignment.

"That's not my name," Amanda whispered, unable to look away from those purple eyes.

The woman turned sharply, toward something in the distance, then smiled and carefully released her hold on Amanda's arm. When Amanda turned, she saw the blond knight from her earlier daydream striding across the meadow at a near run.

"Hey, you there!" He called loudly, closing in.

"I…" Amanda tried to speak again, but this time the fear was too much. With a last lingering look into the comforting purple of the woman's eyes, she spun on a heel and took off running.

"Wait! American, wait!"

The woman's voice joined the knight's yelling, but Amanda did not look back to see if they were both in pursuit. She dug in deeper, using her fear to fuel each desperate step. The trees circled the meadow. *Tuntum. Tuntum.* Her feet pounded. The tree's hum urging her on. *Tuntum. Tuntum.* She veered toward the right, seeing a cluster of large rocks up ahead.

Just when Amanda felt she could not take another step, the attic door appeared a few feet ahead. She zagged toward the welcome sight, twisted the doorknob, and fell over the threshold, collapsing through the dusty attic floor and onto the hard park bench with enough force to knock her off the wooden seat and onto the cold, hard ground.

A slashing pain tore through her head as Amanda blinked up at the trees in silent confusion. She was not in the attic. She was not in a purple meadow. She was back home, in the park. Alone. She gripped her stomach, thinking she might actually be sick. Instead, she slumped against the bench and drifted into a heavy darkness.

When Amanda finally reopened her eyes, the pain and nausea had receded enough to carefully get back to her feet. She looked warily around the empty park.

"Drew?" She called out, softly at first and then again, louder. But there was no response. The sun was far below the trees. Drew was gone. Her backpack was gone.

Wincing against the lingering pain in her head, Amanda managed to shuffle the rest of the way home and into the brightly lit building. She rested her head against the wall of the elevator, unable to understand what had happened or why Drew had left her sleeping in the park.

When Amanda got to her apartment door, she realized her keys were in her backpack—wherever her backpack was. But that wasn't a problem. She had barely reached the door when it was wrenched open with an abrupt jerk.

"She's back," Chad called into the apartment before stepping aside for Amanda to enter. "Your mother has been worried sick."

"What?" Blinking uneasily, Amanda stepped into the apartment just as her mom came rushing at her.

"You're safe!" Patty's arms wrapped around Amanda, crushing her close for one soothing second of relief before thrusting her back out at arm's length. The joy on her mom's face had already been swallowed by a burst of anger.

"Where have you been?"

§

Thirty minutes later, Amanda was in her room, fishing her cell phone out of her backpack. She hadn't eaten anything since lunch, but her stomach was churning too much to want food.

She looked at the cell phone and its long line of text alerts. Six messages from Drew. Two from Trina. Three from Aunt Judy. She didn't feel ready to read them. Her hip was sore from falling off of the park bench and her head was still wobbly.

Though she hadn't made Amanda eat dinner, Patty had given her a pill for her headache, and it was beginning to help. Amanda gingerly stretched out on her bed, above the covers, and closed her eyes as she attempted to make sense of what had happened.

Drew had brought her backpack over, her mom had said, and he'd seemed upset when Amanda wasn't home. He said she'd forgotten her backpack in the park, when they'd stopped there to talk and he'd dozed off on the bench.

"You'd better let him know you're okay," Patty had snapped while handing over the backpack. "He's been out looking for you. And Chad was about to go out searching,

55

too. I've been on the phone to Trina and was just about to call the police."

Amanda hadn't known what to say to any of that. Had Drew fallen asleep on the bench, too? But if he woke up before Amanda, why had he left her there?

"Why were you and Drew in the park? And why would he fall asleep?" Patty's questions had picked up speed. "Did something happen? Were you doing something? Drinking? Or—?"

"No," Amanda interrupted quickly, wanting the noise to end. "I'm just not feeling well. My head really hurts."

Patty paused her interrogation, watching the way Amanda held her head and squinted her eyes. She then started in with a new line of questions.

"Does the light hurt? Do things sound louder than usual? Do you see shiny spots or feel nauseated?"

Amanda could only nod weakly. Next thing she knew, her mom had brought her a pill and sat her on the couch with a cool towel on the back of her neck. She'd dimmed the lights and lightly stroked Amanda's hair.

"Migraines," Patty said at last. "Your father used to get them, too," she added in a low voice. "But not until he was older. For him, they started in college."

"Oh, come on," Chad broke in loudly. "So, that's it? A migraine means she can wander off and come home whenever she wants?" He stood across from the couch, hands on his hips. "She ruined our night, scared you half to death, and we still don't know where she was!"

"Chad, please!" Patty crossed the room, ushering him out with a flurry of hushed whispers. By the time she'd come back, Amanda was feeling better physically, but a lump of fear had lodged in her chest.

"I'm sorry," she'd managed to choke out before bursting into tears and collapsing in her mom's arms, where she was gently held and softly rocked.

Amanda knew she had to tell her mom something, anything that might take away the worry and buy her time to figure out what had really happened in that dream. If it had been a dream.

"We did stop at the park," she began haltingly, trying to bring in as much truth as she could. "Drew and I were talking about my story. I was telling him ideas, and then he just… fell asleep. And, I don't know, I guess it made me mad. Because I thought he was interested, I mean, interested in what I was saying, but…

"Anyway, I walked off, alone, to think, and then my head started to hurt. I guess I lost track of time walking around because it started to get dark, and my head hurt so much… and I wasn't sure where I was. But I wanted to come home, so I turned around and kept walking until I saw the park again…"

"Shhh, shhh." Patty continued to sway. "You're home. Let's get you feeling better first."

Now that she'd been allowed to come back to her room, Amanda was anxious to check in with Drew, but she didn't know what to say.

She was still stretched on her bed, staring at the ceiling and searching for an explanation, when her phone vibrated with an incoming message. Drew again. He had probably seen her lamp turn on through the window.

"I'm home," Amanda texted quickly, without reading his previous texts.

"What happened?!?!?" He texted back immediately, forcing Amanda to sit up and face the situation. Looking down at her feet, she saw her shoes were leaving mud on the bedspread.

"Great," she muttered to herself, swinging her legs off the bed and brushing feebly at the mud and long, broken, blades of grass.

And then she noticed that the grass was purple.

CHAPTER 5

AUNT JUDY RETURNS

"I only want to go for a walk."

"Hmmph," Patty continued scrubbing the sink, though there was nothing left to clean.

"Just half an hour?"

"Amanda." Her name was a warning, but Amanda was not ready to back down. It was Saturday, a day after the park incident. Her mom had refused to talk about it all morning, other than to tell Amanda she should stay inside and rest today. Luckily, Chad had left for work before Amanda had gotten up, and would be gone all day, but Amanda was still unhappy about being confined inside.

"But, mom," she pleaded. "I feel fine now. And I've explained. And I've apologized. And I understand if you're still mad at me, but I just want to get some fresh air."

"Fresh air," Patty scoffed. "With Drew?"

"I—" Amanda hesitated, but Drew *was* waiting for her text to let him know when they could meet.

"That's what I thought." Patty finished her scrubbing and began rinsing the sink.

"I need to explain to him in person," Amanda tried to argue her case with honesty. "I don't want him to be mad at me."

Patty wiped her hands on a dishtowel, still facing the sink. Amanda watched her shoulders lift and lower in time with the sound of a large sigh.

"Are you dating him?"

"What? No."

Amanda's face felt warm when her mom turned around to look her in the eye.

"We're just friends," Amanda insisted.

Patty continued to stare, narrowing her eyes.

"All right, look," Amanda opened her mouth and was surprised at the frustration that poured out. "I know we're teenagers, and apparently that means we're supposed to suddenly be all hormonal and date-crazy or something, but he's *Drew*. I mean, we've been friends since forever and I don't see why everything's supposed to change just because we're 14 now."

Her mom's face softened and the pressure in Amanda's chest released.

"You're right, I'm making assumptions. There's absolutely no reason why anything has to change between you and Drew." She waited a beat. "Does Drew want it to change?"

"No," Amanda answered quickly, still feeling the buzz of unleashing so many spontaneous words. "I mean, I don't think so."

"Hmmm." Patty set down the dishtowel. "You were pretty upset with him yesterday, when he dozed off instead of paying attention to you."

"Oh, well," Amanda stalled, knowing that wasn't what actually happened. "Friends can get into fights."

"True," Patty agreed, as she filled a kettle and set it on the stove. "Tea?"

"Um," Amanda felt the vibration of her phone in her pocket as another text came in. She weighed her options. Having tea would put off meeting Drew for at least twenty more minutes, but it might also increase the chances her mom would say yes to her going out at all.

A knock at the apartment door saved her from answering.

"I'll get it!" Amanda turned for the door, but Patty put a hand on her shoulder.

"You get the teacups," she told Amanda. "I'll get the door."

Amanda stayed in the kitchen, technically, but instead of going to the cabinet to get the cups, she stepped back a few paces to a place where she could watch her mom answer the knock. It wouldn't be Drew, she told herself. He wouldn't show up without getting the okay from Amanda first. Not after yesterday. But no one had called up from the front desk to let them know they had a visitor, and Amanda couldn't imagine who else in the building might be dropping by.

"Patty!"

Judy threw her arms wide, then quickly stepped over the threshold to press her cheek against Patty's cheek, giving her a half-hug in the process. Before Patty could react, Judy spun away and made a beeline for Amanda. She pulled her niece into a full embrace, swaying from side to side before letting her go with a beaming smile.

"You've gotten taller!"

"Yeah, I guess." Amanda stood with a surprised smile of her own, noticing the blue streaks in her aunt's long dark hair and the tangle of beaded necklaces that hung over the collar of her faded concert tee.

"Judy?" Patty still stood beside the open door. "What are you doing here?"

"I told you I was coming for a visit." Judy pivoted to face Patty, letting one arm drape over Amanda's shoulders. "Had to be here for Amanda's fifteenth birthday!"

"But that's next weekend."

Some neighbors walked by, glancing in with polite but awkward smiles before quickly looking away. Patty shut and locked the door.

"Well," Judy shrugged. "Someone needed me here."

Amanda stiffened as her mom's eyes swung her way.

"Did you ask Aunt Judy to come early?"

"No!" Amanda answered so strongly that Judy took a step back to assess the two of them with narrowed eyes.

"What I meant is that someone needed me here *for work*," she clarified. "But I get the feeling I walked into something here."

"Pssh," Patty rolled her eyes. "Don't start analyzing us."

"Occupational hazard," Judy laughed, her eyes tracking between Amanda and her mom inquisitively.

"Yeah, well," Patty sighed, then changed the subject. "You don't have any bags. Where are you staying?"

"I have a place," Judy told them, now squinting through her dark-rimmed glasses and pursing her lips.

"Seriously?" She added after a moment of tense silence. "No one's going to tell me what's going on here?"

The tea kettle whistled. Patty hurried past them both to take it off the heat before reminding Amanda to get the cups.

"Tea, Aunt Judy?" Amanda was reaching down a third cup when Judy's next question made her freeze in place.

"Is Chad actually *living* here now?"

Amanda set the last cup on the counter and cautiously turned around to watch her mom's face tighten into a determined smile. Judy held up some mail with Chad's name on the envelopes.

"Is that a problem?"

"I don't know, is it?" Judy countered, but her gaze had turned toward Amanda, making her concerns clear.

"That's it!" Patty slammed down the box of tea bags and took an angry step toward her sister-in-law. "We're not doing this. You're not here five minutes and you're already questioning my parenting?"

"Not at all! I'm questioning your current taste in men," Judy made such a disgusted face Amanda had to slap a hand over her mouth to keep from laughing out loud.

Her mom was not amused.

"Amanda," she spoke with rigid control. "Why don't you go downstairs for a while?"

"What?" Amanda startled but quickly recovered. "Yeah, okay!"

"Downstairs does not mean outside," Patty clarified, as Amanda bolted for the door. "And be back in one hour!"

Amanda texted Drew on her way to the elevator and had his response by the time she reached the first floor. Someone new was working at the front desk, but Amanda didn't stop to introduce herself. She simply smiled and walked by, passing the library, where Mr. Rudowski was reading the paper, and heading toward the double glass doors at the end of the long hall.

The party room was used for community activities, tenant meetings, and private parties. When there wasn't a scheduled event, any resident could use the space. Yet it mostly sat empty, making it Amanda's favorite place in the building. The spacious room had couches and chairs that were great for lounging or reading, a cluster of tables that offered a place for games or drawing, and a long bar with a mini fridge that was perfect for chilling sodas and candy bars. Amanda had been spending a lot of time in the party room since Chad had moved in.

When Drew entered the room, Amanda was sitting across a lounge chair with her back against one arm and her knees draped over the other. She was mentally replaying the scene between her mom and Aunt Judy and imagining what they were saying to each other now that she was out of earshot.

"Did you bring it?" Drew asked, skipping all formalities and plopping down onto the couch beside her chair.

"Yeah." Amanda sat up and fished a folded plastic bag out of her pocket. She clenched the bag in her hand for a moment, nervous, then unfurled it with a flourish, holding it up so Drew could see the purple blades of grass pressed inside its transparent walls.

"Hmm." Drew reached for the bag and studied the contents with a frown.

There were a few broken blades that were several inches long and many smaller flecks of crumbled purple matter. The inside of the bag was smeared pinkish-gray in the places where the grass had pressed into the plastic. Drew pinched one of the larger blades between his thumb and index finger, watching the way it gradually pulled apart as he rubbed the plastic between his fingers.

"You can open the bag," Amanda offered, but Drew only shook his head, staring down at the grass in amazement.

"There's still mud on my shoes, too," Amanda added, causing his attention to shift to her feet.

"Where?" Drew asked, leaning down as far as he could without moving the coffee table. "There?"

"Here." Amanda crossed one ankle over the opposite knee and pulled off her sneaker without untying the laces. There were thin streaks of mud caked in the treads and against the white parts of the shoe, just above the sole.

"It looks *kind of* purple," Drew agreed, turning the shoe over to check each side. "But it's so dark it looks closer to black. Like really dark dirt."

"Hold on." Amanda hopped up and crossed the room, walking with a slight limp as she still wore only one shoe. She wet a paper towel at the sink in the bar and squeezed out the excess water. When she came back, she dabbed at the shoe and pulled the paper towel away to show a distinctly purple smear.

"Whoa!" Drew slumped into the couch and stared at Amanda with wide eyes. "So that's it. You really were there."

"Well, I don't know..." Amanda trailed off.

"Amanda." Drew lurched forward, waving the plastic bag. "This is proof."

"But that's… impossible." Amanda was starting to feel sick again.

"What other answer is there?"

"Well, being crazy comes to mind." Amanda tried to laugh, but her voice cracked. She had to blink away a rush of nervous tears.

"You're not crazy," Drew told her.

"I could be crazy," Amanda insisted.

"Okay," Drew admitted after careful consideration. "Crazy is always a possibility."

"I may have imagined the whole thing," Amanda nodded, almost liking the idea.

"You could be delusional," Drew agreed.

"Delusional is a little strong," Amanda frowned.

"I don't know," Drew persisted. "You tell nine out of ten people that you meditated your way to an alien world and I'm pretty sure they'd say you were crazy. They'd probably even want to lock you up in a padded room somewhere."

"Gee, thanks," Amanda crossed her arms over her chest, no longer liking this explanation.

"Hey, don't get mad at me," Drew laughed. "You know those nine out of ten people who'd think you're crazy? Well, I'm number ten. I *know* you're not crazy. Well, not for this at least."

Amanda laughed but wasn't ready to move on. She stopped smiling and let herself feel the fear she'd been carrying since last night.

"It seems like a pretty crazy thing."

"Yeah, but this proves you're not crazy," Drew insisted, sitting straight up on the couch and holding the plastic bag between them. "You went somewhere, and this grass came back with you."

"Yeah, but," Amanda's heart raced as her mind pushed back against the idea.

"Are you sure you didn't see anything?"

It was Drew's turn to frown and shake his head.

"I told you, my eyes were closed. You were there and then... you weren't."

Amanda let her eyes roll toward the ceiling before inspiration struck.

"Could I have been sleepwalking?"

"Amanda."

"No, really." Amanda started rubbing her hands on her thighs, warming up to the idea. "You put me into some kind of meditative sleep state, and I was dreaming so deeply I got up and walked away. I wandered off the path and into some weird kind of plant that happens to be purplish."

Drew looked down at the bag in his hands. Amanda watched the light reflecting off his hair as he gently shook his head. When he looked up, his expression was more serious than Amanda had ever seen before.

"You didn't get up off the bench," he told her gravely. "My eyes were closed, but I didn't feel a thing. The bench didn't creak. The air didn't move. You were there, and then you weren't. Just like that. I already told you, I was awake the whole time. I'm sure of it. That sleeping thing was just what I told your mom."

"I…" Amanda didn't know how to finish the thought. The evidence was clear, but also impossible.

"Phasing to another dimension is the only thing that makes sense," Drew continued with a matter-of-fact nod.

"Phasing to a what?" Amanda stumbled over the words.

"Physics tells us there are many different dimensions and, quite probably, many alternate universes to our own," Drew spoke smoothly. "We're typically bound to our own universe, but there must be something different about your genetics that makes you able to look into these other worlds and, apparently, travel there under the right conditions."

"Oh, of course," Amanda agreed sarcastically, but Drew ignored her.

"The real question is whether there are others like you. And, if so, how do we get in touch with them— Hey!" Drew interrupted his own thought. "Maybe the knight you saw is another person who's like you! Maybe he was traveling to Terra-V when he saw you."

"Wait…" Amanda looked down at her hands, trying to process this theory, but Drew was too excited to wait for her to catch up. He got to his feet and paced around the room, becoming more animated by the minute.

"It really does make sense," he told her. "It's the *only* thing that makes sense, actually. You imagined stepping through that door and—*poof*—you disappeared from right beside me. Then you brought back bits of purple mud and grass on your shoes. Actual proof!

"Man." Drew continued to pace, rubbing his hands together. "I wish I'd had my eyes open when you disappeared. If I could see it happen, then we'd really…"

He spun on one heel and gave Amanda a look that made her heart leap into her throat.

"No," she answered before he could even ask the question. "No, way."

"Come on!" Drew crossed back to the couch and reached for her folded hands. "Don't you want to see if you can do it again? And this time, I could actually see it happen. Then we would know, without a doubt."

A memory of nausea and pain came rushing back as Amanda continued to shake her head. She wasn't sure what had happened, but she knew she wasn't in a hurry for it to happen again.

"You don't understand," Amanda began in a small voice. "It wasn't... fun. It was scary, and painful, and I didn't know where I was or what to do. Then, when I did come back, I didn't know what had happened, and you were gone. And my head hurt so much."

"Oh," Drew frowned, looking genuinely remorseful.

They sat together, Drew's hands wrapped around Amanda's, as they each sorted through their own thoughts.

"I'm sorry," Drew said at last. "I didn't mean to push you."

"It's okay," Amanda told him. Drew kept his eyes on their nested hands.

"I'm sorry about something else, too," he said more softly. "I'm sorry I wasn't there when you came back. I'm sorry I left you alone."

"Oh." Amanda sat back in her chair, not quite pulling her hands away. She wished Drew hadn't looked up at her then, but she could not look away from his dark eyes.

"That's okay," she managed at last.

Then her phone buzzed, startling them both.

It was a text from her mom telling her to come home.

"I thought she gave you an hour?" Drew asked while Amanda untied her loose shoe and wedged it back on her foot.

"I guess she changed her mind." She tied her laces and looked toward the glass doors, half expecting her mom, or Aunt Judy, to be standing there watching them.

As they walked down the hall toward the elevators, Amanda told Drew about Aunt Judy's unexpected appearance and the fight that had been brewing when she was asked to leave.

"Strange timing," Drew said, when the elevator stopped on Amanda's floor. She held the door open with one arm before stepping out into the hallway.

"What do you mean?"

"Oh, nothing," Drew shrugged. "Hey, can I keep the evidence for a while? Get a closer look at it?"

"Sure." Amanda reached into her pocket and handed the bag over a little reluctantly. She trusted Drew to keep it safe, but as she walked toward her apartment, she couldn't stop questioning what he'd meant about the timing of Aunt Judy's visit.

§

When Amanda returned to the apartment, she found her mom there alone. Judy had gone back to wherever she was staying, though she had been invited back for dinner. Not knowing what had happened while she was gone, Amanda decided that her safest option was to follow Aunt Judy's lead and retreat to her room while she could.

When she got there, Amanda flopped onto her bed and stared at the cracked ceiling. She didn't want to think about Drew's theory, but she couldn't put it out of her mind. Was it possible that Terra-V was a real place? Was it possible she had actually traveled there? Through her own mind?

As crazy as the idea seemed, Amanda knew it had to be the right answer. Nothing about her visit to Terra-V had felt like a dream. She had *actually* been there, standing in the purple grass and hearing the distant sounds of the tuntum trees. She had talked to the strange woman and she'd felt her heart pound as she'd run from the knight. Besides, the purple grass and mud on her shoes had to have come from somewhere.

As Amanda tried to picture Terra-V, and the woman she'd met there, an image of Aunt Judy unexpectedly intruded.

Strange timing.

Drew had said it was strange timing for Aunt Judy to show up. Could her arrival have something to do with the visit to Terra-V? Amanda hadn't called her, and her mom had been surprised by her arrival. Had she shown up because Amanda hadn't been returning her recent texts? Had she sensed something wasn't right?

Judy a social worker or psychologist. Amanda wasn't sure which. Though she assumed Judy was some kind of expert because she traveled all over the country for what she called "special cases." She would stay with a new client for weeks, or even months, before moving on to her next assignment. Amanda had never heard of other therapists who did that.

Whenever Amanda had asked about her job in the past, Aunt Judy would say she worked with young adults who had special needs and needed help deciding what they wanted to do with their lives. Amanda thought it sounded like a difficult job. She was proud that her aunt was making a difference in people's lives, but she'd never given it much thought beyond that.

Patty seemed to have mixed feelings about Judy's work. When they were getting along, she'd praise her sister-in-law for taking care of people who were often ignored. When they weren't, she was more likely to say Judy helped other people figure out their lives because it kept her from focusing on her own. Once, Amanda had heard her mom tell Chad that Judy's fascination with helping everyone but herself was a family trait.

No matter what Patty said, Amanda loved Aunt Judy and always enjoyed her visits. Judy was just five years younger than her mom, but she acted more like a college kid than an adult who was nearly forty. She knew the best bands, the coolest movies, and the most interesting books. She could sit up half the night talking about anything, and she never made Amanda feel silly or childish.

Yet Amanda hadn't told Judy about her imaginary house or her tendency for daydreams. In fact, when Judy sometimes talked about the old Victorian homes they used to visit when Amanda was very young, Amanda told her she barely remembered them and wasn't all that interested in old houses.

She didn't know why she'd kept the imaginary house a secret from her aunt, but some little voice deep in Amanda had warned her not to tell. Maybe she didn't want her aunt to tell her to get her head out of the clouds the way her mom always did. Or maybe she was afraid that if there was something wrong with her—mentally—Aunt Judy would be the one who would know.

When Judy came back to the apartment that night, there was no chance for Amanda to be alone with her before dinner. Chad was already home from work and was talking to Judy in the same overly-pleasant, condescending tone he often used with Amanda. That might mean her mom had told Chad about their earlier argument, Amanda thought, but it was hard to tell because it was a tone Chad used with a lot of people.

At the table, Amanda had a hard time pretending to be interested in Chad's stories of his work heroics. She faded in and out as he talked about the error he had caught on a purchasing order and the display of paint chips he had saved from a customer's unruly kids. Apparently, every day was an epic series of battles when you were the manager of a local hardware store.

As Chad rambled on, Amanda picked at her dinner and felt her eyes growing heavy. She hadn't slept well and was still feeling the effects of whatever magic had swept her from the park to Terra-V. She didn't mean to slip away, but before she realized what had happened, Amanda was standing back in the attic, staring at six wooden doors.

The door to Terra-V called to her, just as it had before, and Amanda was not surprised to notice a slight rattle in its silvery doorknob. She stepped forward but was stopped by a familiar voice behind her.

"Now is not the best time for that." The voice spoke calmly, and when she turned, Amanda wasn't surprised to see dark-framed glasses, blue-streaked hair, and a faded concert tee.

"I'll explain later," Judy smiled, "I promise. But we really shouldn't leave your mom alone with those horribly obnoxious stories any longer. Okay?"

They were back at the table then.

Chad's voice still droned on. Patty continued to cut and eat her chicken, bite by mechanical bite. Only moments had passed.

Amanda swallowed hard, pressing her palms against her thighs. Her eyes darted across the table.

Aunt Judy smiled with a reassuring nod.

CHAPTER 6
A SECRET SOCIETY

The elevator doors had scarcely closed when Amanda turned on her aunt impatiently.

"Well?"

Amanda twined her fingers together, nervously shifting the grip of her hands. Judy watched the elevator numbers count down to the lobby. Her profile was tense and still.

"Not yet," she answered, after passing another floor.

"Not yet?" Amanda echoed in disbelief. "You showed up inside my head and all you can say is *not yet*?"

"I wasn't inside your head."

Judy's calm response made Amanda more anxious.

She looked past Judy at the elevator's familiar orange walls and flat brass railings. A poster tacked on the side wall—featuring a hand-drawn glass of wine and bottle of beer beside a slice of pizza—advertised a neighborhood social from the week before. A sign next to it reminded guests to ask for a parking pass to avoid being towed. The images blurred as Amanda listened to the *ding* of the elevator passing another floor.

With a swift movement, Judy pressed the emergency button to stop the elevator. Amanda stumbled backward, more from surprise than from the sudden stop, and her aunt steadied her with a hand on each arm. A shrill bell sounded until Judy looked pointedly up at the hidden camera mounted behind a small mirror in the upper corner of the elevator. Once tha alarm stopped, she swung her gaze back to Amanda's pale face.

"Promise me you won't go through any more doors in the house." Her aunt spoke with an intensity she'd never shown before. Her words were just above a whisper, sharp and urgent. "Not unless I'm with you or you've been properly trained and cleared to travel alone. Do you promise?"

"I... Uh... Yes." The promise tumbled out as Amanda felt herself struggle to breathe normally.

"I'm serious." Judy leaned closer, her eyes boring into Amanda's soul. "I need your solemn word on this. You will not, under any circumstances, go through any door in that house until I say you can. Do you understand? Say it."

"I... I won't go through any door until you say I can. I promise."

Judy squinted at Amanda, weighing the sincerity of her words, then gave a small nod and restarted the elevator, watching the numbers above the doors as if nothing had happened. They passed the third floor. Amanda took a deep breath, trying to steady herself.

"I do promise," Amanda began tentatively. "But if I *were* to go through..."

Judy answered matter-of-factly, just before the elevator opened on the ground floor.

"You could be stranded in another world."

They stepped into the open space of the apartment lobby. Amanda glanced toward the reception desk and saw the same man who had been working there earlier in the day, the one she didn't recognize. Her eyes would have slid past him if he hadn't sent a quick nod to her aunt. A nod that reminded her of Judy signaling someone through the camera in the elevator. *Do they know each other?* Amanda remembered how Aunt Judy had shown up at their door without a call from the front desk. But the thought was lost in an echo of what her aunt had just said. *You could be stranded in another world.*

"Is there somewhere private where we can talk?" Judy asked. "A TV room or something?"

Amanda thought of the party room where Drew had planned to wait, in case Amanda could get out after dinner. He might be there now. Amanda could bring Judy there. She could introduce them and explain how Drew had helped her get to Terra-V. But would Judy answer her questions in front of Drew? She couldn't risk that, Amanda decided quickly, feeling a desperate need for answers.

"There's a library," Amanda offered, with just a small prick of conscience. Judy glanced at a trio of laughing friends walking in the front door before gesturing for Amanda to lead the way.

When they got to the library, Amanda hung back while Judy scoped out the small room. It had a wide doorway that opened onto a seating area surrounded by bookcases. Two couches sat in an L-shape in front of an electric fireplace. An oil painting of three boats on a choppy sea hung over the mantle. The room was empty.

"No door," Judy muttered, assessing the space with a neutral expression. "That's okay. We'll keep an eye out and talk quietly."

She gestured Amanda toward one of the couches, then took a seat herself. While Judy's back was turned, Amanda glanced down the hall. She saw Drew watching her through the party room's double glass doors. She held a finger over her lips, warning him to stay quiet, then followed her aunt into the room.

Once Amanda was seated, Judy closed her eyes and took a deep breath. They hesitated on the edge of the moment, feeling its weight.

Until Amanda broke the silence.

"Are you going to tell me what's going on?"

"Yes," Judy nodded. Amanda thought she heard a distant click from the hall, like a door softly closing, but she couldn't be sure.

"When you say stranded…?" Amanda pictured the strange beauty of Terra-V and the terror she'd felt when the attic door disappeared from the purple meadow.

"Later," Judy brushed the question away, along with Amanda's protest. "There are other things to cover first.

"Amanda," her aunt continued gravely. "I promise that I will be honest with you and answer your questions to the very best of my ability. But I need you to swear that you will not tell anyone what I'm about to tell you. Not even your mom. Okay?"

Amanda felt a fluttering in her chest. She didn't know for sure if Drew was in the hallway. Besides, she told herself, Drew listening in wouldn't *technically* be the same as her repeating what Aunt Judy said later on. Though her clenched stomach knew the truth.

Judy frowned, assuming another reason for Amanda's hesitation.

"I wouldn't normally ask you to keep something from your mom, but once you hear what I have to say..." She trailed off, though her voice sounded encouraging.

Amanda nodded weakly. She was about to explain that she wasn't worried about keeping it from her mom, but she didn't get the chance.

"Okay," Judy smiled, assuming Amanda's full agreement. "So, you must have a lot of questions?"

Her body softened, her voice returning to its friendly, almost conspiratorial tone. That stiff, unknown Judy had left the room and Amanda's beloved aunt was finally back by her side. Amanda's relief made it easier to set aside her qualms about the possibility of Drew listening in.

"Well, I have a few," Amanda laughed, releasing some of her tension.

Judy asked how long Amanda had been visiting the house. Amanda told her she honestly wasn't sure. She explained how the daydreams had been happening for a long time but had gotten stronger in the last year. She described the attic doors and how one had been calling out to her, just begging for her to open it and step through.

Judy nodded knowingly.

"And that's how you ended up in that purple meadow?"

"Ye-es," Amanda stretched the word out, glossing over the first time she'd opened the door, her temporary trouble accessing the house, and the way Drew had helped her get past all that. She had questions of her own to ask first. "How did you know I was there?"

"You were seen," Judy answered shortly, quick to move on to another topic, but Amanda wanted to know more.

"By the knight?"

"The knight?" Judy smirked. "Oh, yes. The knight."

"I saw him in the house, too. That same knight. About two weeks ago."

"I know. He didn't see you very well the first time, just a glimpse. But I had my suspicions, so I sent him your picture and he confirmed it was you. After he saw you again in the meadow."

"Oh."

The idea of Aunt Judy and this knight talking about her made Amanda feel oddly exposed.

"What did you think of that experience? Of going through the door?"

An image of Terra-V sprang into Amanda's mind. The purple grass, the twisting trees, the dewy softness of the air. She remembered the searing pain in her head, the nausea that had left her weak and trembling, and the strange woman who had taken that sickness away with a single touch. Just picturing the woman, with her iridescent skin and deep blue hair, brought a faint sensation of the soothing warmth that had spread through her body. Like the vibration of a song she could feel, but barely hear.

Judy frowned.

"Maybe we should back up," she suggested, before pausing to bite her lower lip. "This isn't easy for you, and I wish it were easier for me. I mean, I'm normally very good at it, but this time... Well, I thought I'd have more time to prepare before you... I mean, if you ever...

"Let's just get through the basics, okay?" Judy brushed her scattered emotions away and got to the point. "Amanda, you are part of a special group of people who live all over the world, and blend into all different parts of society, but who have special abilities humans typically do not have. Do you have any idea what that might mean?"

Amanda remembered Drew's hypothesis and hoped he *was* listening to this explanation, even if her aunt didn't want it to leave the room.

"I can phase to other dimensions? Through my mind?"

"Well, sort of." Judy leaned back and gave Amanda a long, assessing look. She seemed both amused and impressed. "Most people in your position worry they've gone crazy, but you seem to be figuring it out."

"Oh, I'm pretty sure I'm going crazy," Amanda admitted with something that tried to be a laugh but came out as a choked cough. Tears pricked the corners of her eyes.

"You are *not* crazy," Judy insisted more intently, reaching to squeeze Amanda's hands. "That I can say for sure."

"Okay." Amanda wasn't entirely convinced. "So, who are these people then?"

"We go by different names. Thought walkers. Mind travelers. Officially, we're the Psychic Traveler Society. Or PTS. Sometimes, in more public interactions, that acronym is changed to stand for something else. Like, when we work through government channels. Stuff like that. There are very few normals who know about us, but we have our liaisons, the people who bridge between our society and the rest of the world. We often just call ourselves travelers."

"Uh, okay." Amanda rolled the name around in her mind. *Travelers.* She had tried to follow the rest of Aunt Judy's answer but too many questions were crowding in. She imagined Drew out in the hall, dying to ask questions of his own.

"We don't entirely know *why* we have this ability," Judy continued, anticipating Amanda's next questions. "And we don't entirely know *where* it is that we go. It could be other dimensions, as you said, or it could be other planets in distant galaxies. Those questions are better left to the scientists. The rest of us have our own jobs and our own place in our society."

It was both what she expected and an entirely surreal answer. Amanda was beginning to feel like she was stuck in a dream. She considered whether she might still be asleep on the park bench with Drew by her side. She *felt* like she was awake, but she wasn't entirely sure she could trust that feeling anymore.

"And the house?"

"You can think of the house as a sort of hub," Judy continued in a practiced way. "When we're in the house, our *bodies* haven't traveled anywhere. Our bodies stay put while our minds enter that shared space. It's the place our minds pass through on our way to somewhere else—like a train station—but it can also be a place to *mentally* meet without our bodies traveling to a different location."

"Like when you talked to me in the attic during dinner."

Amanda was putting the pieces together. Her brain seemed to be both running quickly and working slowly.

"Exactly," Judy smiled. "We call it the birdhouse."

"The birdhouse?" Amanda shook her head in disbelief, again wondering if this conversation was really happening. "Why the birdhouse?"

"Oh, I know, it sounds silly." Judy fluttered her hands. "It's just a nickname we use. Think of it like this: we travel from place to place and that's our home base. Like a nest. But the birdhouse sounds cooler than the nest, right?"

"Uh, I guess so," Amanda recalled the river walk she and her mom had once explored on a summer vacation. The path had been lined with decorative birdhouses and several had been in the shape of ornate Victorian homes. "And your job in the society is…?"

"My job is this," Judy spread her arms toward Amanda making a sweeping, all-encompassing gesture. "I'm a PTS counselor, specializing in initiation and integration. See, these abilities typically run in families, but not always. They can skip over siblings, or generations, and they can show up in people with no family history of psychic travel at all. So, finding and helping new travelers is really important.

"We watch for abilities emerging, which usually happens in young adulthood, then a counselor—like me—is assigned to connect with the traveler and help him or her transition into our society."

"That sounds—" Amanda stopped talking as new thoughts crowded in. "By young adulthood, you mean teenagers?"

"No," Judy frowned. "It's typically people in their mid to late twenties. Occasionally someone develops these abilities in their early twenties, and once it happened with a nineteen-year-old."

"But never younger?"

"Never younger," her aunt agreed. "Until now."

Amanda thought about that. Her palms felt itchy, so she rubbed them on the front of her jeans while she considered the situation. Most travelers were young *adults* when this came up. That meant they were typically ten years older than her. At least.

"But I'm only fourteen."

"Yes," Judy agreed. "You're only fourteen."

"Nearly fifteen," Amanda corrected, on second thought.

"Nearly fifteen," Judy amended. "Which is still much younger than I expected."

"That's why you took me to those old houses when I was little?" Amanda was still looking for pieces she could fit together. "Were you trying to bring this out in me? Or make it happen?"

"No," Judy sighed. "I suppose I just wanted to lay some groundwork. You know, give myself an excuse to ask about historic houses later. Or maybe set myself up as someone you'd talk to if you started dreaming about the house."

They sat quietly again.

Amanda was thinking about everything Aunt Judy had revealed so far.

Judy was giving Amanda time to process the incredible information she'd been given.

And then Judy jumped to her feet.

"Hey!" She rapidly crossed the room until she was in the hall, standing face-to-face with Drew. "Who are you? What are you doing here? Were you listening to us?"

"Aunt Judy, wait!" Amanda rushed to Drew's side. "This is my friend. This is Drew."

§

Until that night, Amanda had never thought of her Aunt Judy as a *real* authority figure. She was an adult, but not an adult like Amanda's mom or one of her teachers. Judy was the kind of adult who seemed more like an extra-old teenager. She'd breeze in, take Amanda out to movies or concerts, or just flop on the bed and chat about whatever was going on in Amanda's life. But there in the hallway, despite her blue-streaked hair and ripped jeans, Judy squared her shoulders and stared them down in a way that left no mistake about her absolute authority.

Drew shrank in a nervous slouch as he shoved his hands deep into his front pockets. Judy shifted her angry stare between Amanda and Drew. She knew about Drew. She'd heard Amanda talk about him often enough. But she was clearly unhappy about his appearance during this particular conversation. Especially as the guilty look on his face made it clear he'd been listening outside the library for quite some time.

"He already knows!" Amanda blurted the words, ready to take responsibility.

"What was that?" Judy directed the full force of her icy stare on her neice, but Amanda was focused on the nervous energy she sensed in Drew.

"He already knows," she repeated quietly. "He's known for a long time now. From before I ever opened that door. Before we had any idea what would happen when…"

As her words trailed to an uncertain halt, some of the tension left the hallway.

Amanda was telling the truth and Judy knew it. She gathered her dark hair in a loose ponytail at the back of her head. She looked up at the ceiling and then down at the floor before dropping her hands by her side. Amanda and Drew gave her time to think, not daring even the slightest glance at each other. Crossing her left arm over her body, Judy stepped back and used her right arm to point emphatically toward the empty library.

"Sit down."

She didn't have to tell them twice.

Amanda and Drew perched on the same couch and launched into the whole story before Judy had a chance to ask another question. Amanda explained how she had told Drew about her recurring dreams of the house. Or the *birdhouse,* as she was trying to think of it now. Drew jumped in when she got to his theory about her subconscious mind working out some deep emotional problem. They told the rest in turns, sometimes talking over each other in their haste to include everything. Through it all, Judy stood with her arms crossed and her lips pursed.

When they were finished, Judy lifted her hands in prayer position, letting them briefly rest over her nose and mouth, then let out a long sigh. She rubbed her temples, checked her watch, then quickly sat on the edge of the opposite couch.

"You brought back some purple grass?"

Her expression was blank. Her tone carefully controlled.

"Yes." Amanda looked at Drew meaningfully. There was only a brief hesitation before he leaned back to pull the rolled-up plastic bag from his front pocket.

Judy took the bag carefully, staring at its smeary contents before silently transferring it to her own pocket. Once the bag was again out of sight, she clasped her hands on her lap.

"Is that everything?"

Amanda and Drew promised there was nothing more to tell. Though Amanda hadn't mentioned overhearing the conversation where her mom had told Chad about her dad's mental illness and his secret job that required a lot of travel. She'd started to piece that together herself, but it didn't feel like the right time to ask for confirmation.

"We've been gone long enough." Judy abruptly stood up, preparing to leave.

"That's it?" Amanda didn't see how the conversation could be over when they'd just gotten to the point where their talk could really begin. Drew seemed unsurprised and nodded lightly when Judy said they would talk more soon. She reminded them this was serious business and made them both promise not to say a word about it to anyone else. They were mostly quiet as they made their way back upstairs. It was an uncomfortable silence.

"Would you have told me about him?" Judy asked Amanda—after Drew got off the elevator on the fourth floor. "If I hadn't caught him listening in?"

"Yes," Amanda answered right away, though her stomach felt uneasy.

They were quiet again until the elevator stopped on the seventh floor. They stepped out into the empty hallway, and Judy reached for Amanda's arm, gently holding her back.

"I know this is overwhelming," she said softly. "But this is only the beginning. Amanda, I need you to be honest and open with me from here on out. I need you to trust me and let me guide you through this. Can you do that?"

Amanda looked into Aunt Judy's serious face and felt like she was looking at a stranger. What did Amanda *really* know about her aunt? What had she *ever* really known about her? Judy had kept all of this from her. She'd hidden this secret society. She'd hidden that Amanda's dad was in this society—if Amanda's suspicions were correct. She'd even lied by telling Amanda's mom they were going out for ice cream instead of having this secret conversation. How did she *really* know that she could trust her aunt now?

But she was Aunt Judy. Amanda wanted to trust her aunt because she'd always trusted her and there were too many other things changing. Besides, Amanda thought, who else did she have to trust?

CHAPTER 7

EXPLORING THE HOUSE

"Tell me what you see."

Amanda and Judy were walking down a long hallway, though their bodies were sitting safely in Judy's locked hotel room. To Amanda, the shared mindspace felt like a vivid dream. It wasn't the same as being awake—or traveling to Terra-V—but it felt *almost* like they were actually in a large Victorian house. She stopped walking and looked along the length of the hallway. There were bedrooms spaced along the hall, each decorated in a different color scheme. She'd wandered through them all, but never found anything of interest. Other than the doors clustered in each bedroom. Doors she'd never opened.

"We're in a house." Amanda studied the burnt orange flowers scrolling over the dark blue wallpaper before adding, "an old house."

"Yes." Judy cocked her head to one side but kept her eyes on Amanda's face. "What do you see in the living room?"

Amanda turned toward the open double doors on her right. She saw the same living room she'd explored dozens of times.

"It has a piano, and couches, and a bunch of small tables. There are some glass cabinets on the walls with books, and knickknacks, and other stuff in them. Wait!"

Amanda looked around again, checking her bearings. They had been in the upstairs hallway an instant before. Now, they stood in the nearly identical hallway on the first floor. The large living room was to the right and three small rooms were arranged in a line at the left of the hall.

"We were upstairs," Amanda said slowly. "We were on the second floor, near the bedrooms, then you asked about the living room. And now we're... here?"

"The birdhouse isn't a physical place," Judy reminded. "It's more like a dream. Have you ever noticed how you move through dreams?"

Amanda thought about it. In her dreams, the locations were strangely connected. Her bedroom closet might open into her English class. She could climb a tree in the park and end up at the top of a skyscraper. Someone could mention a place and they would be there.

"How well do you remember walking around this house?" Judy asked softly. "Do you know where to find the steps to the attic? Have you climbed those steps?"

Amanda thought about the floor plans she'd drawn in her blue notebook. The layouts of the rooms were clear, but she'd struggled to fit each floor into a shape that made sense for the whole house. She'd never figured out exactly how the attic stairs connected to the second floor.

"It's just the way the birdhouse is," Judy reassured. "You'll get used to it with practice."

She stepped closer to the large living room, then turned to face one of the smaller rooms across the hall. She took a single step toward the small room and Amanda instantly found them both standing in what appeared to be a home office. It had a roll-top desk with inlaid wood and ornately scrolled legs. There was a small armchair beside the desk with a wood frame and dark pink upholstery. A carved bookshelf sat on the opposite wall, next to a green velvet loveseat. Layers of heavy, velvet drapes and thin, filmy sheers covered the large windows at the front of the room. There were five doors set in various places around the room, all in white wood with brass handles.

"Can you guess what's behind these doors?"

Amanda watched warily as Judy walked briskly toward a door on the back wall. She turned to face Amanda while resting her hand on the doorknob. Her body language was casual, as if she were standing in front of an ordinary closet door, but there was an adventurous gleam in her eye.

"Another... world?" The word sounded odd to Amanda, but she didn't have a better one.

"Maybe." Judy grinned, lightly testing the turn of the knob. "The doors in the birdhouse do go somewhere else, but not all of them lead to different worlds. Some go to normal places right here, on Earth."

Amanda turned that thought over. She wished Aunt Judy would just give her the answers without these guessing games, but she'd been told it was better for her developing abilities if she puzzled out as much of it as she could herself.

Whatever that meant. Amanda wanted to do well, to figure out the right answers, but a worrying thought kept drifting through her mind. *You could be stranded in another world.* She pushed the thought aside.

"Do *you* know where these doors go?" Amanda asked, testing out an idea at the edge of her understanding. Judy confirmed that she did know where the doors went. Amanda's thought clicked into place. "Do the same doors always go to the same place? Every time?"

"Good question!" Judy let go of the knob, which left Amanda feeling both disappointed and relieved. "The doors do go to specific places. The same doors to the same places, every time."

"And when you get there…" Amanda remembered the imaginary door on Terra-V. The one that had disappeared and reappeared like a mirage. *You could be stranded in another world.*

"That's a little more complicated." Judy brushed off the question, just as she'd sidestepped several earlier questions, then looked back toward the hall. Amanda was getting used to setting aside the questions her aunt wasn't ready to answer, though she wished she had a notepad to write them down for later. Standing in the hall—which was still the first-floor hall—Amanda saw Judy now looking into the large living room with a puckered frown.

"I guess it's time," she muttered, then moved into the room before Amanda could ask, *"Time for what?"*

Amanda followed, cautiously watching as Judy crossed her arms and moved her gaze slowly around the room, pausing here and there for an extended moment. It had been a long afternoon and Amanda could feel her energy lagging. She was tired of exploring the house, guessing at mindboggling answers, and feeling like a lab rat trying to solve some unexplained task.

"What do you see in here?"

"Uh," Amanda sighed, glancing around for something she had missed from the hallway. "I don't know. I already told you, there's a piano and—"

"Are there any people here?" Judy interrupted, in a surprisingly sharp and exasperated tone. "Other than you and me?"

"People?" Amanda felt a prickling on the back of her neck as she looked for bodies crouched behind the couches or eyes peering out from between the large, potted plants.

There was no one else in the room. At least, no one she could see.

Judy stepped closer and held both of Amanda's hands in her own. She looked deeply into Amanda's eyes. Amanda felt compelled to hold her stare, unable to see anything else around them. Her stomach turned over as waves of anxiety vibrated from her core.

"This house is a shared space," Judy reminded gently. "It's a sort of social hub. Travelers can meet here, mentally, from all over, just as we're here now."

"Okay." Amanda wanted to look away, but the intensity of her aunt's gaze held her in place.

"The thing is, the sharing here is voluntary. Do you know what that means?" Amanda shook her head very slightly. The prickling feeling was spreading up the back of her neck. Her cheeks and ears were warm.

"It means," Judy continued pointedly, "you can only see people here if they *want* to be seen. And they can only see you if *you* want to be seen."

"Oh… uh…" Amanda felt a slight tremor run through her body. If that were true, she puzzled, then had she *wanted* the knight to see her? When she'd thought she was hiding from him behind the dusty furniture? And then her face went cold as she realized what Aunt Judy may be trying to tell her. *Were there other people in the room with them right then? Watching? Could they already see Aunt Judy? Were they waiting for Amanda to appear?*

Judy stepped back. She released one of Amanda's hands, giving her more freedom to look around the room. For almost a full minute, Amanda continued to watch her aunt. She was afraid to look around. She didn't want to see. She didn't want to know. Her heart raced. Her mind tried pulling away from the house. The wall behind Judy began to fade and blur. Amanda's head ached.

Judy squeezed her hand and smiled. She whispered, "It's okay. Take another look."

Amanda closed her eyes and swallowed, then looked toward the largest couch. It was empty. Her breath came easier as she checked the neighboring chairs and saw they were empty, too. Slowly, her eyes drifted around the vacant room, feeling a weight begin to lift. They were alone.

Her relief spread until she reached a spot between the piano and a tall curio case. She blinked, recognizing the knight—though he wasn't wearing his armor—and wondered how she hadn't seen him there before. He met her eyes with a carefully blank expression, though Amanda saw that his arms were crossed tightly over his chest, like Aunt Judy's had been when she'd entered the room. He looked angry or frustrated.

A movement near the large couch caught Amanda's attention. There were three people sitting on its plush cushions now: two middle-aged women wearing stylish pantsuits and a slightly younger man with slick, dark hair and gold, wire-rimmed glasses. Amanda's breath caught in her chest. Judy squeezed her hand, but the sensation barely registered. Amanda gazed around the room again, feeling her eyes widen. There were people standing behind the couch, sitting in the adjacent chairs, crowding in the doorway, and gathering around the piano. People stood along every wall. People of every shape and size. People of every age—every *adult* age.

Without thought, Amanda pulled her hand away from Judy and wrapped both arms around her own chest. The gesture wasn't a sign of anger but an attempt to keep her heart from leaping out of her body. She turned her head more rapidly, taking in the sea of faces without registering details. The knight alone stood out, his lips pressed tight, his eyes worried. Even Aunt Judy had blurred into the background of faces and bodies. As Amanda desperately looked back in her direction, an older man stepped forward from the crowd. He had bright eyes, gray hair, and a short, neatly trimmed beard. He wore a dark suit and a heavy frown. He opened his mouth to speak, but Amanda didn't hear whatever he intended to say.

Amanda was sitting on a hotel room bed. Her back rested against the headboard and her body trembled in a cold sweat. There was a fuzzy, tugging blur throughout her mind, a tangle of thoughts, as if she'd just woken from a deep dream. Her aunt was sitting beside her, staring blankly into space. For a startling second, Aunt Judy looked unreal, like a wax figure, and then her eyes blinked open. She reached out for Amanda's arms. Too fast. Too grasping.

"Are you okay?" Her words were worried, her eyes searching.

"I—" Amanda's mouth fell open, but no other sound came out.

§

"I haven't decided what to do about Drew yet."

Judy was driving Amanda home. Her eyes stayed on the road as large raindrops splattered against the windshield. Amanda watched the arc of the wipers swishing rhythmically across the glass. Her head still felt fuzzy after their training session in the house, though it was nothing compared to the migraine symptoms she'd experienced on her trips to and from Terra-V.

"What do you mean?" Amanda had her own suspicions.

"I haven't told anyone about him," Judy clarified, though that didn't entirely answer the question. The wipers cleared the rain away. *Swish. Swish.* They stopped at a red light. The rain seemed to slow down, but the wipers continued at the same pace. *Swish. Swish.*

"It would be better if he didn't know anything," Judy continued. "Though it's too late for that. And he doesn't strike me as the type who would accept a cover story. Maybe if he hadn't seen that purple grass…"

She seemed to be talking to herself as much as she was talking to Amanda. Driving seemed to have that effect on people, Amanda noticed, especially in a light rain. Her mom was the same way. If Amanda stayed quiet long enough, her mom often carried on a whole conversation, saying more than she ever would if Amanda had asked a series of direct questions. It was the way Amanda had learned most of what she knew about her dad. She simply had to plant the idea of him during a car ride, maybe with a seemingly simple question, then let her mom ramble on as the rain created splotched patterns across the windshield.

"But he did see the grass," Judy went on, making her case. "And if he overheard as much as I think he did… Though he seems to be accepting it very well. Much better than most of the normals I've encountered."

"Better than my mom?" Amanda asked quietly. "When she found out about my dad?"

Judy pressed her lips together until they disappeared in a tight, white line. Amanda regretted daring too much. But then her aunt answered.

"Your mom never knew about your dad."

Amanda considered that answer. She'd thought through the situation the night before and realized there were two possibilities: her mom had told Chad what she believed was the truth, or her mom had told Chad a story to hide what she really knew about her dad's psychic travel. Amanda wasn't sure which was better. She didn't like the idea of her mom telling Chad a family secret, but it made her angry to think her dad would keep such an important part of his life from her mom.

"So, my dad *was* a traveler then? The psychic kind."
Amanda needed to hear it confirmed.

"He was a traveler." Judy stopped at another red light but kept her eyes on the road. Amanda did the same, noticing it was easier to not make eye contact during this story. "He was in college when his ability emerged. He was the first traveler in our family, so no one from PTS was watching out for him. Like most travelers who lack PTS guidance, he initially went to doctors who thought he had schizophrenia—that's a mental disorder that commonly appears around the same age.

"But it wasn't long before our counselors got to him and sorted it all out," Judy added quickly. Amanda remembered her mom telling Chad that doctors had gotten her dad's condition under control. "Gabe knew to watch for signs of it in me, so I had a much easier transition."

"Why couldn't my mom know?" Amanda tried to hide the anger building inside, but her words came out with a sharp edge.

They pulled up to the apartment building and Judy navigated the car into a free parking space. She already had a guest parking tag hanging from her rearview mirror. Amanda knew the pass was valid through the weekend, and she fleetingly wondered how long her aunt planned to stay in town.

"It's complicated." Judy put the car in park and switched off the windshield wipers. Though she left the car running as she faced Amanda. "Normal minds usually can't comprehend psychic travel. It's too much. It's too different from their own experience of the world. When they can't accept it, that can become a dangerous situation. For them, and for our whole society."

Amanda thought about that, still staring at the rain gathering on the windshield. She speculated on what Aunt Judy meant by *dangerous*. Would it hurt her mom to try to understand? Would it drive her crazy to believe in something she could never actually see for herself? Couldn't her dad have brought back proof? The way Amanda had brought back the purple grass?

"Drew accepts it," Amanda said shortly, avoiding all the questions she didn't want to ask.

"He does," Judy agreed. "But that doesn't mean he'll be able to accept more than what he already knows. These situations with normals have a way of going badly. Amanda, I know you want to share this with him, but it might be kinder if you don't."

Amanda bit her lip, neither agreeing nor disagreeing. As far as she was concerned, it was too late for that. She couldn't cut him out now. He needed to know, she decided. Though a nagging inner voice questioned whether Drew needed to know as much as *she* needed him to know.

§

Drew had his own ideas on the subject.

"You could be in danger if the wrong people found out." They were walking to the bus stop Monday morning, which was the first chance they'd had to talk in person about what they'd learned. While Amanda and Judy had been worrying about what to tell him, Drew had been stewing in his own anxiety over Amanda's safety.

"I'm serious!" Drew insisted. "There are scientists out there who would love to experiment on a brain like yours, if they knew what you could do."

"There are probably scientists inside PTS who already do that," Amanda countered. It didn't have the calming effect she'd expected.

"Did your aunt tell you that?"

Amanda reminded him that there was a whole society where psychic travel was an accepted ability, and that PTS had been designed to keep travelers safe. They had experience with blending into the *normal* world and they would keep her safe, too.

It was true, she told herself, carefully leaving out her own doubts about this whole new world and what her place might be in it. Drew didn't need to see her fear, and Amanda felt braver with every argument she made in favor of PTS.

They walked quietly for a few minutes before Drew grudgingly admitted that Amanda had made some good points. A few steps later, he caught up with his own predicament.

"But they can't be happy about me knowing all this," he frowned.

Amanda didn't have an answer for that.

§

When they got to school, Trina was not waiting in their usual spot. Amanda thought she caught a glimpse of her just before the first bell, then lost her in the crush of students. They didn't meet up until their second period P.E. class, where Trina had no place to hide in the small locker room. Amanda set her bag on the bench next to Trina and fished out her gym clothes.

"Hey."

"Hey."

Trina had already changed into her gym uniform and was untangling the laces on one of her sneakers. She frowned at a knot that had apparently tied itself while the shoe was still in her bag.

"I looked for you this morning," Amanda offered.

"I waited for you to return my texts all weekend," Trina countered, without looking up.

"Yeah, sorry." Amanda sat on the bench and reached for Trina's shoe. She was better at untangling. "Aunt Judy showed up on Saturday. A week early."

"Uh huh." Trina examined her nails, scraping at some flaking polish. "Did you even ask Drew about the football game?"

"Oh, right." Amanda freed the knot from the lace but let the shoe dangle from one hand.

"Right." Trina took back her shoe and slid it onto her foot. "I get it. It's just a stupid football game. I didn't really want to go either. I mean, just because, like, *everyone* else is going, doesn't mean I should want to go, too. It's just you *said* you were going to set it up, so I thought… But that doesn't matter, I guess. You have Drew and your aunt and other things to do."

"Trina!" Amanda stopped her from leaving, then lowered her voice, very aware of the other girls crowded around them. Just as the travelers had crowded into the living room.

Amanda fought against the pull of the house, blocking the images forming behind her eyes. The brocade couches. The carved wood. The blue and orange wallpaper.

"We're going to the game." Amanda focused on the faint freckles scattered across Trina's cheekbones, using each detail of her friend's face to keep her here. In the locker room. Out of the house. "It's not a stupid game," she insisted. "We're going and it's going to be great."

"And Drew's friends?" Trina raised an eyebrow, still looking uncertain.

"Yes, sure," Amanda agreed, hearing the promises roll out of her mouth. "They'll be there, too. We'll all hang out and it will be the best night ever! You can even spend the night after. It's my birthday weekend, I'm sure my mom won't mind!"

"Really?" Trina smiled, her curly hair bouncing as she tossed her head and laughed brightly. "Okay, fine, you sold me! I'm in!"

Amanda rolled her eyes and laughed with Trina, pushing aside the thought of Aunt Judy and her training. Pushing aside the house. And Terra-V. She deserved a night off for her birthday, Amanda reasoned. She just hoped Aunt Judy agreed.

CHAPTER 8

THE YOUNGEST TRAVELER

Amanda didn't have a chance to tell her aunt about her Friday night plans. She thought she would have more time to talk about it. Maybe after their first day of training. Or their second. But it hadn't worked out that way.

When Amanda got home from school on Monday, her mom was sitting at her small desk, typing on her keyboard. Aunt Judy slouched on the couch, tapping on her smartphone. They both wore headphones and neither looked up when Amanda entered. Her mom looked intent. Her aunt looked bored.

Amanda watched them from the front door, thinking about all the years her mom and aunt had known each other. Aunt Judy was about five years younger than Amanda's parents, and she'd been close with them both. She'd been part of their daily family life until Amanda was seven.

It was soon after Patty had sold their house and moved them to the apartment when Judy said she had to move away for work. She promised to visit often, but that's when the rift began. Watching them now, Amanda flashed back to crouching behind a moving box while her mom yelled at her aunt, *"I can't believe you're leaving now! After all we did for you!"*

"I'm home!" Amanda dropped her backpack loudly to chase away her own memory.

They both looked up, but only her aunt removed her headphones.

"You're home!" Judy echoed with a huge grin. "Your mom says I can take you off her hands tonight. Get dinner, maybe see a movie."

"After homework!" Patty added, without pausing in her typing.

"Right," Judy added. "Dinner and a movie, *after* homework."

She winked and Amanda knew her aunt had entirely different plans.

§

They were soon back in Judy's hotel room, eating Chinese take-out and sorting through the mechanics of psychic travel.

"So… if I go into the house from this hotel room, I wake up from the house in this hotel room." Amanda spoke slowly, looking at the diagram Judy had sketched. "But it was only my mind that was in the house. My body was here the whole time."

"Yes," Judy encouraged, slippery noodles dangling from her plastic fork.

"And if I go through a door in the house, my body—and my mind—physically travel to that place. Wherever it is." Judy nodded, sliding the noodles into her mouth and grabbing a napkin for the sauce that had dribbled onto her chin. "But then to come back…"

Amanda stopped talking, picturing the door that had appeared and disappeared in the purple meadow on Terra-V. She shuddered, now knowing what would have happened if she hadn't used that door to get back into the house. If she had simply imagined herself home.

"To come back…?" Judy prompted.

"An imaginary door shows up in the place where I traveled. That door brings my mind back into the house. Then, when I wake up, my body—and my mind—physically travels back to where I started the trip. So, in this case, the hotel room."

"Very good." Judy put down her paper plate after shifting aside a container of egg rolls. "Now. What happens if you physically travel to another place, and then let your mind go back into the house *without* going through an imaginary door?"

"My mind and body would stay in the new place when I woke up from the house, instead of coming back to where I began."

Amanda shuddered again. *You could be stranded in another world.*

"Think of it this way." Judy picked up an egg roll and used it to gesture as she spoke. "The doors in the house are each connected to a certain spot. But that spot extends for about a twenty-yard radius. That's its *proximity zone.*

"When you pass into the proximity zone from the house, you can see the door you came through, but then it fades away because it isn't physically there. It's a mental gateway. You can explore all over that world, but you have to come back to the same proximity zone for the same door to reappear. We call it a proximal door. It shows up anywhere in that proximity zone. Stepping through it will bring you back into the house where you started."

She took a casual bite of the egg roll as if they were chatting about the weather or current events. Amanda had hardly touched her orange chicken.

"Now, if you went to a *different* proximity zone while you were in that location, the proximal door in that zone would also bring you back in the same way, just through a different door in the house. Then, you'd wake up from the house back in this hotel room. Or wherever you began your journey. Understand?"

"I guess so." Amanda pushed the chicken around her plate, puzzling it together. She hoped it was like a board game where the instructions sounded complicated but were easy once you started playing.

"It's kind of like a chain," Judy tried again. "Your whole psychic travel journey is a chain that starts from wherever you first mentally enter the house.

"The first link in the chain is your origin point. When you move through a door in the house, you add another link to the chain. But that new location is not your origin point, because you used a door to get there. You can use doors in the house, and proximal doors, to travel to several locations without changing your origin point.

"But, as soon as you mentally go back to the house—without using a proximal door—you've broken the chain. You set a new origin point and that's where you'll be when you wake up from the house. Does that help?"

"Ye-es," Amanda nodded slowly, but she didn't feel confident that she *really* understood.

Judy finished her egg roll and brushed off her hands.

"Ready to test it out?" Her eyes gleamed with an excitement Amanda didn't feel.

"I guess?" Amanda glanced at her uneaten dinner, remembering the travel sickness she'd had on her trip to Terra-V.

"Take this." Judy fished a small white tablet from a plastic bottle. "Let it dissolve on your tongue and it will help with the nausea you had last time."

"Aren't you going to take one?" Amanda examined the letters etched into the pill, then carefully set it on her tongue. It dissolved with a fizzy sensation and a faint taste of chalky mint.

"I don't need it."

Judy explained that her body had gotten used to the effects of psychic travel and that soon Amanda would travel easily as well. It was hard to believe, until Amanda realized that simply moving in and out of the house had already gotten easier. Judy said that was because Amanda had stopped resisting it. "Acceptance makes a huge difference in how your body feels."

They went into the birdhouse together, appearing in the living room. There didn't seem to be anyone else there, but Amanda couldn't shake the uneasy feeling of being watched. Aunt Judy had said no one could see her unless she wanted to be seen, Amanda reminded herself. But had she really wanted to be seen before? Was it something she could actually control?

Judy pointed to the doors in the living room, explaining that they each went to different places right here on Earth. Some went to foreign countries. Three went to cities in the United States: New York, Chicago, and San Francisco. They were taking the door to Chicago, which led directly into The Psychic Traveler Society's main headquarters.

The door to Chicago was to the right of the piano. Like the other doors in the living room, it was stained a deep, rich brown. A large, raised panel covered the top two-thirds of the door while a smaller, matching panel decorated the lower portion. Each panel was framed by a thick border of inlaid wood with lighter wood scrolling through a dark background. Carved molding lined the door, and its handle was an antique brass lever.

When Judy opened the door, Amanda saw people in business attire hurrying through a vast atrium. The walls and floor were white marble with gold accents. The ceiling was high, giving the space a light and airy feel, while ornamental trees grew from large, evenly spaced planters.

Despite the old-fashioned marble and gold, Amanda thought it looked like a scene from a modern movie. Adult professionals in a big city law firm, or advertising agency, or something equally fancy. Except the scene was unfolding through the doorway of a Victorian living room and no one in the atrium seemed to be aware of Amanda and Judy's presence on this side of the door.

With a nudge from her aunt, Amanda felt her feet moving over the threshold, and then… Nothing.

For a split second, everything went white. A roaring *whoosh* of air seemed to blow through Amanda's mind. Her body stumbled on ground that tilted from one direction to another. A sharp odor flashed beneath her nose. Amanda felt Aunt Judy's arm around her waist, steadying her. Several people stopped to stare, some with sympathetic smiles, others exchanging surprised whispers.

As she stood straighter, Amanda saw her aunt cap a glass vial and slip it into her pocket. She looked for the door they'd passed through, but it had already faded away. Instead, she saw dozens of identical doors popping up all around them. The doors had the same mirage-like quality as the attic door in the meadow at Terra-V.

Proximal doors, Amanda thought to herself with a sense of amazement.

As she watched, people slipped through doors that promptly disappeared, making space for new doors to greet approaching travelers.

"It's the end of the day," Judy explained, maneuvering Amanda out of traffic and toward a quieter side of the spacious room. "Time to go home, and many people who work here commute."

Commute. Amanda pictured cars or buses, before realizing what it meant for a psychic traveler to commute to work.

Many people who had witnessed Amanda's rocky arrival continued to watch her from a discreet distance. Additional passersby had then paused to see what was drawing their attention. Some had moved on quickly but most of them had gathered in a curious crowd.

"Nothing to see here!"

Judy stepped toward them, waving her arms, but only a few were prompted to leave. The rest whispered to each other more urgently, exchanging knowing looks. One man stared at Amanda so intently his bag slipped from his fingers and landed on the floor with an ominous crack.

"Ignore them," Judy told Amanda with a toss of her head

"Why are they…?" Amanda didn't finish her question. *I'm a kid,* she realized. *I'm the youngest traveler they've ever seen.* She remembered the crowd gathered in the house and how annoyed Aunt Judy had been at those who had come to gawk at her.

Ignoring them—and trying to control a motion-sick headache that threatened despite the white tablet—Amanda let her eyes wander. The room was even larger than it had appeared through the doorway. There were tall, arched windows rising from the floor up to the two-story ceiling, but the bottom two-thirds of the glass was opaque. Only the upper portions of the windows held clear glass and even that seemed to have a softening effect. The light filtering in created a hazy glow around them, tinted pink and orange by the setting sun. Amanda's distressed eyes appreciated the softness of the light.

The atrium was an enormous square, large enough to include the entire proximity zone, Amanda supposed. Windows spanned three walls, while the fourth featured three arched doorways.

When Judy led the way through one of the doorways, they faced another wall with two pairs of double doors. Those doors were offset from the arched doorways in a way that would keep anyone from seeing directly into the atrium when they were open.

Amanda noted security guards at the doors, nodding some people through and checking others' badges. They paid no attention to Amanda as she followed her aunt through one set of doors.

Amanda then found herself in a much smaller lobby. A bank of elevators was on her right and an information desk stood to the left. A revolving glass door, flanked by smaller glass doors, was ahead of them. Through the glass, Amanda saw a busy city street.

I'm in Chicago, Amanda marveled, feeling nearly as amazed as she had been in the purple meadow on Terra-V. Perhaps even more amazed, since Chicago was a place she could find on a map and Terra-V seemed more like a dream. This was real. Chicago was real. And Amanda was there, hundreds of miles from home, yet only a moment away.

"There are training facilities on the fifth floor," Judy explained, pressing the button to call an elevator. "The sixth floor has an impressive library with some items you'll find quite interesting."

Before she could say more about the building's many departments, an elevator door opened to reveal a thin, nervous man standing inside. He held the door open with one arm and gave Judy an apologetic half-smile.

"He wants to see you," the man said, before quickly darting his eyes toward Amanda. "Now."

It clearly wasn't a question, but there was no force behind the command. Amanda expected Judy to ignore him, maybe with some snarky retort. She was surprised to see her aunt's shoulders droop in resignation.

"Okay," she muttered under her breath, before ushering Amanda into the elevator.

They rode all the way up to the top floor, which didn't help Amanda's queasy stomach. She leaned lightly against the elevator wall, trying to remember the healing touch of the woman in Terra-V. *What had she done?* Amanda wondered. *How had her simple touch made this sickness go away?*

When they finally stepped out of the elevator, Amanda was left in a posh waiting room while the thin man led Judy through another set of double doors. He soon came back out to sit behind a cluttered desk. He didn't seem keen on conversation, which suited Amanda just fine. She sat in her armchair and buried her face in her hands. The travel sickness she felt now was nothing compared to her round trip to Terra-V, but her body still felt weary and shaky from the experience.

Amanda lost all sense of time as she waited. It was enough to inhabit the blissful darkness behind her closed eyes and feel the frayed nerves throughout her body releasing their electric tension. After a while, her body settled enough for her mind to feel more aware of her surroundings. She could hear the tap of the thin man's typing. She could see the gleam of the warm hardwood floor between her cracked fingers. Her entire body settled more heavily and easily into the armchair.

The sound of raised voices caught her attention.

"That is not your decision!" A deep voice boomed from behind the double doors.

"And it's not yours either!" Judy shouted back with equal passion.

One of the doors jerked open. Judy stormed out, then turned back toward whomever remained in the room.

"It's a decision for the High Council," she continued briskly, "and I will appeal your ruling."

She crossed quickly toward the elevator, calling Amanda to her side, but they had nowhere to go until the elevator arrived.

The man who followed Judy into the waiting area was familiar to Amanda, though she couldn't immediately place him. He was tall and imposing with gray hair and a trim beard. His dark suit and a patterned blue tie added to his dignified appearance. When he opened his mouth to speak, Amanda recognized him as the man from the house. The one who had been about to say something when she'd woken up in Aunt Judy's hotel room.

"She's fourteen years old," he told Judy, ignoring Amanda and the thin man who now stood by his desk.

"Almost fifteen," Amanda corrected automatically.

Judy smirked her way, but the older man continued to act as if Amanda were not there. Given the strangeness of her recent circumstances, Amanda considered whether she might actually be invisible. But that only happened in the house, she reminded herself. If she could learn how to control her visibility.

Amanda's head continued to pound.

"She's a psychic traveler," Judy told the man. "It's her ability that matters, not her age."

He finally looked toward Amanda, assessing her at a glance.

"We're not equipped for a child's needs."

Amanda was getting tired of being called a *child*. Fifteen was closer to an adult than a child. She could cook for herself, clean for herself, ride the bus around town. She did more to help her mom than most of the kids she knew, and she was used to adults commenting on how grown-up and responsible she was for her age. Yet here was a man she'd never met calling her a child!

"I'm equipped to train her," Judy shot back. "And we can adapt for the rest."

"No." The man shook his head firmly. "It can wait until she's older."

The elevator doors opened, but Judy let them close without giving up her ground. She took a step closer to him and Amanda was surprised to see him shrink away.

"You know how important she may be."

Amanda had to strain to hear her aunt's whispered words, and she wasn't sure she'd heard them correctly. *Why would she be any more important than any other traveler?*

"No." The shaking of his head picked up speed. "No, no, no. That's nothing but conjecture. I deal in facts and facts only."

"Fine." Judy pressed the elevator call button again. "We'll see what the High Council has to say."

The elevator doors opened more quickly this time. As they rode back down to the lobby, Amanda bit her lip, resisting the urge to ask for answers. She knew Aunt Judy would explain when she was ready.

§

The seriousness of her situation hadn't sunk in when Aunt Judy first admitted to being forbidden to train Amanda. *Temporarily forbidden,* she'd clarified with a smile that had wiped away Amanda's concern. She'd explained how some people, including Director Alvarsson, were uneasy about a teenager developing psychic travel abilities. But he had many outdated ideas, according to her aunt, and the decision wasn't up to him. The case would be presented to something called the High Council, and Judy was confident they would approve Amanda's training.

"This is just a bump in the road," she had insisted. "A small delay."

By Friday, five days had passed without another visit from her aunt. Amanda had texted her daily and received variations on the same reply: *No news yet, be in touch soon.*

When Amanda complained to her mom, she was reminded that Aunt Judy couldn't visit them every day when she had work to do with her client.

"She'll be here for your birthday on Saturday," Patty reassured.

There was no way for Amanda to explain that *she* was the client Aunt Judy was supposed to be helping, so she stomped off in a sulk.

Amanda went back to visiting the house on her own. She wandered around the empty rooms aimlessly. She willed her aunt to appear in the house with her, but she never did.

At times, Amanda remembered the blond knight, and his worried frown as he stood by the piano. But he never made an appearance either. As far as Amanda could tell, she was the only traveler in the house. Whether that was because she didn't want to be seen or because there was actually no one else there was a mystery.

Her mood grew darker with each passing day. Drew encouraged her to be patient, but that only made her feel worse. *He can't understand,* she thought morosely. Aunt Judy had been right. Normals couldn't understand what it meant to be a psychic traveler.

As Amanda became more anxious, Trina's mood soared. By Friday afternoon, she was giddy about going to the football game, and every smile, every giggle, irritated Amanda. Spending the night after the game, meant Trina riding the bus home from school with Amanda and Drew. Wanting to make things easier on Amanda, Drew turned on an uncharacteristic charm. He teased. He told joke. He laughed at everything Trina said.

Amanda felt sick by the time they got off the bus.

She didn't think the day could get worse until her mom said Chad would be driving them to the game.

"I'm sorry, Amanda," Patty said from her desk. "There's a rush on this transcription and a bonus if I can finish it tonight. I can't afford to pass that up."

"But you promised." Amanda was embarrassed by the whine in her own voice.

"I know," Patty frowned. "It's a short ride and Chad is just driving you. It's not like he's staying to watch the game with you."

"Oh, I don't know," Chad interrupted, tossing his keys from one hand to the other. "She's not fifteen yet, maybe I should stay and chaperone."

His wink nearly pushed Amanda over the edge, until Trina broke up laughing, as if Chad had told the most amazing joke she'd ever heard.

Amanda noticed it was the same high-pitched, overly loud laugh Trina had used with Drew on the bus. It made her think Trina was more nervous than she let on, and the thought brought a wave of compassion. Amanda pushed aside her own bad mood and decided to make the best of the evening.

Drew was right. Aunt Judy was doing the best she could. She would be back to resume Amanda's training as soon as she possibly could.

Yet later that night, as the game dragged on past halftime, the worry crept back into Amanda's heart.

They were sitting at the very top of the bleachers with a large group of freshmen students, including Drew and his friends. Trina and the others were cheering another touchdown, while the marching band struck up the school fight song.

The dark sky had a white glow from the field lights, and the fall air felt crisp against her skin. All around her, people were happy and having fun.

Under different circumstances, Amanda might have enjoyed the excitement of the game. Instead, she felt detached and alone. She waited until Drew and Trina were distracted by the action on the field, then hurried down the metal steps to walk around by herself.

After circling the football field, and navigating her way around clusters of happy teenagers, Amanda slipped into a quiet, shadowy place under the bleachers. She sat on the cold, hard grass and leaned against a metal support beam. The band played a brassy tune and feet stomped overhead. Between the rows of seats, Amanda could see glimpses of the playing field. The announcer shouted something about a twenty-yard gain, and Amanda thought of a proximity zone. *A point extending in a twenty-yard radius, holding space where a proximal door could appear.*

Letting the field blur in front of her eyes, Amanda stepped into the dusty attic.

The second door from the left beckoned.

Amanda stepped close enough to rest her forehead on its rough, wooden surface. She felt warmth through the door as she pictured the purple meadow on the other side. Her hand itched to turn the doorknob. She could see the woman from Terra-V looking at her with an unlimited well of kindness. She could feel the soothing vibration of the woman's light touch spreading throughout her body.

"You shouldn't be here."

Amanda kept her forehead on the door, even as her shoulders tensed. She recognized that voice. The last time she'd heard it, it had been shouting at her across the purple meadow. Calling for her to stop, to wait, to come back.

Hearing the voice now, Amanda mentally connected it to the worried expression the knight had worn as he'd stood by the piano. *He was trying to help,* she realized. *He was afraid I'd be stranded in Terra-V.*

"I know."

Amanda turned to face the blond man and saw he was again dressed in chainmail and a blue tunic. It was odd but somehow comforting.

"We haven't really met," he offered without a smile. "I'm Cameron."

"Amanda," she returned, then felt like an idiot. *He already knows who I am.*

"Hi, Amanda." Cameron leaned against the same covered chair that had once been Amanda's hiding place. "What are you doing here?"

"Looking for my aunt," Amanda answered quickly, though it wasn't entirely true.

"Not sneaking back to Terra-V?"

"No." Amanda had heard a warning in his voice, but she also sensed an understanding.

"Why are you dressed like that?"

"It's part of my job," Cameron answered with ease.

"You're a knight?"

"Something like that."

Amanda considered his answer, fleetingly questioning whether he could be *from* Terra-V before realizing he looked nothing like the woman with the iridescent skin and willowy limbs. He looked human. He also spoke English. But so had the woman from Terra-V.

"Amanda?"

Drew's voice echoed through Amanda's head. She turned quickly, searching the attic, but not seeing any trace of him.

"What's wrong?" Cameron narrowed his eyes.

"Amanda?" Drew sounded more insistent.

"I can hear my friend… he's calling my name." Amanda turned her head from side-to-side, checking every inch of the space around her. He sounded so close.

"He's not here." Cameron stepped closer, speaking urgently. "You need to go back."

"No, I can hear him… he's right…"

Drew crouched in front of Amanda.

She blinked again and again, letting the features of his face become clearer with each flicker.

She turned her head slowly, checking out her shadowy surroundings. They were under the bleachers. A loud cheer echoed from above as the band played the school fight song. Again.

"Where did you go?" Drew's voice was soft, worried.

"Nowhere," Amanda sighed. "I'm not going anywhere."

CHAPTER 9
A HEARING AND A REVELATION

"You're the first of us to turn fifteen," Trina told Amanda, as if it were a fact she didn't already know. "You'll be the first to turn sixteen and the first to drive."

"I guess." Amanda yawned.

They were still nestled under their covers. Amanda in her own bed, Trina on the single air mattress set up in the middle of Amanda's bedroom floor.

"Izzy said she'd take me out driving, once I get my permit."

"Mm, hmm." Amanda burrowed deeper in her covers. Sixteen seemed so far away. There was no need to worry about driving now. Beside, she secretly doubted Trina's sister would teach her to drive. Izzy often made big promises, until something better came along.

"Think you'll have a party next year?"

Birthday parties were big in Trina's family. Year after year, her parents had invited Trina's entire homeroom to her parties. It was at one of those parties when Trina decided to make Amanda her best friend.

"Nope." Amanda stretched her arms overhead, thinking about breakfast. "I'm happy with pizza and cake."

"And Drew?"

Amanda stopped mid-stretch.

"And a few friends," she corrected curtly.

They were both quiet then. Amanda willed Trina to drop her prodding about Drew and just be *normal* about things for once. She eyed her phone sitting on her desk across the room and hoped Aunt Judy had texted while they were asleep.

"You're really not going to tell me, are you?" Trina sounded more resigned than annoyed. "About where you and Drew disappeared to together?"

Amanda sighed and pushed herself up to a seat.

"We did not disappear together. I went to the bathroom and ran into him on my way back to the bleachers."

"Okay." Trina sounded unconvinced, which irritated Amanda more than she wanted to admit. Partially because she was lying, but also because she didn't owe Trina an explanation for every little second of her time.

Amanda climbed out of bed and skirted Trina's mattress to get to her phone. No messages. When she turned around, Trina was studying her disappointed expression with a knowing look. Amanda rolled her eyes and went to brush her teeth.

She was still in the bathroom when a nagging, insistent thought pushed into her mind. It was a hazy image of her aunt sitting on the canopied bed in the house's blue-themed bedroom. *Amanda.* Her aunt's voice echoed through her mind. After the fifth repetition, Amanda sat on the edge of the bathtub and let her eyes go out of focus.

Aunt Judy sat on the blue-covered bed. Her hair was pulled back in a messy ponytail and she looked tired. She wore a pair of gray sweatpants and a pink hoodie.

"How did you do that?" Amanda recalled how she'd heard Drew when she was in the house during the game.

"Later." Judy waved off the question as another mystery to be explained later. "We have plans to make."

Amanda sat on the bed beside her.

"About my training?"

"The High Council wants to meet with you. Today, at noon. I pushed for tomorrow, but then Alvarsson, the Director, tried to use that as proof that you don't have enough freedom to be part of the Society. You know, because you are a minor and under your mom's parental control. As if adult travelers never have conflicts to work around!"

The anger in her outburst showed how tense these last few days had been.

"It's okay, though," Judy resumed more calmly. "Your birthday lunch is at one, and I doubt the hearing will last more than an hour. We'll tell your mom I want to take you out for a quick shopping trip before."

"About that," Amanda faltered. "Trina's already here. She spent the night, and I can't just leave her here before the party. Not without it being really weird."

Judy's eyes fluttered shut and her slow breath suggested she was counting to ten. It was the same thing her mom did when Amanda said something especially annoying.

Amanda worried that maybe she didn't have enough freedom to manage the double life of a Society traveler. Unless…?

"I can get Drew to distract Trina." She suggested, hoping to prove she was up to the challenge. Judy frowned. She didn't like the idea of Drew being involved any more than he had been, but it was a plan that could work.

Amanda and Trina went down to the party room around eleven. It wasn't where Amanda's birthday lunch would be, but it was a good, parent-free place to hang out. Amanda had texted Drew about the plan while Trina was in the shower, and he'd beaten them there.

When they walked in, they saw a 500-piece jigsaw puzzle from the game cabinet scattered across one of the tables. Drew held up the box to show a picture of kittens in a wicker basket.

"Wanna see how many pieces are actually in here?"

Most of the puzzles in the game cabinet had pieces that were missing or mixed into the wrong boxes. Before their friendship's middle school hiatus, Amanda and Drew had once discovered three pieces of blue sky in a puzzle comprised entirely of teddy bears. They'd never found the puzzle where that blue sky belonged.

Trina shrugged as she walked over to the table, and Amanda was surprised to see a faint blush on her cheeks. She couldn't imagine anyone being nervous around Drew. But then she remembered the times in middle school when she'd loitered in the apartment lobby, out-of-sight, waiting for him to walk a minute or two ahead of her before she left for school alone.

Shaking away the awkward memory, Amanda followed Trina to the table. It was just Drew, she told herself, again wishing Trina would just be normal.

As they settled into chairs, Amanda had second thoughts about slipping away for an hour. What would Trina say when she didn't come back for so long? But then Drew launched into a steady stream of conversation, entertaining Trina just as he had on the bus. Trina relaxed, and Amanda felt both relieved and uneasy.

About forty-five minutes later, Amanda's phone buzzed with a text from Aunt Judy. It was time.

"Oh, geez." Amanda tried to sound natural. "Grandma's on the phone and Mom wants me to go talk to her."

She was proud of the excuse, but just Trina waved Amanda away with an offhand *okay*. She was busy laughing at Drew's story in that loud, high-pitched way that set Amanda's teeth on edge.

As she left the room, Amanda glanced into the library and her stomach sank. Mr. Rudowski was there, reading a book and running his free hand over his thick mustache. She'd thought the library would be a good place to make their exit. But when she met Judy in the lobby, her aunt was unconcerned. The man behind the front desk quietly led them through a door and into a storage room. As he closed them in, Amanda recalled how he'd shown up at the building just before Aunt Judy's visit.

"Wait! He's a traveler?"

"We position travelers where they may be useful," Judy answered shortly, handing Amanda a white tablet and urging her to hurry. Amanda frowned at the pill. She didn't like being pulled along without answers, but she set the tablet on her tongue and kept her irritation to herself.

When Amanda and Judy stepped into the Chicago headquarters, the atrium was nearly empty. One woman stepped through another door moments after they entered, taking no notice of their appearance. They passed only a few people on their way to the elevators and Amanda was surprised, despite it being a Saturday.

"I expected another crowd," Amanda confided once they were alone in the elevator.

"The meeting time was kept private." Judy watched the numbers above the elevator doors. "That's partly why they wanted it on a Saturday."

Amanda relaxed a litte. Meeting the High Council was nerve-racking enough, especially with Director Alvarsson set against her training. She didn't need more strangers gawking at her. On the other hand... she wondered if drawing a crowd would have somehow shown support for her training from the other travelers.

They stepped out of the elevator and followed a winding hallway to a wide conference room with a frosted glass door. Amanda had expected something more formal, like a TV courtroom, but this was a simple room. A rectangular table filled the space, with one of its longest sides facing the door. Seven people sat along the far side of the table, studying Amanda and Judy intently. Two empty chairs waited across from them, close to the door. Director Alvarsson sat alone at one short end of the table. His assistant sat at a small desk on the opposite side of the room, ready to take notes on his laptop.

Amanda recognized some of the High Council members from the living room on the night she'd been surrounded by the crowd of travelers. Knowing they'd seen her flee in fear was mortifying, but defiant anger quickly replaced Amanda's embarrassment. Of course she'd fled, she thought defensively, anyone would have been overwhelmed in that situation.

Director Alvarsson stood up to greet them, smiling graciously, as if they were old friends.

"Amanda." He reached out, shaking her hand before turning to her aunt. "Judy. Thank you for joining us on such short notice. I'm sure it was difficult to get away."

"It's fine," Amanda answered, wishing her voice didn't sound so small.

"We're happy to meet you, Amanda." The woman at the center of the table smiled warmly. "Please have a seat."

Amanda expected the council members to introduce themselves, but they didn't.

"You're fifteen today?" The same woman asked. "Happy birthday."

"Thank you." Amanda spoke around the lump that had formed in her throat.

The woman's eyes softened in sympathy.

"Fifteen. This must be such an overwhelming experience for you."

It was overwhelming, Amanda thought, but not in the way this older, self-assured woman made it sound. As if it was too much for a girl her age. Amanda could sense her aunt tensing by her side, getting ready to reply. Amanda hurried to speak first.

"Not really." She cleared her throat. "It's more of a relief than anything else."

"A relief?"

Amanda saw two council members lean in and another tilt her head thoughtfully.

"Yeah, well, I'd been wandering through the house for so long. And I somehow knew it was more than a normal daydream, even if I didn't know why or who to ask about it. So... yeah. Finally getting some answers is a relief."

Several council members nodded, remembering their own early experiences with psychic travel. The woman in the center lost her smile as she shuffled a stack of papers. Amanda chanced a quick glance at her aunt and Judy gave her a proud wink.

"We can understand that," the woman resumed briskly, "but there is more to our society than simply providing answers for those with psychic abilities. We also have to ensure that our members understand *their* responsibilities and place in our world. We have strict rules, for all of our safety, and those rules must be carefully followed."

Amanda squirmed in her seat. She couldn't be held responsible for breaking rules before she'd even learned what they were, could she?

"*The Sheltering Arms of the Tuntum Trees*," the woman read from a piece of paper at the top of her pile. "That is a short story you wrote? And turned in as a homework assignment?"

"How did you—?"

"Madam Ellis," Judy interrupted Amanda. "That was written before Amanda traveled to Terra-V Before she had any idea that the house, and the door she looked through, were anything more than a daydream."

"Didn't Amanda just testify that she'd always suspected it was more than a daydream?" Director Alvarsson asked mildly.

"Oh, please," Judy scoffed, showing her typical spirit, before addressing the council again. "You can't fault Amanda for things that happened before she understood what she was doing?"

"Such as an unauthorized visit to *Terra Violavita?*"

Amanda blinked at the foreign-sounding name before concluding it was an official term for Terra-V.

"Yes." Judy spoke through lightly clenched teeth. "Amanda couldn't have known what would happen if she stepped through a door in what seemed to be a daydream."

She shot a look at Director Alvarsson before adding, "Even if it was a very vivid, unusual daydream."

"I suppose," Madam Ellis agreed, though without much conviction. "Still, one could argue her visit suggests a lack of self-control."

"A lack of self-control?" Judy challenged. "It takes strength and courage to travel the first time, and perhaps enhanced abilities."

A murmur rippled across the table.

"It is rare," Madam Ellis granted, ignoring the other coucil members' unsettled mutterings. "Usually there is internal resistance to that sort of exploration, especially without training. Those few who have pushed through on their own have often proven to be our more reckless adventurers."

"And some of our strongest assets," Judy countered.

Tension crackled across the table. Amanda realized she was missing some unspoken meaning in their debate.

While she still held the floor, Judy pulled a sealed petri dish from her pocket and held it up for everyone to see. Amanda recognized strands of purple grass and smears of dark violet mud.

The silence in the room was absolute.

"I'm sure your investigation turned up this as well?"

Judy passed the dish across the table. Madam Ellis refused to look at it, even as everyone else in the room leaned in for a better view.

"You brought this sample back?" She asked Amanda, narrowing her eyes. "By yourself?"

"Yes." Amanda was confused by their reaction. "It was stuck on my shoes."

"On her shoes!" The other council members were talking among themselves. *"On her first trip! And Alone! Before she even knew!"*

The buzz in the room grew. Amanda's eyes ached and her whole body trembled. From a distance, she heard the councilwoman calling for quiet. The room was shifting, dimming. The last thing Amanda saw was Director Alvarsson's alarmed expression as he studied her flushed face.

And then everything went dark.

§

"Amanda! Amanda!"

She heard her name and felt the pressure of firm hands on her shoulders.

There it was again. That pungent scent that settled her stomach and slowed the spinning in her head. Someone pressed a cold cloth against the back of her neck.

When she opened her eyes, Amanda saw Aunt Judy hovering above, her face white with worry. Director Alvarsson was next to her, holding the cloth against her neck and nodding his head in small, compassionate bobs. Amanda realized she was on the floor. They were still in the conference room. As Aunt Judy and the director helped her to her feet, Amanda saw the entire High Council standing to watch the drama unfold. Amanda sat gingerly, insisting she was fine.

"Just dizzy for a second," she explained weakly, before closing her eyes to hold back tears. This was worse than fading out of the house in front of them, she thought. It was her body giving out. A clear sign that she wasn't ready for this, no matter what she might say.

The High Council gradually retook their seats. Director Alvarsson sat as well. Judy pulled her own chair closer to Amanda, running a hand lightly over her niece's back.

"*It is hard on the system, at first.*" Amanda heard voices talking around her. "*And without training... But with practice... Unless she needs more time before... We've never had... Maybe it's different when...*"

She wanted to listen, but Amanda was preoccupied with the voice in her own head. The one telling her she had failed. The council wouldn't let her be trained. Not after this. She'd have to wait until she was older. But how old? Eighteen? Or twenty-one? Surely, they wouldn't make her wait that long! Maybe when she was sixteen?

"Amanda?" Judy's voice cut through the worried thoughts, and Amanda opened her eyes. The council had been quietly conferring among themselves and were ready to respond.

"Amanda." Madam Ellis' sad smile said it all. Amanda studied her hands as the councilwoman droned on.

"Given the unusual circumstances, and the stressful nature of exploring one's developing abilities, we feel it would be best to limit your training at this time. We do wish to encourage your abilities, but with caution and care for your own safety.

"For now, your aunt may teach you about our society and meet with you in the shared mindspace of the house, as you've already experienced. However, you are not authorized for full psychic travel at this time. You will not open *any* doors in the house. You will not be taught about what may reside beyond those doors. We will revisit this matter in six months."

Amanda nodded numbly. *Six months?* It wasn't as long as she'd feared, but it felt like a lifetime. In her mind, Amanda saw the twisting trunks of the tuntum trees, gradually sinking as their boughs formed a protective barrier around the purple meadow. She heard their steady thrum. *Tuntum. Tuntum.* She saw the encouraging grin and gleaming violet eyes of the woman she had met there. The woman who had called her American and taken away her pain. Could she survive six months without going back to Terra-V? Without even learning more about that magical place?

There was a sharp knock.

The conference room door opened.

Amanda turned to see Cameron, the knight of her dream world, sweep into the room.

"I have news from Terra-V," Cameron told them gravely. "News you need to hear before you make any decisions."

§

"This is preposterous!" Director Alvarsson was on his feet, arguing against the revelation Cameron had just shared.

"She's not ready!" Madam Ellis insisted, though many on the council seemed less sure of their earlier decision.

"Then we'll get her ready," Cameron replied calmly.

Amanda watched them all, afraid to say a word. Judy seemed similarly restrained, waiting to see how this would play out. Or maybe still making sense of what Cameron had revealed.

"Can't you explain this… this *mistake* to the Vherahna?" Cameron smirked at the Director.

"Clearly you've never met the Vherahna." He spoke with the authority of experience.

Director Alvarsson shook his head, bringing one hand to cradle his bearded chin.

"We need that relationship," he said to no one in particular. Everyone in the room understood the truth of his words. Everyone except Amanda.

"Can we put them off for a while?" One of the council members asked hopefully. "For six months? Or a year?"

Cameron shook his head grimly.

"I can hold them off a month, at most, as we make our plans."

"And we can't send someone else?" Another council member ventured.

Cameron looked at Amanda. She felt every other pair of eyes follow.

"No," he answered shortly. "Alira met Amanda and believes she alone is the answer to their most sacred prophecy. They won't accept anyone else."

Amanda shrank in her chair.

"Amanda, what did you say to Alira?" Judy prompted gently.

"Um." Amanda turned toward her aunt, speaking softly. "Alira was the woman in Terra-V?"

Someone behind her groaned softly.

"Yes," Judy confirmed, resting her palms on Amanda's knees to keep her from swiveling the chair away. "What did you say to her? Exactly?"

Amanda bit her lower lip, trying to remember anything beyond the soothing vibration of the woman's healing energy. "I don't know. It wasn't much. She said I was young, and uh, I said I was American, and she thought that was my name. I think. But then I felt sick and she did… something. She hummed a song or something that made me better. And I think that was it.

"I didn't really think it was real," Amanda added pleadingly. "I thought I was dreaming."

"And you told her that." Cameron was already nodding, confirming a suspicion. "That's why they think you're the *waking dreamer* they've been waiting for."

"The waking dreamer?" Judy asked before anyone else had a chance.

"It's part of the prophecy. It says a *waking dreamer* will lead them on a sacred journey."

"They want Amanda to lead them?" Judy's concern deepened. "Beyond the trees?"

"It would be a short journey," Cameron reassured, speaking to Judy directly as if she were the only one in the room. "And Amanda wouldn't be alone. I would be with her the entire time, along with a tactical team to keep everyone safe. I wouldn't let anything happen to her."

"You want to do this?" Madam Ellis asked incredulously.

Cameron considered his words.

"This quest may be as beneficial to us as it is to the Vherahna."

"And why is that?" Director Alvarsson sounded impatient and slightly sarcastic.

Cameron widened his stance and let his eyes sweep across the room before answering.

"For one thing, this sacred prophecy was by Edmund Robinson."

"Edmund…? A prophecy by Edmund… When did he…? I thought it was a Vherahna prophecy… But could it mean…? And for it to be her… But you don't think…?"

Amanda only caught snippets of the discussions that had broken out around the table. The energy in the room pulsed with speculation, and the excited chatter only stoked the anxiety churning through Amanda's body. She was still making sense of the basics. The woman she met was part of an alien race. *The Vherahna.*

"For another thing." Cameron's clear voice cut through the din. "We still don't know what happened to—"

"No!" Director Alvarsson insisted, shaking his head. "We know what happened to him. Despite the rumors."

"Do we?" Cameron rushed on quickly, "Terra-V is the last place he was seen. Officially."

"Enough." Madam Ellis flashed her eyes from Amanda to Cameron. "This is not the appropriate forum for that debate."

Cameron also glanced at Amanda before returning a stiff nod of agreement.

"All right." Director Alvarsson dropped his arms by his sides. "We have a lot to discuss. Amanda, you can go for now. And, Judy, we'll be in touch soon."

As Amanda stepped out of the room, her head swam with questions and possibilities. *Who was Edmund Robinson? What had happened to him? And would they really let her travel because she fit some prophecy he'd made a million years ago?* Amanda told herself nothing had been decided yet. That as far as she knew, her sentence to six-months of limited training would hold. That it was too soon to get her hopes up. Yet she felt lighter. Happier.

There was one thought repeating in her mind: *I'm going back to Terra-V.*

CHAPTER 10
AFTER THE PARTY

It was nearly one o-clock when Amanda and Judy left the hearing. While Amanda was full of questions, Judy cared more about hurrying back for Amanda's birthday party.

"We can't afford to upset your mom now!" she insisted while jogging through the PTS front lobby and into the proximity zone. "Come on!"

When a door to the house appeared, Judy looped her arm through Amanda's and pulled them both through.

The rapid journey did nothing to help Amanda's travel sickness. She felt green as she wobbled back into the party room, doubting whether her body *could* handle a trip back to Terra-V. But the Vherahna were in Terra-V, Amanda reminded herself, silently rolling the name she'd learned over her tongue. *Alira.*

Amanda pictured Alira's angular features and long limbs as she stood with her back to a row of twisting, purple trees. *Tuntum. Tuntum.* She imagined the healing vibration of her song, longing for it to settle her frazzled nerves. She longed to see more of the violet world, too. Exploring *beyond the trees*, as Aunt Judy had said.

Drew and Trina were still sitting at the game table, though they hadn't made much progress on the puzzle. They stopped talking when Amanda walked in, and Drew quickly stood up.

"Amanda!" He rubbed his palms on his jeans, shifted from one foot to the other, then buried both hands in his pockets. "How was the, uh, call? With your grandma?"

"Fine," Amanda answered briefly.

She couldn't talk about the hearing in front of Trina and her head hurt too much to come up with a coded answer for Drew. She sat down heavily and rubbed her temples, breathing through the nausea that was building in subtle waves.

"Are you okay?" Trina sounded concerned but impatient. Her bright, darting eyes bothered Amanda, but she didn't have the energy to care.

"It didn't go well?" Drew moved closer, hovering over Amanda. "The, uh, call with your grandma?"

"No, it's not that." Amanda shook her head, then instantly regretted the dizzying movement. She couldn't tell Drew it was the travel that was making her sick, not with Trina sitting beside them. Though he should already know that, she thought irritably. If he'd listened to what she'd told him about her travel sickness before.

"Am I late?"

Judy breezed into the room carrying a small, brightly wrapped present and a shiny purple balloon. Trina and

Drew turned toward her, while Amanda lowered her head into her hands. "Amanda, what's wrong?"

The question further annoyed Amanda, though she knew it was asked for Trina's benefit.

"Just a headache," she mumbled, without uncovering her eyes.

"This will help!" Judy leaned close enough to waft her glass vial under Amanda's covered face. One quick pass and Amanda felt her shoulders soften. After a second pass, she felt well enough to lift her head, though the sickness hadn't been entirely erased.

Judy winked toward Trina, "Essential oils! They do wonders!"

She then started chatting with Trina, asking if she remembered when they'd met a few years ago. It was during a visit when Trina had come out with them for ice cream. *Or was it frozen yogurt?*

Their voices were light, unbothered by Amanda's apparent misery. Amanda slumped back in her chair. She was preparing to shoot Drew a snarky comment, when his hand grazed her upper back, just above her shirt's scooped neckline. He shifted away quickly but kept his hand on Amanda's chair. Close enough to raise the hairs on the back of her neck.

Amanda forgot what she was about to say. Her body felt hollow, tingling with a rush of energy. Was it the glass vial? It felt similar to the wordless joy she'd felt in Terra-V, and Amanda flashed again to the shimmering woman in the purple field. *Alira.* Who *was* she? And who did she think Amanda might be?

"We should get upstairs." Judy broke into Amanda's thoughts. "It's after one."

"Oh, yeah, your mom's been texting!" Drew pulled Amanda's phone from his pocket but froze halfway between handing it to Amanda.

He glanced toward Trina. "You left it here when you went upstairs. And I saw your mom— I mean, your aunt— texting earlier. When you were gone... with your mom. And then your mom texted just a minute ago. When you had your head down."

Amanda pressed her lips together and widened her eyes at Drew. He was usually a better liar, she thought, remembering the scrapes they'd gotten out of as kids. As she reached for her phone, a question nagged. *Were there times when Drew had lied to her?*

Judy and Trina continued to talk all the way upstairs. While they were in the elevator, Amanda checked her phone. She saw texts from her mom asking if she'd heard from Aunt Judy and reminding her to come up at one. There was a return *"Okay!"* message that Drew must have sent while she was gone.

Amanda tried to catch Drew's eye, to thank him for covering, but he was biting one finger while staring at the elevator doors. There was something different about him, and Amanda couldn't tell what had changed.

Back in the apartment, Amanda's birthday party was simple: pizza, cake, and presents with her family and friends. And Chad.

As she looked at the fifteen tiny candles glowing on her vanilla cake, Amanda tried to be grateful for this low-key party. It was the kind of celebrating she preferred—but without Chad's obnoxiously loud singing and tasteless comments. Her mom snapped at him for an inappropriate joke about whether Amanda was too old, or not old enough, for a birthday spanking. Snapping at him was good, Amanda told herself grudgingly, but it wasn't enough. Her mom was still the reason he was there at all.

Aunt Judy had missed that exchange, as she quietly sat with her eyes only slightly out of focus.

That was lucky for Chad, Amanda thought.

Studying the flickering candles, Amanda knew she could wish for whatever she wanted. A better job for her mom. Or for Chad to go away forever. That idea made her chest pound with hopeful excitement. Until an even better idea filtered in. *Tuntum. Tuntum.*

Amanda's mind was back in Terra-V. She could feel purple bark beneath her hands and hear the soft whooshing of a tree's warm sap. *Tuntum. Tuntum.*

She closed her eyes and made her birthday wish.

§

Mr. Hewlett called Amanda up to his desk during their quiet reading time. She and Trina had been caught passing notes at the beginning of class, and it didn't seem fair that he was singling her out again.

Though it was fitting for the day she was having. The weekend had passed without an answer from the High Council. The waiting had triggered stress acne along her jawline, and it felt like everyone in the hallway had been staring and whispering about her.

On top of all that, Trina had come to class mad at her and wouldn't tell her why.

Amanda dragged her feet, thinking about Trina's bad mood. She'd seemed fine before school, but when they'd met up in English, Trina wouldn't even look at Amanda. She'd even shifted her desk a few inches away to show she couldn't stand to be near her.

When Amanda had passed a note asking what was wrong, Trina wrote back, *"Like you don't already know."*

Amanda had tried again, swearing that she didn't know. She watched Trina scribble a response and fold it in a square. That's when Mr. Hewlett had stepped in to take the note out of her hand.

"I applaud your old school efforts at actually writing with pen and paper." Mr. Hewlett lifted the tightly folded note for the class to see. "However, passed notes are just as unwelcome as cellphones in my classroom. Which you already know by now."

He'd taken Trina's note with him, and Amanda saw no sign of it when she reached his desk.

"How are you getting on with your story?"

Mr. Hewlett's casual question and friendly attitude caught Amanda off guard.

"My story?"

"The Sheltering Arms of the Tuntum Trees," Mr. Hewlett clarified, using the whispery, lilting voice he reserved for reading poetry. "You were going to expand on it? For the writing contest?"

With each sentence, his expression shifted from happy expectation to perplexed concern.

"If you're having trouble with it," he guessed, "I'm happy to help."

"Oh, uh, no." Amanda twined her fingers, remembering the look on Madam Ellis' face when she'd asked about the story. Amanda didn't know how the High Council knew about her homework assignments, but Judy had once said travelers were placed where they may be useful.

Could Mr. Hewlett be a traveler? Amanda shook off the thought.

"I've decided not to do that," she admitted, talking to Mr. Hewlett's chin. He offered his help again, telling Amanda she may not want to waste this opportunity.

"Thanks, but I'm just not that interested in writing." Amanda glanced up long enough to see the disappointment etched across her teacher's face. He couldn't be a traveler, she reasoned, or he would know why she shouldn't write this story.

"I'm really more of a math person," she added weakly, now looking at his tie.

"I see." He sounded genuinely hurt.

Amanda's eyes flew back to his face.

"It's not you," she babbled nervously. "Your class is great! I'm just more of a reader than a writer, and even then, I'm—"

"More of a math person," Mr. Hewlett finished her sentence with a resigned sigh.

"Yeah."

"Is there any other reason?"

Amanda hesitated. There *was* a reason. A good reason. But if she told her English teacher that submitting her short story to a local contest could expose her secret thought walking ability—and jeopardize the ultra-secret Psychic Traveler Society she'd recently joined—he'd think she was crazy. Or he'd laugh and say she had the imagination of a writer.

"I'm just not that interested in writing," she repeated dully.

Mr. Hewlett nodded slowly.

"Friends are important, Amanda." He'd shifted to that overly sympathetic voice adults use when *relating* to teen-agers. "But I hope you'll consider your priorities carefully when making decisions that could affect your future."

That's what I'm doing! Amanda longed to tell him, but she didn't.

§

After the final bell, Amanda hurried to track down Trina outside the school entrance. There were only a few minutes before she'd have to catch her bus. She had no time to waste and jumped right in.

"What is your problem?"

"My problem?" Trina put one hand on her hip and pointed at Amanda with the other. "You're my problem."

Amanda's mouth dropped open. A group of passing students gawked at them, then giggled and whispered as they walked on.

"Don't play dumb with me." Trina crossed her arms over her chest.

The day was overcast, and a brittle breeze stung their cheeks. Amanda shook her head helplessly. She could see her bus in the distance. Drew waved at her from his place in line, but she ignored him.

"Trey saw you," Trina accused angrily. "He saw you and Drew coming out from under the bleachers. After you were making out, or whatever."

"What?"

A horn sounded in the distance. Amanda saw that Drew and the others had gotten onto their bus and the door had closed.

"Don't you have to go?" Trina asked, turning to see the last few kids hurrying to climb on buses.

Amanda swallowed over a lump in her throat.

"Screw that," she told Trina. "This is more important!"

"Go catch your bus!" Trina insisted, but the line of buses had already begun inching away from the school. The wind blew Trina's curls over her face, making her uncross her arms to tuck the stray hair back behind her ear.

"No."

Amanda took a few steps back to lean against the low brick wall near the school entrance. More than ever, she wished for Aunt Judy's magic glass vial to calm her mind and soothe her nausea. She pictured Drew and his friends, shoving and laughing as they walked through the halls. Is that what they'd been thinking about her and Drew since school started? Is that what Drew had let them think?

"Trina, it's not—" Amanda could hardly get the words out. "That's not true! Didn't Drew say it wasn't true?"

Trina glared, then softened.

"I don't know." She leaned against the wall beside Amanda.

A few kids straggled out of the building, heading toward the cars that were now waiting where the buses had been. Some looked their way before rushing past. Amanda was sure they all knew. They all believed Trey's lies without a second thought. Just like Trina had.

"I haven't asked Drew about it," Trina confessed.

The raw embarrassment in her voice made Amanda wonder why Trina was this upset about a rumor that didn't concern her. Unless it did. Amanda remembered how Drew and Trina had jumped apart when she'd walked in on them in the party room. She remembered Drew's fidgeting and stammering.

"Uh, Trina." Amanda felt her own embarrassment deepen. "Is there something…? Are you and Drew…?"

She didn't know what to ask.

"Sort of." Trina smiled weakly, then burst into tears.

"I don't know!" she added with an anguished sob. "I've liked Trey for so long, but then Drew was so sweet on the bus to your place. And at the game. And then, when we were alone…"

Amanda!

Judy's voice flooded through Amanda's mind.

Amanda!

She was in the small den this time, sitting in the green chair by the fancy little desk. She was again a blur, but Amanda instinctively knew it was her aunt.

Amanda!

Amanda tried to send a message back: *Not now!* But she was already having trouble listening to Trina while the house—while Aunt Judy's voice—was calling out to her so

146

strongly. Trina began to fade away, even as Amanda fought to see and hear her.

And then something new happened.

It felt as if Amanda's mind had somehow split in two. She was leaning against the wall with Trina, listening to her say, *"I'd never noticed the unusual color of his eyes..."* but she was also in the den with Aunt Judy, hearing her say, "The High Council has made their decision."

"And then his arm brushed against mine on the table..." Trina sounded further away.

"They're letting you go to Terra-V!"

Amanda sat on the loveseat across from Judy, letting the announcement wash over her. She was going back to Terra-V! Back to the tuntum trees and the purple meadow. Back to Alira and the Vherahna. Her thoughts spun in a hundred directions.

"We'll have to rush your training to get you ready, and we'll have to work out a story for your mom. I have some ideas, but we'll talk more later. Maybe tomorrow. Or Wednesday. There's so much to do!"

Amanda?

"Amanda!" Trina was flush with anger as she shook Amanda's arm.

The house was gone. Aunt Judy was gone.

They were leaning against a cold, brick wall, while leaves skittered across the cement walk and car doors slammed in the nearby parking lot. The car line was empty.

"Were you even listening to me?"

Trina hitched her backpack on one shoulder and glared at Amanda with pure disgust. Her tears had stopped, but

147

Amanda saw where they'd left faint lines to shimmer in the shifting sunlight. They reminded Amanda of Alira's opalescent skin.

"Of course, I was listening!"

Amanda scanned her memory, looking for the last snatches of conversation she'd heard before transitioning into the house.

"His arm brushed against yours on the table!" Amanda exclaimed triumphantly.

She was glad to have pulled up a piece of Trina's story. Until the words sank in, along with the shivery memory of Drew's hand grazing the back of her own neck.

But his arm brushing Trina's didn't mean anything, Amanda told herself. Just like it didn't mean anything when he'd touched the back of her neck.

They were friends and sometimes friends bumped into each other. She was sure that touch only stood out because she'd been struggling against travel sickness when it happened. In those few minutes of misery, every sensation in her body had felt heightened. It had nothing to do with Drew or any deeper meaning.

Trina rolled her eyes, lifting her hands in the air with spread fingers.

"You are unbelievable!"

Izzy came outside then, swinging her keys by their ring. A crystal keychain caught the light as it whirled around her finger. Amanda blinked at its rapid flashes.

"Hey, Amanda," Izzy greeted. "Need a ride home?"

Amanda started to agree, relieved she wouldn't have to bother her mom with a call about missing the bus.

Trina coldly cut her off.

"No, Amanda would rather be alone with her own precious thoughts."

§

Two days later, Judy was waiting in their apartment when Amanda got home from school. She was wearing the same gray sweats and pink hoodie she'd worn to meet Amanda in the house's upstairs bedroom. Her blue-streaked hair was pulled back in a ballerina bun, showing a tribal tattoo that curved delicately around the back of her ear. She wasn't wearing any jewelry or make-up.

"Aunt Judy has news," Patty announced in a carefully controlled voice.

She was in the kitchen, leaning against the counter while dunking a teabag in her mug of hot water. Her eyes watched the teabag bob up and down. Her hand swirled gently to vary its movement.

Judy ignored her and rushed over to take Amanda's backpack off her shoulders.

"News?" Amanda's heart lifted. Her aunt hadn't responded to any of her texts since their last house visit, and Amanda had begun to worry that she'd imagined the whole thing. It was hard to trust a meeting that happened inside your head.

"Yes, news!" Judy confirmed. "And something to show you!"

Amanda had unzipped her jacket and was starting to take it off when Judy stepped across the entryway to open the apartment door.

"Oh, are we going out?" Amanda shrugged the jacket back up her shoulders.

"You won't need that," Patty interjected, her voice now brittle.

"No, you won't!" Judy shot Patty a hopeful, almost pleading smile. "You're coming, aren't you?"

Patty let out a long exhale, set down her tea, and pushed herself away from the counter.

"I suppose."

Amanda kept her mouth shut, speculating on what might be happening now. Had Aunt Judy told her mom about psychic travel? That wasn't likely, even considering her mom's strange behavior.

Amanda was even more confused when they stepped into the elevator and Judy pressed the button to take them up to the top floor of the building.

"Tada!" Judy pulled out a set of keys and opened the door to apartment 1208.

Amanda lingered in the hallway. She looked at her mom for an answer, but Patty only gestured for Amanda to follow her aunt inside.

"This is… your apartment?"

Amanda's eyes widened at the spacious living room and open kitchen. Floor-to-ceiling windows and a sliding glass door led from the living area onto a covered balcony. The kitchen was large enough for a dining table, and French doors connected the kitchen to another room.

"Yes!" Judy beamed. "It turns out my work will keep me in the area for quite a while, so my company is moving me here. I know, it's big for one person, but it was the only apartment currently available in your building. And if I was going to stay in the area, I wanted to be as close as possible to my favorite niece!"

"I'm your only niece," Amanda answered automatically, overwhelmed by what she was seeing.

The apartment was already furnished. The décor matched Judy's style, but the furniture looked too new to have been brought from Judy's last home. In the living area, there was a bright blue couch, adjacent to an orange loveseat. Both were scattered with brightly patterned throw pillows. Large pictures on the wall featured modern, graphic designs with bold shapes and touches of graffiti art. Amanda could see ceramic dishes in a variety of colors stacked in the glass-fronted kitchen cabinets, and there was a large, decorative bowl centered on the kitchen table.

"Come on, I'll give you the tour!"

Amanda followed eagerly as Judy opened a door on the other side of the living room, away from the kitchen. It was a sunny, corner bedroom with large windows on two walls. The furniture was dark and modern, with white bedding and more pillows in a range of colors. Amanda recognized some of her aunt's jewelry hanging from a metal, tree-shaped rack on the dresser. The open closet showed some familiar clothing, including the deep blue sweater Amanda had given Judy last Christmas.

Beyond the living area and Judy's bedroom, the apartment turned a corner that led down a narrow hallway. Two more bedrooms were on the outside of the building, where the windows faced into the interior L-shape of the building, just like they did in Amanda's bedroom.

In the first bedroom, Amanda looked down and counted windows to find Drew's apartment. It was easy to find but looked strange from this height.

Both bedrooms were unfurnished and had empty closets. Across the hall, there were two full bathrooms and a closet that contained a stacked washer and dryer.

Heading back through the living area and kitchen, Judy led them to the French doors Amanda had noticed from the entryway. She opened them now to reveal a home office, complete with a wide desk, a leather recliner, and bookshelves that nearly filled one wall. A new computer sat on the desk.

Dazzled, Amanda turned to see her mom's reaction to this cozy office set-up. But Patty was no longer behind her. She'd walked back into the kitchen where she was running one finger thoughtfully over the electric kettle.

Amanda pictured the small, secondhand desk crammed into their crowded living room and the ancient computer where her mom typed day after day.

"Your work is paying for this?" Patty had gone back to her flat, neutral voice. This time, Amanda heard the masked pain in it. And maybe a touch of jealousy.

"Yes," Judy spoke with a level effort, perhaps willing Patty to be more accepting. "I thought it would be nice for us to be in the same building. And for Amanda to have another place to do her homework while you work. Or to spend the night occasionally."

"Hmmm." Patty studied Amanda with an assessing eye before turning back to her sister-in-law.

This was part of her aunt's plan.

Amanda realized that PTS was paying for this apartment to support *her* training. It was almost like it was *her* new apartment, too.

"You want Amanda to spend the night here?" Patty repeated. "Occasionally?"

"Well, your place has gotten pretty crowded lately."

Patty's eyes flashed in anger.

Amanda bit her lip.

Judy stood her ground.

"Has it?" Patty flared, then looked at Amanda and the fire went out of her eyes. She let her gaze drift around the open living area, then out onto the balcony. Her voice was very quiet when she continued.

"Not all of us can afford this much space."

Amanda felt a flutter in her chest. In that moment, she was seeing her mom as an entirely different person. One who didn't have all the answers. One who might not be as confident as she seemed.

Judy stepped closer to Patty, reaching for her hands before Patty could think to pull away.

"There are ways to afford it." She spoke softly, mirroring Patty's voice and stance.

Amanda watched a silent conversation flash between them, subtle movements crinkling their eyes and softening their lips. If she didn't know better, Amanda might have thought they were the ones with a psychic connection. She felt awkward and left out. Her body tensed.

Was this about Chad? she wondered. Her mom had tried to hide it, but Amanda knew she was having trouble affording their apartment without his help. If Aunt Judy was offering to chip in, they wouldn't need Chad's money. Amanda's heart leaped at the idea of going back to Terra-V *and* getting rid of Chad.

"I'm here now."

Judy extended one hand, but her fingertips only briefly hooked around Patty's hand before Patty straightened up and pulled away.

"For how long?" The words were raspy, as if passed over broken glass. "You're here now, but how long until you're off again with another client? Doing some other important job that you can't talk about?"

Patty looked around the apartment one more time, this time in outright disgust.

"Come on, Amanda," she said with authority. "You have homework to do. At home."

CHAPTER 11

PREPARATIONS AND PROPHECY

Stepping through the attic door was easier this time around. Amanda lifted the glass vial to her nose, then deftly tucked it into her pocket. As she checked her gear, she silently admired her growing skills. One month ago, she had stumbled into this meadow, sick and terrified. She hadn't known where she was or how she had gotten there. She hadn't known how lucky she'd been to show up with her clothes and shoes intact, or how impressive it had been to bring them back with her, let alone carrying some purple grass along for the ride.

In the last few weeks, Amanda had learned many things about psychic travel. Carrying items through the house was one of her earliest lessons. As Judy had explained, psychic travel required intense mental clarity. For anything to come through the house, to a new destination, a traveler had to be keenly aware of bringing that item with them. As if it were an extension of the traveler's own body.

Clothes were relatively easy to carry through.

"We tend to picture ourselves clothed," Judy had explained, "even in our dreams."

A novice traveler's brain usually carried their clothing quite naturally, she said, though shoes were sometimes a challenge. Other items took more work. The first few times Amanda tried to bring her PTS-issued glass vial of Vhelox through the house, she would study the bottle with minute care, clutch it tightly in her fist, and still show up in Chicago empty-handed. Yet here she was, in Terra-V, with her vial and other gear safely transported.

It had been hard work, and Judy was pleased with Amanda's dedication. The many practice trips had also begun to condition her body against travel sickness, which made Amanda very happy.

After a single whiff of Vhelox, Amanda could stand tall as she scanned the purple meadow stretched around her. The reality of Terra-V matched her memory almost exactly. Though there were changes, given that they had arrived at midday.

The tuntum trees stood at their tallest height. Without their humming movement, it was quiet enough to hear their leaves rustling lightly in the wind. Amanda heard other sounds as well. A bird-like cooing in the distant trees. The chirp and buzz of smaller creatures hiding in the long purple grass.

Amanda didn't watch the proximal door fade away behind them. She'd gotten used to doors disappearing and reappearing during her training trips to the PTS centers in Chicago, New York, and Los Angeles. Instead, she turned her face to the sky, noting its pinkish cast and how the color paled around the soft yellow of the glowing sun. A different sky, a different sun, a different world.

"Ready?" Cameron wore his chainmail armor as if it were pajamas. He wasn't adjusting his belt or tugging at his tunic the way Amanda kept fidgeting with the vial in her pocket. At the sight of his patient waiting, Amanda felt foolish for turning and gaping at the world around her. There would be time for that on their actual journey, she told herself. Though she couldn't tamp down the excitement she felt over every new sight or sound.

They crossed the meadow toward a break in the trees that led to the larger Vherahna community. As they walked, Amanda slipped a hand across her waist to furtively check that her small steel knife was still attached to her belt. She was still getting used to the sensation of it resting against her hip.

"How are you feeling?" Cameron kept his eyes forward and his pace steady.

"Pretty good," Amanda told him, glad her answer was mostly true.

The lemony sun was high overhead, casting the meadow in a soft, shimmery glow. The tuntum trees, at their full height, were narrower than Amanda had ever seen them. There were slivers of space between their twin trunks, now that they were untwisted. With each step, Amanda could make out more signs of structures and movement beyond the thinner lines of trees. Just being here, breathing in the sweet, damp air made it easier for Amanda to set aside the lingering effects of her travel sickness.

"The Vhelox works pretty well," Cameron agreed. "But Alira will fix you up the rest of the way soon."

As if summoned by the sound of her name, Alira appeared at the edge of the meadow. Three other Vherahna stood with her. At the sight of them, Amanda's nerves chased away the joy of her return. The happy sensations were replaced with a wave of self-doubt. *What am I doing here?* She worried. *I'm not ready for this. How could I be ready for this?*

Sensing the shift in Amanda's confidence, Cameron slowed his steps. He softly reminded her that she was an honored guest of the Vherahna and that he would be with her throughout the visit.

Amanda nodded rapidly. She doubted that she would survive the actual journey when she was this nervous about their planning meeting.

"America!" Alira stepped forward as they neared, reaching out her slim arms with her palms upturned. She seemed to radiate light from her very being.

"*Amanda*," Cameron corrected gently before greeting Alira with a deferential nod.

"Amanda," Alira repeated with a small frown, as if she preferred the sound of America. But then she looked Amanda up and down, shook her head, and lowered her arms. "You are unwell from the travel. May I help?"

Alira put one hand on Amanda's upper arm and closed her eyes. Behind her, the other Vherahna crossed their hands over their hearts and closed their eyes as well. As she let her own eyelids drift shut, Amanda heard—and felt—a low hum building around and inside her.

The sun felt warmer on her face. Her shoulders felt lighter. The queasiness of her stomach settled, and the faint pounding in her head receded. Amanda felt as if she'd stepped into a warm bath. Her whole body was softening, yet also growing stronger.

As the vibrating tone ebbed to silence, Amanda felt the air moving more freely through her lungs. Her feet planted more firmly on the ground. Her blood fizzed with a surge of energy. She opened her eyes and thanked Alira, extending the message to the other Vherahna as well.

"Ah, yes, these are my friends." Alira gestured toward them with a glint in her eye.

She introduced them one by one, noting that Cameron already knew the two men—Hais and Tras—from his previous visits.

Amanda noticed only slight differences between the Vherahna men and women. The men were shorter and broader than Alira. They wore their hair much longer. Like humans, the men were less curvy through their torsos, their shoulders tapering to slim waists and hips.

The third Vherahna, Caeph, was a woman with similar proportions to Alira. She was taller than the men, though smaller, and perhaps younger, than Alira. Her name was a gentle whisper that sounded to Amanda like *Say-if.*

With a pleasant smile, Caeph was introduced as the adept who would accompany them on their journey.

"Accompanying us?" Cameron's friendly smile fell away. "We did not discuss an adept joining us."

"We agreed I would travel with a companion," Alira smiled.

"Yes." Cameron glanced toward Hais and Tras before continuing, "But I thought only elders left the forest?"

"Only elders leave the forest to attend summits with the Churukh," Alira corrected. "This journey is not for a summit meeting."

Alira began to turn away, as if the matter were settled, but Cameron stopped her.

"An adept though?"

Amanda watched as Alira's smile froze and her eyes flashed. The other Vherahna held neutral expressions. Yet in their intent stillness Amanda noticed an odd double-blink of their eyes. It was a quick, barely perceptible motion. *Blink-blink. Blink-blink.*

In seeing it again, Amanda remembered noticing the same quirk when she'd met Alira on her first trip to Terra-V. There had been so much to process that this small detail had slipped her memory.

"As an adept, Caeph has completed our highest training. She is prepared for this journey."

"Yeah, but..." Cameron hesitated, letting his gaze pass over Amanda thoughtfully. Alira kept her eyes focused on Cameron alone. *Blink-blink. Blink-blink.*

Amanda looked at Caeph again, wondering if she was considered an adult or if the Vherahna had teenagers in their society. If she'd finished school, she must be an adult, Amanda reasoned. Though it was hard to tell how much of an age difference there might be between Caeph and the other Vherahna.

"Age is not always an indication of ability." Alira spoke simply yet her words carried weight.

"Touché." Cameron laughed lightly. Alira offered an amused smile in return.

"We will discuss our plans in more detail today," she added. "Now, come! Let us show Ameri— *Amanda* our home."

Cameron agreed, but his smile faded the moment Alira's back turned. Amanda noticed the other Vherahna pull slightly away from him. Only Alira slowed to walk close by his side as they moved toward the village. Caeph walked silently beside Amanda, while Hais and Tras trailed slightly behind.

Though they were quiet, the Vherahna created an aura of calm that slowed the nervous beating of Amanda's heart. Despite moving deeper into an alien world, she felt a sense of peace and acceptance rolling over and around her.

A wide stream flowed through the edge of the meadow and into the forest beyond. As Alira led them over a curved bridge, Amanda noticed that its wood was not the same lavender as the tuntum trees. It was a more silvery-blue, closer to the aged wood back in the attic.

Once they'd crossed the bridge, Amanda stepped closer to the nearest tuntum tree, comparing the difference. Alira moved to her side. The rest of the party halted, watching their exchange.

"Go on," Alira encouraged. "You can feel it."

Amanda hesitated, torn between her desire to touch a tuntum tree and her determination to not be a distraction. Alira stood close by her side. Her opal skin glittered more subtly outside of the sunny meadow clearing. Under the dense cluster of trees, Amanda thought she saw faint flashes of light beneath the shifting greens and purples of her skin. Like electric charges sparking.

Though the beat of the trees was not currently sounding, the double-blink of Alira's eyes echoed their rhythm. *Blink-blink. Blink-blink.* Amanda made herself look away. She felt embarrassed for staring but encouraged by the kindness she'd seen in Alira's purple eyes.

With her heart in her throat, Amanda turned to see Cameron nodding his approval.

As she inched closer, Amanda felt the energy of the tuntum tree. It had an invisible resistance, like when pressing magnets toward each other. But with little effort that resistance gave way to an enveloping warmth.

Amanda tentatively laid one hand against the bark, surprised that it felt similar to trees back home. The bark was smoother, with a sort of sandy feel, but it was firm beneath her palm. Below that tough exterior, Amanda could feel a distant thrumming. *Tuntum. Tuntum.*

She pressed her cheek into one of the tree's twin trunks, closing her eyes to better focus on the sound. *Tuntum. Tuntum.* It was the same sound she'd heard before, weaker now that the trees were still.

Amanda stepped back, letting her fingers trail around the curving line of one trunk. Though it was fully extended toward the sky, she could feel the direction the twist would take when it was time for the tree to descend.

She wasn't sure how long she lingered at the base of the tree. But when Amanda turned back to the group, the Vherahna had their heads bowed over templed fingers. A whispered chant cradled the air. It brought inexplicable tears to the corners of Amanda's eyes, and she knew she would never forget this magical moment.

Cameron stepped forward, a knight in the midst of a fantasy realm, and shook his head with a soft laugh.

"Come on, kid, there's a lot more to see."

§

Amid the purple grass and otherworldly trees, the Vherahna community looked a lot like the primitive forest villages Amanda had seen in many movies. A winding stream cut through the length of the forest, dotted with silvery-blue wooden bridges. On one side, simple wooden homes scattered around lush gardens, featuring a variety of unusual plants. Across the stream, larger public structures included bathhouses, a meeting center, and a laundry building.

Deeper into the village, Alira showed Amanda the largest building within the forest. They went inside, where Amanda admired row after row of wooden shelves, each stocked with stands of glass vials in dozens of colors and styles. Some were small, similar to the glass vial Amanda had in her own pocket. Others were the size of an average perfume bottle. There were wooden boxes on the shelves as well, each painted with ornate dots and swirls.

In a sizable workspace beside the shelves, about two dozen Vherahna were kneeling at low desks where they mixed concoctions of either a thick paste or a viscous liquid. Amanda flattened her hand over her pocket, feeling the glass vial inside, as she watched them work. Periodically, a Vherahna worker would sit very still, rest one hand above the product in progress, and emit a low tone like the one Alira had used to heal Amanda in the meadow.

As they worked at different rates, the tones ebbed and flowed around the room. The soothing sounds vibrated throughout the space, washing over Amanda, weakening her knees, and muddying her thoughts. She tried to capture the feeling in words, wanting to share the experience with Drew later and wishing he could experience the magic of Terra-V for himself.

She pushed those thoughts out of her mind.

Back outside, in the fresh air, Amanda considered what she had seen and remembered what she had been taught about the Vherana.

"That's vhe," she sighed wistfully.

"In one form," Alira agreed. "Vhe is all around us. It is in the air, the ground, and the tuntum trees. It is in us, in all of us, and flows throughout our world."

"With your help," Amanda added. She'd learned all about vhe in her training, and the concept had seemed deceptively simple.

Vhe was an energy, a life-force. In Terra-V, there were two intelligent races: Vherahna and Churukh. Both races needed vhe to live, but only the Vherahna could produce and share vhe. Either through vibrational song and touch or through their infused salve and ether.

Later in the visit, during a feast in their honor, Amanda heard stories about a time when the Vherahna had traveled freely throughout the Churukh communities. In those days, they would routinely pass from village to village, replenishing vhe through song, healing those with wounds or illnesses, and leaving a store of salves and ethers to last until their next visit.

"That was long ago," Alira clarified. Those around her wore melancholy smiles. "It was before our time, and before the English came to greet our people."

Amanda looked toward Cameron. She remembered the Terra-V history she had learned in her PTS lessons, and worried that early travelers may have had something to do with the change that now kept the Vherahna in their forest home. Alira held out a pacifying hand and continued to explain.

"Long before the English arrived, thieves among the Churukh recognized a path to gain power over the others. They could control money exchanged for goods and services." She spoke of money as if it were a foreign concept, and Amanda wondered whether the Vherahna had a currency system of their own.

"In time, the thieves realized they would have even greater power if they controlled the vhe as well," Alira continued, in a more somber tone.

A hush fell around the table as every head bowed. Cameron and the handful of knights who had joined the feast followed suit, and Amanda quickly bowed her head, too. After a weighty pause, Amanda sensed movement as every head lifted. She cautiously raised her eyes, unsure what had happened.

Alira resumed her story.

"It became unsafe for the Vherahna to move freely beyond the protection of our forest. Churukh pilgrims came to us instead, bringing their sick and collecting as many vhe treatments as they could carry home. Though not all had the strength to make the journey, and our own numbers had been halved, making it quite difficult to keep up with their needs."

The table was quiet. Attention hung on her every word.

Amanda felt a shift in the energy around her. There was a building of anticipation as if a storm were about to break. She glanced at Cameron who flashed a small but encouraging smile.

"When the English came, our burdens were lessened." Alira's words released a sigh of contentment throughout the party. The Vherahna resumed eating, and drinking, and lightly murmuring among themselves.

"Your people have done what they can to negotiate peace with the Churukh thieves and help the oppressed Churukh people," Alira continued. "They have become friends of the Vherahna. They offer additional protection to our forest—though our sacred tuntum trees keep us safe from outside harm."

She winked at Cameron then, before lovingly sweeping her gaze over the tuntum trees that bordered their festival area. Amanda heard Cameron laugh in response. He lifted his glass in tribute to Alira.

"The Vherahna have been dear friends to our people. May our friendship continue to flourish!"

The other knights held up their glasses, calling *Hear! Hear!* The Vherahna drank together in response, and Amanda hastily joined in.

As the feast went on, Amanda considered the glass vial tucked in her pocket.

She'd been told the Vhelox was an attempt at synthesizing the vhe-infused ether made by the Vherahna. It was not as effective, but it had similar benefits in helping with nausea and pain. And it was the best they'd managed after finding that vhe-infused products degraded rapidly after being carried through the house.

Amanda looked around, wondering what other benefits the travelers were getting from the people of Terra-V.

§

As the conversation turned to their upcoming journey, it was decided that their party would include Amanda, Alira, Caeph, Cameron, and six of his fellow knights. Cameron had argued to keep their number small, saying it would be an easier journey with fewer people to manage. Alira had agreed, as long Caeph was included in their number.

Their argument on that point had facinated Amanda. With every reason Cameron presented against bringing the adept, Alira had kindly agreed. *Blink-blink.* Before politely adding, "But Caeph will join us on the journey."

After several minutes, Cameron had caved. With Caeph along, he would need six knights instead of four, raising their total number to a party of ten.

"We have horses for ten," Alira had smiled. *Blink-blink.* And the matter was settled.

To end the feast, Alira stood to recite the *Prophecy of the Waking Dreamer.*

Though Amanda knew the prophecy was the purpose of their journey, she'd never heard the foretelling recited in full. Her palms felt clammy as a renewed hush fell over the party. She swallowed a gulp of the sweet tonic that filled her glass, then trained her eyes on Alira, trying to appear thoughtful and calm, despite the jittering tremor of her heart.

"The *Prophecy of the Waking Dreamer*." Alira announced, her clear voice carrying across the festival."As gifted to us by our mutual friend, the honored Edmund Robinson."

> When the waking dreamer stumbles in,
> the world begins anew.
> Give her shelter, food and drink,
> she'll lead your journey true.
> Beyond the trees, you shall explore
> to bridge what's grown apart.
> The special gift you've scarcely known
> was missing from your heart.

An unfamiliar yet pleasing rustling filled the clearing. It was almost, but not entirely, like the chirping of crickets. Amanda swiveled to see Vherahna and traveler alike holding up their hands and rapidly brushing their thumbs against their fingertips. It looked like a snapping motion but without the sharp force.

Amanda lifted her hands to try the gesture for herself. The sound of her fingers was not as pronounced as the melodic swish that rang from the Vherahna, but she enjoyed both the tingling sensation in her fingertips and the feeling of inclusion within the group.

Minutes later, after the chirruping applause had faded away, Amanda felt the weight of the prophecy and a keen sense of disappointment. It didn't say *anything*. Leading a journey, bridging something, finding a special gift. It was nonsense. Vague, semi-poetic nonsense. There was nothing in the prophecy that told Amanda what she was actually supposed to do.

As the Vherahna cleared dishes from the feast and talked among themselves in their whispery, songlike language, Amanda found herself alone with Cameron.

"How are you holding up?" He sat on the purple ground beside her, near the wide base of a tuntum tree. "Being in a different world for an extended period of time can be hard on your body."

"It's not that," Amanda answered. Though she *was* feeling the effects of the alien world. The slight differences in gravity, atmosphere, and general surroundings came together in a physically unsettling way, despite the mental excitement of traveling. It created a low-level buzz that simmered and sizzled deep in her body.

"You're worried about the journey?"

Amanda shrugged.

The journey was what she had wanted and waited for. For weeks, she'd worried that the trip wouldn't happen. She thought the council wouldn't allow it, or they wouldn't find a way for her to leave home without her mom knowing. But Aunt Judy had stepped in, convincing Patty that Amanda would be happier at home over the Thanksgiving break instead of going with her to meet Chad's parents. Chad had eagerly agreed.

Once it was decided, Amanda had spent every spare moment in training. She learned psychic travel techniques and special skills she might need to stay safe. Her confidence had grown with each lesson. Yet here in Terra-V, just days ahead of their departure, new fears were creeping in. Amanda sat in the shade of the tuntum trees and realized how much of this mission rested on her inexperienced shoulders. *The waking dreamer stumbles in... She'll lead your journey true...*

"I don't know what I'm doing."

Amanda braced her arms over her bent knees and looked at Cameron helplessly. Before the feast, Cameron had tried to discuss a route for their journey, but Alira had been unwilling to collaborate.

"Amanda will know where to lead us," she had repeated firmly. "She will choose a direction, and we will follow."

"But what if I choose the wrong direction?" Amanda had asked.

"You cannot."

"What if I choose a direction that leads us into danger?"

"Then we are meant to encounter danger."

Amanda had expected Cameron to step in then, but he only listened to their exchange play out.

"What if I fail?" Amanda had stumbled over the words, but Alira answered without a trace of doubt.

"The prophecy says that you will be successful."

"What if the prophecy is wrong?"

"Prophecy is never wrong," Alira had told her calmly. "It is only our interpretation of a prophecy that could be wrong."

Amanda had widened her eyes at Cameron, frustrated by his continued silence.

"Well, what if your *interpretation* of the prophecy is wrong?"

The question had come out in a rush, leaving Amanda terrified that she'd crossed the line of polite behavior. But Alira had only smiled.

"Then that is not your responsibility. You are only being asked to choose a direction. You are not being asked to assess the risk of our journey or interpret our prophecy. You are only being asked to choose a direction."

Replaying that conversation in her thoughts now, Amanda felt the same unease.

"I don't know what I'm doing," she repeated, enjoying a strange freedom in saying the awful words out loud.

"Neither do I," Cameron nodded, twining a long strand of purple grass around his fingers.

Amanda looked up sharply. Cameron had more experience in Terra-V than any other traveler. She might be the journey's leader in the Vherahna's eyes, but Cameron was the *actual* leader who was expected to keep them safe.

"I know Terra-V well enough," he conceded. "I'm confident that my team can keep us safe for a short journey, and I trust that Alira will accept whatever we accomplish in the time we've allotted.

"But there are many things I don't know. I don't know our exact route, who we'll encounter, or what we'll find. If we find anything at all. But those are things that I don't need to know. Sometimes, being aware of what you don't know is as important as having a plan.

"Only a fool thinks he knows everything and can be prepared for anything. It is the acceptance of *not knowing* that keeps you sharp—and safe."

"You sound like Alira." Amanda rolled her eyes, but his answer had made her feel better. Even if she didn't entirely understand it.

"I've spent enough time with her," Cameron granted. "And with the Vherahna."

As Amanda considered that, a sharp crack rippled through the forest, followed by a creaking hum. She looked up, then back at the trees behind them.

"The trees!" She pressed her hands against the pulsating trunk. A new, stronger vibration spread beneath her palms. "They're moving!"

"Yes," Cameron laughed. "They do that."

Amanda ignored him, leaning close to better feel the bark shifting slightly beneath her palms. She closed her eyes, grateful to simply be in this amazing new world.

§

On the Tuesday before Thanksgiving, students and teachers alike were ready for the holiday break. In Amanda's Spanish class, they watched videos while their teacher obsessively checked flight statuses from her phone. In P.E., they were given the choice between flag football in the main gym or free time in the weight room. Amanda chose the weight room, working out while Trina and the others lounged and chatted on the equipment.

Amanda's art teacher had already left town for the holiday break. Instead of hiring a sub, one of the assistant principals came in to sit with them while they continued previous projects or started on something new. Amanda wanted to draw a forest of tuntum trees, but—having learned from her short story—she drew a room with a series of doors instead.

As she sketched, she felt relieved that it was a B day on their block schedule. Her B schedule meant no English class with disappointed looks from Mr. Hewlett, and no Earth Science with Trey and his friends smirking her way.

Of course, a B day also meant no class with Drew, and Amanda had mixed feelings about that.

Amanda and Drew hadn't talked much over the last few weeks. Now that Drew was dating Trina, and Amanda was busy with her training.

Judy often brought Amanda to and from school, using the time to quiz her on psychic travel or scenarios that could be dangerous on Terra-V. At longer red lights, she even had Amanda practice sending her telepathic messages through the house. It was a difficult skill and one Amanda had not yet mastered.

When Amanda and Drew did talk, they avoided the rumor Trey had started about them. They had talked about it once when Amanda had first found out. Drew insisted he'd told Trey and Trina that it wasn't true. That they'd been talking under the bleachers and nothing more. He promised that he'd say the same to anyone who asked.

Amanda had believed him. She knew he'd had nothing to do with Trey starting the rumor. But she also knew there were plenty of people who hadn't asked him—and wouldn't ask him—before assuming it was true.

Even if it wasn't Drew's fault, Amanda felt the rumor between them.

Still, it felt odd to not see Drew on the last day before the Thanksgiving break. Partly because Amanda was leaving for Terra-V in the morning, and partly because it was Drew's birthday.

Amanda thought about adjusting her route to World History so they would cross paths, but when the time came, she didn't have to. When she left Art, Drew was waiting outside the door.

"Hey." He ignored the other students weaving around them.

"Hey." Amanda shifted her books in her arms before adding, "Happy Birthday."

"Thanks."

"I meant to get you a card, but…"

"You've been really busy," Drew finished with a forced smile. "It's okay."

Amanda wondered if Trina had gotten him a card, but she didn't ask.

They walked down the hallway, in the direction of Amanda's World History class. It would take Drew out of his way to Algebra, but he didn't seem to mind.

"Are you ready for your trip?"

Drew's direct question, in public, startled Amanda. She glanced around nervously, before remembering travel was a normal topic right before a holiday weekend.

Amanda said she was ready, without elaborating. She'd briefly told Drew about her training and plans to visit Terra-V, but she hadn't opened up to him about her worries.

Deeper conversations with him felt awkward now that he had a girlfriend.

"Look, Amanda." Drew stopped a few feet from her classroom door. "I get why you want to do this... but maybe you shouldn't."

Amanda blinked up at him. His expression was neutral, but his eyes screamed fear.

"Drew, I—"

"I know, you've been cleared and all, but why are they letting you do this? Why do they think you can? After a few weeks of training? It's crazy."

Cheeks burning, Amanda clenched her jaw and looked sharply away. Two of Trina's friends were standing across the hall, obviously watching their exchange.

"I'm worried about you," Drew tried again, leaning in as she pulled away.

"You don't get to worry about me," Amanda hissed. "And you don't get to tell me what to do!"

I'm not your girlfriend, she added silently, then rolled her eyes at her own thought.

"Fine," Drew snapped. He spoke quickly, knowing the bell was about to ring. "Be mad at me. About this, or about whatever, but don't rush into this trip because you're trying to prove something."

"Prove something?" Amanda stormed, ignoring the whispers from across the hall. "You don't know what you're talking about!"

"I know it could be dangerous." Drew lowered his voice, controlling his emotion. "I know that I don't want you to get hurt."

"Really?" Amanda turned toward Trina's spying friends and waved her arms, unconsciously channeling her Aunt Judy as she called out, "Nothing to see here!"

The girls dropped their mouths in mock outrage, then hurried away, gossiping about everything they'd seen.

Drew watched them go, shaking his head.

"If you don't want me to be hurt," Amanda warned, "then stop feeding their rumors. I have real problems to worry about, not your girlfriend's drama."

The bell rang and Amanda went into her next class, leaving Drew in the hallway alone.

CHAPTER 12
BEYOND THE TREES

Less than thirty minutes after Amanda said goodbye to her mom and Chad, Cameron showed up at Judy's door. They'd decided to begin their journey to Terra-V from a shared origin point, and Judy's apartment offered the easiest place to get Amanda home before her mom returned. Cameron arrived in jeans and a sweater—not his armor or the black tracksuit he'd worn at the PTS training facilities—and he carried a duffel bag with some personal items he'd planned to leave with Judy.

"For when there's time to sneak back for a real shower," he laughed.

Watching him hang up his jacket, Amanda imagined where he might live when he wasn't leading his team in Terra-V. The details of his personal life had never come up during their time in training, and she'd never asked.

Amanda had packed a suitcase as well so she wouldn't have to run down to her own apartment during travel breaks.

Air beds were set up in each of Judy's spare bedrooms and the kitchen was stocked with food that would be quick to heat and easily portable if time was short. The uncertain nature of their trip made it hard to schedule check-ins, and Judy would be on standby for whatever they might need. She'd wanted to go with them, but the council—and Cameron—had insisted her support from home would be more valuable.

Once he'd seen the apartment layout, Cameron went into his assigned bedroom to change. He came out minutes later wearing a tactical suit that looked like long underwear with thin metal plates embedded over his chest and back. It was the protective gear the knights in Terra-V wore under their chainmail and tunics.

Amanda would also wear a tactical suit, along with a simple spun-linen tunic and pants set. She'd hoped to dress like a knight, but Cameron said the chainmail would be too heavy. He and his team of knights spent months building up the endurance needed to wear their armor daily. He let her try on a chainmail shirt to feel the weight of it for herself, and she never asked to wear it again.

After changing, Cameron traveled through the house to pick up the items that would have been difficult to bring through the airlines. Amanda watched his body fade away. She had rarely seen travelers disappear without using a proximal door and the experience was still unsettling.

She knew normals were often incapable of seeing a traveler disappear. Their brains would create elaborate excuses to process what they couldn't understand. Sometimes they'd faint, or even experience a mental break.

Of course, many normals could process it safely with advance training, but it was still risky. Knowing that, Amanda had resolved to not travel in front of any normals. Even if she thought Drew could handle it.

"What's the number one rule?" Judy quizzed the moment they were alone.

"No going to the house without a proximal door," Amanda responded on cue.

"Not even for messages," Judy insisted. "Right?"

Amanda hesitated.

"I've gotten so much better at them."

"Amanda," Judy warned. "It's too risky."

"But what if—"

"Messages will be sent by Cameron or his team. Period."

Amanda nodded glumly.

Sending a message through the house was complicated. It required keeping part of the mind firmly rooted in the physical world while letting another part move into the house. Receiving messages was hard enough. It often pulled Amanda into the house completely—like the time she'd been arguing with Trina outside the school and her mind had ended up with Aunt Judy in the house. Sending a message meant keeping her mind in two places, while *also* sending mental calls to a specific traveler.

"I won't send messages," Amanda promised.

"What happens if you slip into the house without using a proximal door?" Judy quizzed.

"My origin point is reset to Terra-V. I'd have to go through the house to New York and fly back here before Mom gets home."

"Right. If this apartment stops being your origin point, the journey ends for you. Got it? You head to New York, I meet you there, and we fly back together. Right?"

"Right," Amanda sighed. She knew her aunt meant well, but she was sick of the same questions.

Besides, screwing up her origin point didn't seem like that big of a problem. It was a pain that New York was the nearest proximal door to home but traveling home from New York in a *normal* way seemed safer than traveling to *another world* in a *psychic* way.

Why was Aunt Judy so worried? It was another question her aunt had put off for some other time.

"One other thing," Judy warned. "If there's any moment you're in danger, you forget all about origin points and go through the house to New York. Promise?"

Amanda promised, then went to her room to change into her travel clothes. She pulled the loose tunic and pants over her form fitting tactical suit, then belted the small metal knife around her waist.

Judy had just finished braiding Amanda's hair in two long plaits when Cameron reappeared in the living room, now dressed in his familiar chainmail and pale blue tunic. He carried his own weapons and pack, along with a simple longbow and a quiver of arrows.

Along with her PTS training, Amanda had learned other skills for their journey, like horseback riding, basic fencing, and self-defense. Fortunately, Amanda and Trina had spent the last two summers volunteering at a nearby stable in exchange for riding lessons. They had also learned some simple archery when it was the cool club to join in middle school. While that helped with her PTS lessons, Amanda was still much more comfortable on a horse than she'd been in her weapons training.

The sight of the bow and quiver turned Amanda's stomach to jelly.

"You won't need them," Cameron reassured. "But it's good to be prepared."

Amanda knew why they were limited to armor and historical weapons. PTS had rules about bringing advanced technologies into other worlds. Her lessons had hinted at missteps in the past, insisting it was best to be cautious with any exchange of knowledge or technological advancement, especially in more primitive worlds. Amanda understood their reasoning but wished she'd taken that year in her archery club more seriously.

Judy squeezed Amanda's hand. The time had come.

§

After their meeting with the Vherahna, Cameron and Amanda had discussed their options and agreed that she should request they begin their journey with a visit to Sage Village. Cameron said was a logical starting point and a relatively safe one.

The Churukh in Sage Village kept to themselves. They dedicated their lives to the pursuit of wisdom, and they interacted peacefully with any who made a pilgrimage to their walled home. They maintained the largest library in all of Terra-V, safeguarding resources on farming, trade, and healing arts, along with Vherahna prophecies and the lineage charts of Churukh royalty.

Biennial summits between the Churukh ruling class and the Vherahna elders were held in Sage Village as well, with PTS representative providing moderation. Outside of these summits, Vherahna leaders also made infrequent visits to confer with the elders in Sage Village.

The Churukh royals—those the Vherahna referred to as the Churukh thieves—accepted these visits as a ritual that did not threaten their own power, and the well-traveled road from the Vherahna Forest to the Sage Village was relatively safe. It was also long. Cameron explained that they would spend the night in a Churukh farming hamlet along their route, then arrive in Sage Village the following afternoon. It was a trip he'd taken before and felt comfortable repeating, and Amanda was glad to have that much of their journey settled in advance.

They arrived in the meadow in Terra-V without a hitch, soon after the trees had risen, and gathered with the rest of Cameron's team at the edge of the Vherahna Forest. Alira and Caeph were there, along with the Vherahna who had come to see them off. As a Vherahna elder, Alira had made the trip to the Sage Village many times before. However, this would be Caeph's first trip beyond the shelter of the tuntum trees. Hais, Tras, and some of the other Vherahna elders were speaking softly with her in turn, offering their guidance and encouragement.

The magnetic force that Amanda had sensed around individual tuntum trees was much stronger at their outermost ring. It formed an energy barrier that could be felt but not seen. Through her lessons about Terra-V, Amanda knew the mystical barrier kept outsiders from crossing under the tuntum trees without permission from the Vherahna. It was strongest at night, but even now, in the early light of day—and even with her permission to be there—Amanda could feel its power.

Beyond the tuntum trees, Amanda saw purple fields cut through with dirt roads that branched in three directions. The road to the right was narrow and overgrown. Cameron said it led to ancient ruins that were of no consequence now. The center path was wide and deeply rutted. It was the path used by Churukh representatives who came in carts and carriages to collect their tribes' monthly supply of vhe-infused products. As it stretched past the purple grass, that road cut through a wide expanse of rocky desert—an area Cameron said was full of bandits waiting to steal the precious vhe for themselves.

To Amanda's far left, a dark road snaked along the border of tuntum trees leading toward a distant, bluish-lilac forest of trees that stood upright all through the day and night. That was their path to Sage Village. Amanda danced with excitement, eager to be on their way.

Until the horses were brought into sight.

"Those aren't horses," Amanda gasped.

Cameron and the other knights laughed.

"I said they were *like* horses," Cameron corrected, "except faster."

"Yeah, but…" Amanda trailed off, staring at the animals before her.

Calling these creatures *horses* seemed absurd to Amanda. They were generally horse-shaped, she conceded, though their elongated backs and narrow flanks reminded her more of an oversized greyhound or cheetah. Their long faces and pointed ears were distinctly horse-like. Yet instead of manes, they sported thick plumes like the crest of a cockatoo.

As they came closer, Amanda saw their bodies were covered in short feathers that gleamed with the sleekness of dragon scales. She watched in astonishment as one of the so-called horses lifted its tail, displaying a fan of gold-streaked quills that would put any peacock to shame.

Rory, a knight in their tactical team, led one of the creatures to Amanda with a friendly laugh and patted the animal's neck affectionately. Its downy feathers were tinged with pale rose, while a deeper red flashed at its crown and through the ornate tail that now trailed above the ground like the train of a dress.

"Don't worry," she encouraged. "Once you get settled, it's just like riding a horse."

"Really?" Amanda shied away but peered intently at its paw-like feet.

"Sure," Rory grinned. "Like a horse that goes about twice as fast and bounds along like a gazelle, but yeah. Close enough."

"Oh." Amanda felt her face pale as Alira approached.

Stepping easily between the jewel-hued animals, Alira laid one hand on the creature Rory had presented and reached toward Amanda with her free hand.

"This is Iveryn," she introduced gently. The animal turned a deep violet eye on Amanda assessingly. "He is a good horse. Iveryn, this is Amanda. She is precious to us and in need of your service. Will you accept her care?"

Amanda let Alira guide her hand toward Iveryn's warm, feathery side. The creature bowed its head, allowing Amanda's tentative touch. *Iveryn,* Amanda whispered to herself. *My horse.* She stumbled over the word, thinking these creatures deserved a more magical name.

Cameron soon came over to help Amanda into Iveryn's small leather saddle.

Fortunately, the saddle was familiar to Amanda. The *actual* horse in her PTS training sessions had worn the same style saddle. Though she noticed it sat further forward on this creature, leaving more space for its flexible back to move unencumbered.

Amanda tucked her boots into the attached stirrups and took hold of the reins. Then leaned back, avoiding the gold-tipped plume that unfurled before resettling against the animal's head.

"Why didn't anyone tell me?" Amanda asked Cameron as he secured her pack to the saddle.

"And miss the look on your face?" He laughed. "Never!"

§

While it wasn't exactly like riding a horse, Amanda soon adjusted to Iveryn's loping gait. His long body and extended stride created an effortless glide which—along with his feathery coat—made Amanda feel as if they were flying. The horses rode in a diamond-shaped formation with Amanda, Alira, and Caeph surrounded by Cameron and his team of knights. Each horse was a different color yet together they blended into a fluid mosaic of complementary tones.

Though Amanda had expected to be amazed by every moment in this alien world, hours on their mounted journey eventually dulled her astonishment.

The dirt road they traveled was wide and even. It wound through a wooded area, occasionally opening onto clearings and small ponds where they would stop to rest. Away from the Vherahna Forest, the trees and plants reminded Amanda of common woodlands in her own world. Except everything that would be green was color-shifted toward blues and purples. The silvery-gray trees matched the wood she'd seen in the attic of the birdhouse. Her first glimpses of forest creatures—which were similiar to rabbits, birds, and squirrels—had revived Amanda's excitement but soon seemed commonplace. The only creatures that never failed to bring giddy smiles were the large butterflies with gently glowing bodies and gossamer wings.

As the wooded area transitioned to open plains, Amanda knew they were getting close to the farming hamlet where they would rest for the night. She was both eager and reluctant to arrive. They'd passed very few Churukh on the road and hadn't stopped to talk with any of them. When their paths had crossed, Amanda had tried not to stare. While the Vherahna had lithe and willowy bodies, the Churukh were stout and compact. They had mottled skin in shades of gray and jet-black hair. Their emerald green eyes dimmed and glowed depending on the amount of vhe in their bodies. Beyond those features, they looked more human than the Vherahna. Amanda mentioned that observation to Rory, who was riding beside her, and asked what the Churukh were like in person.

"They are a lot like humans," Rory agreed. "If you go back to humans in the Dark Ages. They're what you've read about in your PTS lessons. Primitive. Animal-like. They're all about survival, so there're some pretty huge differences in how they behave, depending on their circumstances. Which is pretty human-like, too."

"They aren't that bad," Dimitri broke in from his position just behind Rory and Amanda. "There are good and bad Churukh, just like with any people."

"That's what I said," Rory frowned, peering into a patch of trees they were passing.

"In your cynical way maybe," Dimitri laughed. "Amanda, many Churukh struggle against sickness and hardship. It takes a toll and leaves little time for education and progressive thought. Now, the Churukh you'll meet in this farming community are better off than most, and those in Sage Village have the luxury of spending their time in the pursuit of wisdom and elevated ideals."

Rory scoffed.

"Elevated thinking can have its bad side, too." She shook her head, still scanning the road ahead and the woods beside them. "Education can be twisted to prove any point."

"Yeah," Dimitri responded uneasily, before resuming his genial attitude. "No need to worry about that now though. Amanda, the Churukh farmers are quite friendly, and you'll see that for yourself soon enough."

Amanda noticed that Alira and Caeph were very quiet during this exchange, though they rode close enough to hear. At the head of their party, Cameron rode quietly, too. Amanda tried to remember what he'd told her about the Churukh. He'd seemed neutral on the subject, adding that most societies were complex, and it was rarer to find a straightforward, single-minded community like the Vherahna.

Around the next bend, the road opened onto a ridge overlooking a valley checkered with crops and dotted with farmhouses. Closer in, at the bottom of their steep downward path, homes and public buildings clustered to form a crude town square.

They paused at the top of the ridge, taking in the scenic vista. The sun was low in the sky and Amanda longed to be back among the descending tuntum trees. As she turned to say as much to the Vherahna, she saw Alira draw her horse close enough to link arms with Caeph and twine their fingers together. There were tears silently shimmering on Caeph's cheeks, blending in with the iridescence of her pale skin in the softening light. It was her first night away from the shelter of the tuntum trees.

Awkwardly nudging Iveryn closer to Caeph's other side, Amanda tentatively reached out her arm. Both Vherahna turned their heads her way at once, startling Amanda into drawing back her hand. *Am I intruding?* She worried. But then a kindness in Alira's eyes gave Amanda the courage to thread her own elbow around the crook in Caeph's free arm and offer her hand. Caeph interlaced their fingers and they wordlessly turned back toward the valley below.

The paused that way for several minutes. The Vherahna double-blinking into the silence. Amanda capturing a mental snapshot of the horizon and filling the memory with the warmth of the moment.

When the party resumed their downward path, Cameron brought his deep purple horse alongside Iveryn to offer their assistance on the steep terrain. Amanda was intent on holding on but nodded bravely, saying she was okay when the horse's paws skittered over some loose rock. The current of energy that had passed through Alira and Caeph still sang through Amanda's veins, lending her strength. At the bottom of the path, where the road leveled out and led into the farm hamlet, Cameron placed his fingertips lightly on Amanda's arm.

"Well done," he complimented, before riding back to the head of the party. Amanda flushed with pride, knowing he meant more than the way she had handled her horse.

§

As full dark set in, their party settled into a barn-like structure. Feather-stuffed pallets were spread out for sleeping, along with hand-woven blankets in a variety of colors and styles. Open windows in the loft let silvery light from the twin moons stream softly through the space.

Amanda crept from her pallet to lean against a rough, wooden wall. Her mind was abuzz, and she didn't feel the least bit tired. It didn't help that she knew it wasn't really nighttime. At least, not according to the amount of time that had passed since she'd left home.

Though Amanda didn't have a watch of her own, she knew the days in Terra-V were shorter than days on Earth. A full Terra-V day was approximately eighteen hours long, which meant four days in Terra-V would pass in about the same time as three days on Earth.

Her training had warned that the days and nights in Terra-V wouldn't match her own internal clock. But she'd been too focused on the world's other differences—like its slight decrease in gravity and multiple moons—to notice. Until she tried to sleep.

Amanda watched the others, marveling that they had drifted off so quickly. But then, she told herself, they were used to the passage of time in this world. The knights in their team were stationed on Terra-V and only went home for brief visits once a month. She wondered if they had trouble staying awake during the longer Earth days.

Cameron was the only other member of their party who was still awake. He'd gone outside, saying he wanted a quiet place to message Judy their status. Waiting for him to return, Amanda wondered if the Churukh were asleep as well. There was a public house that served food and drinks, but maybe it closed early. It was a farming community, and she assumed the Churkh needed to make the most of their daylight hours.

Cameron came in and stopped short at the sight of Amanda sitting against the wall. With a gesture for her to follow, they quietly went back outside and settled on the ground several yards from the barn. The moonlight cast a bluish glow over the sleeping community as some unknown creatures chirped in the night.

"Can't sleep?" Cameron pulled out a flask of water and offered Amanda a drink. "Judy sends her love and says she's proud of how well you're doing."

"Oh." Amanda handed the flask back uncertainly. "Okay."

"I'm proud of you, too," Cameron added, looking up at the stars. "To be clear."

"Thanks."

They were quiet then, breathing in the night air. Amanda felt awkward, sitting alone with Cameron in a starlit field. She realized that she didn't know much about him. Like how long he'd been stationed in Terra-V or if he'd worked on other worlds before this assignment. She didn't even know how old he was when his psychic travel abilities kicked in or how long he'd known Judy.

Cameron was about the same age as her dad would be now, Amanda realized with a start. And they'd both spent time in Terra-V…

"Uh, Cameron?"

"Yeah."

The question was on the tip of her tongue, but Amanda couldn't put together the right combination of words. The silence stretched between them while Cameron waited patiently.

"What time is it?" she asked instead. "Back home?"

Cameron squinted at her in the dark. Despite the ban on advanced technology, Amanda knew he wore a special watch chained to a pocket inside his tunic. It helped him track Universal Earth Time (UET).

"About six-thirty your time," he answered without checking the hidden watch. "Dinner time there, bedtime here. I know you're not tired now, but when the sun comes up here it will be about one a.m. your time. And we'll need to get back on the road, so you won't have a chance to sleep when you finally are tired. Got it?"

"Yeah," Amanda sighed. Then she rushed on before Cameron could get to his feet, "Answer one question and I'll go to right sleep. Okay?"

Cameron settled back onto the ground. He looked at her without expression.

"One question."

Amanda hesitated. She was on the brink of asking about her dad, but her mind jumped in with an entirely different question.

"What's with the pineapples?"

Cameron laughed. When they'd arrived, the Churukh had greeted their party with smiles and gestures of welcome. They'd met Vherahna and English visitors many times before—including Alira, Cameron, and several in his team—and were honored to have them stay the night.

Most Churukh did not speak English, but Cameron and the other travelers spoke enough Churukh to get by. As Amanda had learned in her lessons, the Churukh language was difficult but possible to learn, unlike the Vherahna language which included sounds that humans (and Churukh) could not physically make.

The Vherahna spoke all three languages fluently.

Amanda had stood by Iveryn and watched the Churukh's welcome. Up close, it was easier to compare their physical traits to humans. In addition to their compact bodies, they had fuller faces and complexions that swirled with various hues of matte gray. Their eyes were small with dark lashes, emerald irises, and gray-blue pupils. Most eyes were dull, but some held a distinct gleam. They blinked at a single rate, unlike the Vherahna.

As she watched, Amanda had listened to the guttural exchange between Cameron and the Churukh with as little understanding as her horse. Possibly less, she thought, as Iveryn had an uncanny way of appearing to know what was happening around him without the benefit of language. Yet, as they spoke, Amanda had distinctly heard one English word in the choppy stream of Churukh: *Pineapple.*

She'd assumed it was an odd coincidence until one of the Churukh had come out of the public house bearing three pineapples wrapped in coarse cloth. Cameron, Alira, and Caeph had each accepted a pineapple with gracious thanks, while Amanda searched for any sign of confusion among the knights. Clearly, she'd been the only one surprised to see pineapples on Terra-V.

Sitting under the stars, Cameron explained that the pineapples were a serendipitous misstep by the earliest travelers to visit Terra-V. In their time, pineapples were considered a symbol of welcome, which had made them seem an ideal gift to the new world. As it turned out, the pineapples were inedible for both the Churukh and the Vherahna. In fact, they created a sickness that had nearly driven the English travelers out of Terra-V forever. But then the Vherahna withstood the illness, healed the affected Churukh, and discovered new value in the tropical fruit.

Apparently, pineapples contained an acid that perfectly balanced much of the soil in Terra-V, turning many barren areas into fertile farmlands. Pineapples could also be used to clean the metals the Churukh used for tools and weapons. And they became a favorite treat for horses and other native animals.

While pineapples did not grow in Churukh farmlands, the conditions were right in Sage Village. That coincidence had only added to the mythos of pineapples being an emblem of both the highest wisdom and most common practicality.

"So, pineapples are grown in Sage Village?" Amanda had never seen pineapples being grown anywhere. The idea of them being grown on an alien planet seemed unreal.

"Yes, pineapples are grown in Sage Village," Cameron confirmed. "Now, I have answered your one question, which means it's time for bed."

Amanda stood up, knowing that it was too late to push for more answers tonight. *Another time*, she promised herself, picturing her dad walking through this same purple world and imagining that he'd slept in this same barn on a journey of his own.

CHAPTER 13
EDMUND ROBINSON

Cameron was right about Amanda being tired at sunrise. She felt like she'd closed her eyes minutes before Rory woke her up. The others were already outside as Rory repacked her bag, urging Amanda to stop dragging her feet. As Amanda pulled on her boots, she thought of Judy asleep at home and wished she were back in her own bed. Even the house would be a welcome retreat. She pictured the blue bedroom with its soft canopy bed and plush carpets.

"Hey!" A sharp tug on one braid woke Amanda up.

"No daydreaming," Rory ordered, crouching in front of Amanda to stare her straight in the eye.

"I wasn't going to—" Amanda blushed, realizing how close she'd been to drifting back into the house. After her weeks of training and all of Aunt Judy's harping.

"It's harder to resist when you're tired. Try harder."

Rory stood up and brushed off her tunic.

"Right." Amanda bit her lip. "I will."

"If you screw up your origin point, that means the end of the mission," Rory reminded. "For both of us."

"Why both of us?"

"Because if you have to go home through New York, I'm the one getting you there safely and explaining what happened. I do not need that hassle."

Amanda swallowed back swift tears. She'd liked talking to Rory on the road, but now she knew that was just an effort to keep her from drifting back to the house. Because Rory knew she needed a babysitter to keep her in line. Not even a full Terra-V day and she was screwing up already. Amanda laced her boots quickly, resolving to prove Rory wrong.

But Amanda wasn't the only one holding them up.

Though Cameron had planned to leave at first light, Alira and Caeph were tending Churukh farmers long after the sun had risen. It had begun with those gathered outside the barn, but Alira had worried about those who were too sick to come to them. Cameron sent three knights with them to visit the farms and stewed over when they'd return.

"They'll wear themselves out before we even get to Sage Village," Cameron muttered as he parried Amanda's attack. They were fitting in some fencing practice, though Amanda would have rather gone with the Vherahna to see the Churukh in their homes.

"But they want to help." Amanda spun quickly, then lost her footing. In a flash, Cameron sent her sword tumbling into the grass. Amanda was about to retrieve it when Cameron charged, flashing his blade inches from her face.

"What are you—" Amanda scrambled backward, her heart racing and mind reeling. He continued to advance while Amanda darted her eyes toward the knights who were lounging in the field, watching without worry.

"Don't look at them!" Cameron barked. "They aren't going to help you!"

Amanda froze. This wasn't the Cameron she knew. He was huffing with anger, piercing her with his steely gaze. Her mind went blank, and her muscles tensed. When he lunged, she sprang to the left, wanting to put distance between them. She ran, twisting back to keep him in her sight. Other ideas flashed by in quick snatches. *Was he drugged? Or under a spell? Could the Churukh do that? Why weren't the others helping her? Was this their chance to get rid of her while Alira was away?*

Amanda didn't see the barn until she almost ran into it. She pivoted and lifted her arms to shield her face.

Cameron was toying with her, swinging his blade and stalking closer. Amanda peeked around her arms, inching away until her back hit the wall. He dropped his sword and rushed her, pinning her in place with a hand on each of her upper arms. He was bigger, stronger, taller. He squinted down at her, his hot breath on her face.

"What are you going to do now?" He taunted, as Amanda jerked her head away. *I'm going to die,* she answered silently, feeling tears slip from her eyes.

He squeezed her arms. Once. Not hard, but with a quick shake that caught her attention.

"Amanda," his voice was steady, softer, and he added an encouraging nod. "What are you going to do now?"

"Oh!" Amanda blinked rapidly, catching her breath with a flood of relief. *It's a test! We've practiced this!*

"I, uh, I—" Amanda cleared her throat and considered their positions. "I clasp my hands above your elbow, pull down hard to break your hold, and pull you forward. Then, uh, elbow you in the head, kick you, shove you. Whatever it takes to get myself clear."

"Don't tell me." Cameron kept his eyes locked on hers, not moving an inch. "Show me."

Amanda nodded as heat flared up from the pit of her stomach. *Don't think,* A voice inside yelled. *Do it!* With the swift movement they'd practiced in training, Amanda broke his hold, elbowed his temple, and shoved Cameron off-balance. He stumbled but didn't go down. Instead of ducking away, she braced herself against the rough wall and used that leverage to kick his side, hard, knocking him to his knees before he thudded to the ground on one hip.

Amanda leaped forward, prepared to kick him in the face, when Cameron held up his hands and yelled, "Okay! Stop! Stop!"

Still shaking, Amanda let her arms fall to her side. She heard cheering and laughing from across the field.

Her head was still spinning as Cameron broke into a smile from his place on the ground.

"Not bad," he conceded. "Eventually. But a real enemy isn't going to give you so many openings. And he won't wait for you to figure out how to fight back."

"Yeah," Amanda felt the shakiness of her breath as she wiped her tears with the back of her hand. Cameron got to his feet and gently straightened her collar. His face softened as he peered into her eyes.

"Are you okay?"

Amanda squared her shoulders and said she was fine. Cameron cuffed her shoulder affectionately. "Yeah, you are! You're tough, just need some practice."

They walked back toward the others slowly. Cameron scanned the horizon and frowned when there was no sign of the Vherahna and knights. "Like herding cats," he muttered to himself.

"You really want to get on the road," Amanda observed. Though Cameron shook his head.

"Not particularly. But if we're going, I'd rather get there before dark. Plus, Judy will be expecting our check-in from the door at Sage Village."

Amanda considered that. She thought Cameron would be eager to get to the library and plan the rest of their route. Their time was limited if Amanda was going to get home before her mom returned on Sunday afternoon. When she asked Cameron about it, he stopped walking some distance from the rest of his team.

"We can learn a lot at Sage Village," he said thoughtfully. "And it would be better—safer—if our journey doesn't lead much farther than that."

"But then…" Amanda stopped, wondering if Cameron wanted her to keep Alira and Caeph there, no matter what they found out, but she was hesitant to ask.

"Look, the Vherahna haven't gone beyond these farmlands and Sage Village in decades. They're, well, not exactly in-touch with how Terra-V has changed over the last century."

"But the Churukh need them to survive, right?" Amanda felt like she was missing some vital piece of information. "The Churukh need vhe to live, and vhe comes from the Vherahna. How can they be so out of touch?"

Cameron shrugged. "There are a lot more Churukh now, while the Vherahna population hasn't increased since we've known them. Before that, there was a dark period when their healing excursions left them open to kidnapping by ruthless Churukh who wanted more power in their tribes. We put a stop to that, but before we showed up, they were decimated year after year."

Amanda recalled the brief history she'd learned about Terra-V. It had mentioned some ancient tragedy that had thrown off the balance of Vherahna to Churukh but hadn't explained it in any depth.

"Now, the Vherahna stay safe inside the magic barrier of their tuntum trees, with us to help patrol their borders. They treat the pilgrims who make the trek to them, but mostly send vhe out in their salves and ethers. It's not so bad for the Churukh here, closer to the Vherahna, but as we move farther away—"

"Hey!" Rory waved and pointed as she called out to them. "They're coming back!"

"Finally!" Cameron returned her wave, then spoke urgently to Amanda, "Go get that sword you dropped. If we hurry, we may get there before the sun goes down."

§

As they were preparing to leave, the Churukh gave them each a large cup of chunked pineapple for their horses. Amanda fed a piece to Iveryn and laughed as he tossed his head in pleasure.

"It's good, right?" Amanda lifted the next piece toward her own mouth, thinking how good some pineapple would be after the bowl of strange grains and roots she'd had for breakfast. But a nicker from Iveryn stopped her.

"Oh, come on," she pleaded as he stared her down. "One for you, one for me, then the rest for you. That's more than fair!"

Iveryn's steady violet eye disagreed.

"Fine!" Amanda fed him the remaining fruit. "You know, we're going to a place where they grow their own pineapples. Maybe you'll feel more like sharing when we have a lot to spare."

Iveryn whinnied over the last bite, spread his tail feathers, then settled lower to the ground so Amanda could climb onto his back more easily.

"Thanks." Amanda rubbed behind his ears, sending a happy ripple down his neck. "You're a good horse," she told him. Silently adding, *even if you aren't really a horse.*

As Iveryn trotted in formation, Amanda noticed the knights were more alert on this leg of the journey. The Churukh farmers had warned of thieves that had been recently seen in the area.

"Thieves who rob people on the roadways," Cameron had clarified, out of Alira's hearing. "Not the Churukh royals who the Vherahna call thieves."

Amanda pondered that as the hours dragged on. She'd already asked Alira why she called the Churukh rulers thieves and had been told it was because they stole from the people who contributed to their society. The royals did not raise crops, or catch fish, or create goods, yet they took a large portion of those resources for themselves. According to Alira, the royals claimed to be stronger and wiser by birth, making them inherent leaders. They also claimed to offer value through their guidance and the protection of their soldiers. Yet the Vherahna believed most Churukh would be better off without those things.

"It sounds like politics back home," Amanda had told Cameron during one of their breaks. He'd shrugged.

"If you travel to enough worlds, you'll see that politics always comes down to a balance of power and freedom. Even in the best circumstances, no system is perfect."

When Amanda rode beside Caeph, she asked about the class system among the Churukh. The discussion soon diverted to the Churukh monks in Sage Village and the Vherahna prophecies stored in their sacred library.

"We have had many honored Vherahna seers in our history," Caeph shared in her mild, lyrical voice. "But none as deeply respected as your Edmund Robinson."

She bowed her head when speaking his name.

"He's the one who wrote the prophecy about the, uh, waking dreamer?" Amanda stopped herself from saying *the prophecy about me.*

"Oh, yes," Caeph's eyes lit up. "Though he spoke many other truths as well."

"He did?"

"Yes, of course! The *Prophecy of the Waking Dreamer* was Edmund's last foretelling, but he gifted us with many others. And all of his visions have come to pass."

"All of them?" Amanda did not believe in seeing the future. But six weeks ago she hadn't believed in psychic travel either. She asked Caeph to tell her more about the prophecies that had come true.

"Surely you know of Edmund's significance to our people? And to your own?" The rise in Caeph's lilting voice caught the attention of Davis, the knight riding on her far side. Amanda saw him turn their way as Caeph went on rapturously.

"Edmund's first vision brought us the truth of the mystical pineapple fruit. If he had not envisioned our adding it to the barren ground, we—and the Churukh—may have never discovered its wealth of benefits."

"Uh huh." Amanda tried to appear impressed, but it seemed much more likely that Edmund had used science to come to that conclusion, even if he'd called it prophecy. Maybe he was a botanist or had a garden back home.

"Did he make these prophecies to the Vherahna? Or did he travel to Sage Village?"

Caeph looked at Amanda with surprise again.

"Edmund spent many years traveling throughout Terra-V, both with the Vherahna and the Churukh." She smiled sadly. "He honored us all by spending the remainder of his life in Sage Village."

"Oh." Amanda scanned her memory but knew that hadn't been in her PTS training. All she'd been told about Edmund Robinson was that he was an important traveler from the Victorian era and there would be time to learn more about him later.

"Oy," Davis addressed Amanda with a bemused grin. "How is it *you* don't know about Edmund? I'd've thought you'd—"

"Davis!" Cameron interrupted from his place in the row behind them. "Why don't you take point for a while? Give Haruki a break, okay?"

"Yes, sir!"

Davis moved his horse to the front of the formation with a deft flick of his reins. Cameron trotted into the space he'd left open and the rest of the team shifted accordingly. The conversation about Edmund Robinson died in the tumult of realignment, but it did not leave Amanda's thoughts.

At their next rest break, Amanda found out Cameron was still thinking about it, too. He came over to where Amanda and Iveryn were sitting by the bend in a small stream, settled in the lilac grass beside them, and spoke without preamble.

"Edmund Robinson was an architect."

Amanda blinked at him.

"Okay?"

Cameron sighed.

"The Council thought it would be best to focus on this mission and explain the deeper elements of psychic travel later. When you were safely home again. Or maybe when you were older. I don't know."

He leaned back on his hands, looking out over the stream. The rest of their party lounged in pairs or small groups. Some were eating, others resting, while Haruki and Neela took their turn patrolling the perimeter of the clearing. Amanda let her hand gently rest on Iveryn's warm neck as he dozed by her side.

"The birdhouse was built by an architect," Cameron continued. Then quickly clarified, "by Edmund."

Amanda held her breath. She didn't want to say anything that might interrupt his revelations.

"Don't bother asking how an architect builds a house like that, in the mindspace, or how he connects doors to these distant places. That's way above my pay grade. In fact, common knowledge says that's a mystery to everyone at PTS. Except for the architects themselves."

Cameron was quiet then, watching the stream pass by or maybe watching Rory and Davis snickering over some private joke. Amanda weighed her options, wondering if he was more likely to continue talking with prompting or with silence. She took a chance with a direct question.

"Are there many architects?"

"No."

Cameron pushed himself to an upright seat and brushed his hands together.

Amanda waited. Cameron was giving her information no one else in PTS would tell her. Not even Aunt Judy.

"Architects come along very rarely," he said. "Once in a generation. At most."

Amanda's mind raced too quickly to pin down another question. Her body tensed, aware of every passing sensation. It felt a lot like their earlier sparring session, though she didn't know why.

"Edmund was our last architect," Cameron continued. "And he's been gone for nearly 100 years."

Sitting straighter, Amanda remembered the murmurs throughout the High Council during her hearing.

"So." She swallowed, clearing her throat. "We're due for a new architect?"

Cameron stood up. When he looked down at Amanda, he was a dark silhouette with the pale-yellow sun glowing behind him.

"Maybe."

Amanda squinted up at him, unable to ask more.

"We should get back on the road," Cameron said, making a sweeping gesture to gather the others. "We want to get there before dark."

"Yeah," Amanda nodded uncertainly and reached for Iveryn's reins.

They still had a long way to go.

§

As they neared their destination, the climate shifted from the cool, open plains of the farm region to a warmer, humid setting. The purple foliage switched to a mix of broad leaves and succulent spears, all in deeper jewel tones ranging from magenta and amethyst to dark plum and eggplant. The pale pink sky faded to a near white, streaked with coral and orange as the sun dropped toward the horizon.

Though she knew it was a walled city, Amanda was unprepared for her first sight of Sage Village. The towering walls gleamed like polished slate with marbled streaks of violet and mauve swirled through each stacked block. Stained-glass panels hung from open slits spaced along the top edge of the wall, while massive doors in rich blue-gray wood created an impressive entrance.

Beyond their elegance, the walls impressed Amanda with their sheer size. Even from a distance, it was difficult to see where the walls ended as they spread evenly from the central doors. Riding closer, Amanda felt breathless at their enormity.

Smaller doors cut into the large city gates were propped open, allowing visitors easy access to the village. Once inside, Amanda nearly forgot the walls were there at all. She was too busy staring from one direction to the next.

The village flourished within those expansive walls. Small trees and bushes grew in clusters. Graceful stone buildings featured columned porches and balconies draped in baskets of flowering plants. Large slabs of stone created smooth streets where Churukh monks in silken robes moved throughout the community. The surroundings and brilliantly gowned people reminded Amanda of the exotic tales her dad had loved to read to her.

A group of Churukh monks welcomed them at the door and asked about their trip from the forest. Their horses were taken to the village stables, and they were shown to private rooms in a comfortable guest house. Two bedrooms had been prepared for their stay, along with an adjoining sitting room.

Mhevek, the leader of Sage Village, came to greet them personally, expressing honor at having both Vherahna and English visitors. He greeted them in English, though Alira switched to Churukh for her reply. Amanda assumed it was a gesture of respect and tried not to worry about what was being said. She guessed from their body language, and their few words in English, that Alira was presenting Amanda as the *waking dreamer* of Edmund's last prophecy.

"You are most welcome among us, Amanda." Mhevek bowed deeply.

"Hello." Amanda shuffled her feet. She tried to meet Mhevek's emerald eyes, but the weary exhaustion of two days on horseback, in an alien world, was taking its toll. It felt like years instead of hours since she'd slept. Cameron stepped in to explain their long trek, and Mhevek offered compassion for their journey.

"We will have food and drink brought to you this evening, and there will be time for us to have a lengthy visit in the light of day."

In the bedroom she would share with the women in their party—Alira, Caeph, Rory, and Neela—Amanda stood before six narrow feather beds. Each were set on a raised wooden platform and covered by a canopy with sheer curtains. A round table with six wooden chairs was decorated with a silver bowl of flowers, and woven tapestries hung from each of the walls.

Wanting nothing more than sleep, Amanda unstrapped her bow and quiver, dropped her pack on the floor, and stretched out on the nearest bed. She closed her eyes, ignoring the knock on the door, and appreciated the softness of this mattress after her dense pallet in the barn. She was nearly asleep when Cameron shook her arm.

"Not quite yet," he prodded. "Just a little longer and you'll be asleep in your own bed."

"This is a good bed," Amanda mumbled, barely able to process anything more.

But Cameron was insistent.

When Amanda grudgingly sat up, she saw a shimmering, barely visible door in the center of the room. *"Is that?"* She didn't have to finish the question before Cameron was explaining that their guest suites, as well as a section of the adjacent library, fell within the Sage Village proximity zone.

"Come on," he nudged. "Aunt Judy awaits!"

Walking through the attic and waking in Aunt Judy's living room filled Amanda with a shot of adrenaline. She stared wordlessly at the modern furniture, trying to catch her bearings as Judy rocked her in a crushing hug.

"Let her breathe," Cameron laughed, smiling at the happy tears in Judy's eyes.

"You're safe!" Judy repeated again and again with laughter of her own.

"If you don't suffocate me!" Amanda pulled away, embarrassed but happy to be back.

"Right, sorry!" Judy rocked on her heels, pressing her fingertips to her mouth before a sudden thought made her rush for her phone.

"I know you're exhausted," she began, intent on the phone screen. "But we need to call your mom before anything else. She's been texting all morning and I promised to video chat as soon as you woke up."

"That's my cue," Cameron retreated to take a shower and give them their space.

"What time is it?" Amanda blinked toward the window, vaguely unsettled by the blue sky and green leaves outside the glass.

"About 11:30," Judy told her. "In the morning."

"Uh huh," Amanda nodded, feeling as if everything around her was moving too fast. "And, uh, what day is it?"

Sitting her down at the kitchen table, Judy brought Amanda a glass of water.

It was Thursday—Thanksgiving—and she'd been in Terra-V nearly twenty-seven hours. After wiping her face with a damp cloth, and inhaling a blueberry muffin, Amanda put on a bright smile, and they called to wish her mom a Happy Thanksgiving.

About seven hours later, after sleep and a hot shower, Amanda was back at the table eating a huge slice of lasagna and drinking her third glass of iced tea. Cameron had eaten earlier and gone back to Terra-V, leaving Amanda to tell her aunt about their adventure so far.

"I've seen drawings of the library at Sage Village," Judy said dreamily as she cut two thick slices of chocolate cake. "I've always wanted to go there, but I don't have many opportunities to travel off-world."

"I guess I'll see it when I go back," Amanda answered, though her mind was on other things.

Judy passed her niece a piece of cake with a worried frown.

"You're holding up okay?" she asked, again, earning a groaning eye roll from Amanda.

"Don't I look okay?" Amanda stabbed at her cake, though she was already full from dinner.

"You look better now," Judy answered honestly. "After some sleep and food."

She had already played the PTS counselor, asking probing questions, checking Amanda's vitals, then giving her vitamins and another white tablet to prepare for her return trip. She'd said Amanda was doing very well in an extraordinary situation, but she was still worried over where the journey would lead.

"Where's my phone?" Amanda pushed the cake away, unable to take another bite.

"Your phone?" Judy hesitated before retrieving it from the coffee table. "Before you look at it, you should know that Drew has been texting."

"Okay…" Amanda held out her hand, unsure why that would be surprising.

"And I've been responding," Judy added quickly. "As myself, I mean! Not as you. I told him it was me, and I reassured him you were okay."

"Oh, uh, okay." Amanda scrolled through the messages. They showed Drew asking about Amanda and Judy updating him after the few messages she'd received from Cameron during their journey. They were simple texts, rarely more than *she's okay* or *still okay*.

"I almost gave him my number," Judy went on. "But then I thought it might be better to use your phone, so you'd know exactly what we said while you were gone."

"Uh, yeah, okay." Her aunt seemed afraid Amanda would be upset, but Amanda felt nothing as she scrolled through her messages. *Not even one from Trina,* she noticed. Though that was expected.

"I thought you didn't want Drew involved?" Amanda asked after setting her phone on the table.

Judy picked at her cake, then set her fork down.

"I don't. Or *maybe* I don't. I'm not sure."

Judy pushed her plate away.

"I've had a lot of time to think while you've been gone," she continued. "And your situation is so unusual. You're so much younger than everyone else in PTS."

"Are you just noticing that?" Amanda broke off a piece of cake with her fingers.

"Well, no. But in a way, maybe," Judy admitted, reaching for another bite of cake, too. "I've just been thinking that you don't have any peers at PTS, not that are close to your age, and you won't for some time. So maybe it's not so bad to have someone to talk to who *is* your age, even if he isn't a traveler."

"Hmm," Amanda frowned but nodded, acknowledging her aunt's point without expressly agreeing. She hadn't told Judy how things had been changing with Drew and Trina. It felt like the wrong time to bring it up now.

"I thought that's what you wanted?" Judy narrowed her eyes, assessing Amanda's blank expression. "Didn't you want Drew to be a part of this? In any way he could be?"

"Uh, yeah, I did. I mean, I do."

"Okay…?"

They sat quietly for several seconds, knowing that their time was short. Cameron would be back any minute for their return trip to Terra-V. It could be another day—or more—before they had another chance to talk.

Amanda looked up suddenly.

"Am I the next architect?"

CHAPTER 14

THE LIBRARY AT SAGE VILLAGE

Slender arches of pale-gray stone rose in a ribbed canopy across the vaulted ceiling. Celestial murals filled the space between each rib, the subtle art only highlighting the architectural beauty of the polished stone. From the delicate taper at their lofty heights to the engraved pillars supporting their weight, these magnificent arches inspired awe in the hearts of those who visited the library at Sage Village.

Branching from the airy central hall, similar stone archways opened into divided sections where bookshelves lined the walls and gleaming tables offered space to study in comfort. The upper walls, extending above carved shelves and cabinets to the base of the vaulted ceiling, featured massive stained-glass panels that infused the space with a pastel glow.

In the central hall, Amanda sat at a low, round table with Alira, Caeph, and Mhevek, the leader of Sage Village. After several minutes of chanting meditation, Mhevek poured steaming blue tea into each of their pale green cups. Amanda watched herbs lift from the depth of her cup to swirl into the motion of the poured tea and settle across its surface. Alira then offered a small flower bud to place inside her cup. The waxy flower was heavier than Amanda expected. It dropped deeply into the hot tea before bobbing to the surface where its delicate pink petals gently unfurled to reveal a heart of midnight blue.

Entranced by its beauty, Amanda glanced up to see flowers opening in the cups around the table. Alira smiled softly. Mhevek lifted his cup, letting the steam rise before his face. The Vherahna raised their cups and Amanda followed their lead. The steam was pleasantly warm against her skin, and it carried the familiar scent of honeysuckle. The others slowed their breath, inhaling and gently releasing the sweet steam. Amanda slowed her breath as well, feeling her body warm and soften with a sensation of gentle relaxation.

Amanda opened her eyes to see Mhevek briefly bow his head before taking his first sip. Having been previously assured the tea was harmless, Amanda sipped cautiously from her cup. The tip of a flower petal tickled her upper lip. The liquid was sweet and warm on her tongue. As it traveled down her throat, Amanda felt its heat spreading from her core. With each sip, the warmth spread farther into her arms and legs. By the time she'd half-finished the cup, Amanda's entire body felt snugly settled, warm and smooth. Melting into her cushioned seat, she closed her eyes and listened to the rhythmic chanting resume around her.

"Oh, wisdom within," Mhevek beseeched above the Vherahna's gentle humming, "rise to fill our waking dreamer.

Let her see the path that unfolds before her. Let her know the direction to lead. Release her from fear and doubt; reveal the future that is to come."

As Mhevek spoke, his words felt like tiny strikes against Amanda's calm. A nervous, twittering sensation snaked from her belly. There were dark, jagged shapes looming in her imagination. Rocking nausea crept into her body. Amanda tried to breathe, ignoring her growing unease. But the heavy calm fizzled away, leaving her alert and anxious behind her closed eyes.

She heard Mhevek's voice continue, now intoning the *Prophecy of the Waking Dreamer*. Amanda thought of Mr. Hewlett trying so hard to find symbolism in the stories they read. There was nothing hidden in this prophecy. She knew it in her heart and in her mind. The prophecy was a group of pretty words about a quest for treasure. Nothing more. Edmund likely wrote it to inspire hope, and he'd kept it vague enough that the Vherahna could interpret it any way they chose. It was a kind gesture for a society he'd come to care about, and that was all. She was sure of it.

Unless, Amanda thought with a trembling heart, Edmund had possessed some additional perception that came with being an architect of psychic travel. Maybe he could sense something about where and when the next architect would develop her skills. Maybe this prophecy was a set of instructions meant to lead Amanda to her destiny.

But that's crazy, Amanda told herself.

She didn't even know if she *was* the next architect. When she'd asked her aunt, Judy said that no one knew. There were suspicions circling, but only because Edmund

Robinson was nineteen when his psychic travel abilities emerged. The youngest traveler on record. Until now.

Until Amanda.

Amanda pushed those thoughts away, realizing the chanting had stopped. There was silence around the table. When she opened her eyes, the shining hope in Alira's eyes made her heart sink.

§

Amanda left the tea ceremony without any insight on where they should go next. No voice of wisdom had spoken in her head. Alira and Mhevek were unconcerned. They said the seed of knowledge had been watered and needed space to grow. Caeph was silent.

Amanda found Cameron poring over a large map in a quiet section of the library.

"How did it go?" Cameron grinned, remembering his own experience with Mhevek's sacred tea ceremonies.

But Amanda wasn't interested in discussing tea, or chants, or meditation. Her heart had skipped at the sight of the map. With a map, she could weigh their options and make a logical plan for where to lead their journey.

"This is a map! A map of Terra-V!" Amanda hurried to Cameron's side, an accusation clear in her tone. "Why haven't we looked at a map before?"

Cameron stepped back, giving her space.

"I've looked at a map before," he answered lightly. "Many maps, actually, including this one."

"But we can use this to see which way to—" Amanda stopped talking. She chanced a sideways glance at Cameron's amused face. "And that's exactly why you got this map out. You were waiting for them to finish so we could come up with our actual plan."

"Something like that."

Cameron pointed to an area on the painted map.

"Now this map isn't exactly to scale, but… This is the Vherahna Forest, where we began."

"Oh, look!" Amanda squinted at the simple drawings. "The trees there are all twisted up."

"Yes," Cameron sighed. "Here are the farmlands where we camped, west of the tuntum trees. And this is Sage Village, north of the farms. See the large swath of nothing that separates the Vherahna from everything else to the north and east of their forest? That's an immense rocky desert that extends all the way up over here and off the map into the northeast."

"What's south of the Vherahna Forest?" Amanda saw a thin blue line that bordered the bottom edge of the map, swept along the left edge, and curved up into a wide band at the top of the map. "Is that water? Is Terra-V an island?"

"A peninsula," Cameron corrected.

Amanda saw tall mountains drawn in the upper right corner of the map, beside the large band of blue. Settlements dotted the coast, at the base of the mountains, and on one of the mountain peaks. A much larger walled city sprawled at the center of the map, separated from the Vherahna Forest by the rocky desert.

"All of these Churukh lands haven't been visited by the Vherahna in current memory. Representatives from each area's tribes have made pilgrimages to the Vherahna Forest

217

instead. Bringing Alira and Caeph into these areas is risky. Though the honor of seeing the Vherahna in person may provide some protection if we pass quickly. Lingering would be a bad idea. We don't want to give dangerous people time to hatch any plans."

"But that's the entire map! You're pointing at everywhere except the places we've already been."

"Yes," Cameron agreed.

Amanda frowned, then thought of a possibility.

"Where are the proximal doors? There's one here in Sage Village, and another in the Vherahna Forest, but there are six doors in the attic. So, where are the other four?"

"One is nearly at the top of this peak, in a place known as the Aerie." Cameron pointed at the top of the westernmost mountain, then trailed his finger to a settlement lower down on a mountain to the east. "Another is within this settlement of artisans. Both are inaccessible by horse and too far to be of any help to us.

"Another is just as far, in some ruins deep in the rocky desert. It's so far east that it's not even on this map. And there's nothing out there anymore anyway."

"That's only three." Amanda held up five fingers. "Five all together. Where's the sixth door?"

Cameron placed his finger flat on the castle drawn within the walled city at the center of the map. It seemed like a good destination for their journey. The Vherahna couldn't use the door, but it would quickly bring PTS reinforcements if they needed help. Cameron dashed that hope.

"We have an uneasy relationship with the Churukh royals who live in that castle. There's a proximity zone beneath the castle in what used to be the dungeon—which is a story for another time—but soon after it was created, we signed a treaty with the royals that promised—among other things—that we'd never use that door again."

"But if—"

"And then they packed the entire dungeon with dirt and stone to make sure. That door's gone."

"Oh." Amanda's face fell as she realized how much she didn't know about this strange world. Or about psychic travel. She hadn't even known it was possible to block a proximity zone. Cameron waited a beat, letting the message sink in, then offered his own plan.

"The fishing community just north of Sage Village would be the least risky place to go. It's about two hours by horse, so the Churukh who live there have had more opportunity to visit Sage Village. Some of them have met the Vherahna during their occasional summits.

"We—meaning me and my team—have been to the fishing village many times, and they're nearly as welcoming as the Churukh in the farmlands. I think it would be safe enough to bring Alira and Caeph there for a day trip. A view of the sea and mountains would impress them and maybe even be enough to end this journey."

Amanda studied Cameron's expression critically.

"At the High Council hearing, you said this journey was as important for us as it was for the Vherahna. Now it sounds like you're just humoring them."

Cameron shifted his tunic and chainmail, looking beyond the archway to ensure they were still alone. While he fidgeted, Amanda replayed her memory of the hearing.

"You said no one knew what happened to… *someone*… I thought you meant Edmund, but when Mhevek showed me the statue they put up here when he died, you told me his body had been retrieved by PTS. So, you weren't talking about him…?"

"Amanda." Cameron put his hand on her shoulder. When he looked into her eyes, he seemed to reconsider his planned answer. "Do you trust me?"

"I—" Amanda remembered her first sight of Cameron in the attic, his concern when she saw him among the crowd in the house, the way he'd swept into her hearing, and their weeks of training for this journey. In a flash, she pictured his crazed eyes as he chased her across the meadow and pinned her against the barn. And then the softness as he encouraged her to break free and knock him to the ground. Even when he seemed tough, he wanted her to be safe. She could see it in his eyes and hear it in the way he had reassured Judy before they left home.

He reminded her of Drew.

"I trust you," she answered carefully.

Cameron lowered his eyes and Amanda saw his shoulders droop before he looked up again.

"You're doing very well. But, Amanda, you're young, and you have a lot to learn. About PTS, about yourself, about everything. Can you trust that I'll tell you what you need to know when you're ready to know it?"

"I, uh." Amanda swallowed hard, suddenly unsure. "Yes."

"Good girl." Cameron patted her arm and turned to roll up the map.

Amanda didn't ask anything else, but questions swirled in her mind. *Who was he talking about at the hearing? If it wasn't Edmund, was it another traveler?* She remembered the conversation she'd overheard between her mom and Chad. *If my dad died when he was away…?* She couldn't continue the thought, but it was there now. Waiting.

§

Standing on the shore of the fishing village, Amanda looked out over the bright blue waves and felt almost as if she were back home. The water was a more vibrant blue than the water at Virginia Beach, but it looked like pictures she'd seen of the Caribbean. The sky was bluer here as well, with less of the pinks and corals that colored the sky above Sage Village. Even the rocky peaks in the distance reminded her of the Blue Ridge Mountains, only taller with steep tips that disappeared behind wispy clouds.

Closing her eyes, Amanda listened to the waves lapping against the pier and let the breeze cool her sun-warmed cheeks. The only thing missing was the salty sea air.

"Hey, look sharp!"

Amanda swiveled to see Rory behind her, one hand on her knife hilt, her eyes scanning the bustling seaport. Cameron stood a short distance away, talking with some Churukh who were docking their ship. Amanda knew very little about boats, but the Churukh's wooden ships looked like boats she'd seen before. Except for their silvery-blue wood and bright, patchwork sails.

Rory and Brendan had stayed at the seaport with Amanda and Cameron while the other knights escorted the Vherahna to visit those in need. Amanda knew firsthand that the vhe they delivered through song and touch was far more powerful than their vhe-infused products, and she could see how their healing efforts were taking a toll on Alira and Caeph. Like Cameron, she worried how long they could last away from the tuntum trees.

"Are we going somewhere?" Amanda called, noticing how Rory's eyes kept moving over the scene around them. Brendan was several paces away, patrolling the pier.

"Not yet, but it would make my job easier if you'd keep your eyes open."

Amanda pressed her lips together, holding back a retort. As the days went on, Rory seemed more impatient with their mission. And with Amanda. She was increasingly tense and had stayed within a few steps of Amanda ever since they'd left Sage Village.

It was on the tip of Amanda's tongue to tell Rory that she could take care of herself. She'd stayed alert on their ride from the shore and hadn't even come close to daydreaming since her visit home. Besides, it was the Vherahna who drew the Churukh's attention. Amanda was just another *English* to them. Even if her smaller size and plain tunic, without chainmail, attracted some attention from the more curious Churukh.

"This isn't Sage Village," Rory added unnecessarily. "We aren't behind any walls and don't know who could be lurking around."

"Yeah, these villagers are super shifty," Amanda snarked as a group of Churukh passed with nods of polite greeting. Cameron had warned her about the risk to the Vherahna, but Amanda had seen nothing but awe and respect from the Churukh they'd met so far.

"And you have so much experience in Terra-V now," Rory mocked before speaking seriously. "I've told you, they have a primitive culture here and that includes a system where the weakest end up as slave labor. If you can't protect yourself here, they think you *deserve* to be a slave."

Amanda looked around uneasily. There were obvious marks of a class system among the Churukh. Those with better clothes and brighter eyes often had dull-eyed servants carrying their packs and driving their carts. Alira and Caeph had ignored those ranks, giving more vhe to those in the greatest need, but Amanda knew that vitality wouldn't last long once the Vherahna left the village. Those in a higher class would still have more vhe-infused products to keep up their health, while their servants would slink back into weakness.

"You also said they're afraid of the English," Amanda mumbled under her breath.

"What was that?" Rory stepped closer with her eyes flashing. "Yes, the Churukh usually leave us alone. Because they know we're superior fighters and because—in their view—we have magic powers that let us disappear at will. But that doesn't mean we're not at risk here."

"Is there a problem?" Brendan had made his way back along the pier and stopped with his hands on his hips, inches from his sword.

"No problem," Rory replied with a meaningful look at Amanda before turning to face Brendan. "Stay with the kid for a few, okay? I'll take the next pass."

"Sure," Brendan agreed, as Rory walked away.

"What's with her?" he asked Amanda.

"She's worried about kidnappers."

Brendan raised an eyebrow.

"She was telling me how Churukh have slaves," Amanda explained, "which is awful, but it's not like they'll go after me with all of you around."

"Perhaps not," Brendan answered slowly. He chose his words carefully, the way some adults did when they talked to kids. He was one of the older knights, and Amanda wasn't as bothered by the way he talked down to her. Maybe because he spoke to Rory the same way.

"You think the Vherahna are a more likely target?" he asked. "Because Churukh in the past kidnapped so many of them? That was a dark time for sure, and the more desperate Churukh might get some bad ideas seeing Alira and Caeph here now. But them being at risk, doesn't mean you're at any less risk, now does it? The Churukh aren't stupid. They can see you're different than us. Smaller, no armor, and all that. Better we be careful."

Amanda understood Brendan's point, but most of the Churukh had accepted vhe from Alira and Caeph with tears of gratitude, offering them fruits, nuts, or small trinkets. Of course, the Vherahna refused any gifts, insisting that it was their joy and honor to bestow vhe freely.

Some had tried to shove their way ahead, and then fumed when the Vherahna calmly asked them to wait their turn—usually it was Churukh who already had the brightest eyes—but they hadn't done anything worse than grumble to each other. Thinking of them, Amanda remembered what

Cameron had said about not giving dangerous people time to hatch plans.

When the Vherahna and knights returned to the pier, Alira spoke to Cameron sharply.

"Did you know how great the need for vhe is in this community? There are Churukh wasting from want while others sell their ethers for exorbitant amounts of food or goods. This situation is untenable. If it continues, many Churukh will die."

Cameron took Alira and Caeph aside, leaving Amanda to hear Rory's concerns.

"This journey will be the end of them," she predicted darkly. "Cameron thinks he can satisfy some prophecy, but he hasn't spent that much time with Alira in the last few years. She won't keep the Vherahna safe in the forest after seeing so many in need. And she won't let it go when she finds out how much of their products are stolen before they can make it all the way home from the Vherahna Forest. She's too kind to understand how this will end."

Amanda sat on the pier and felt the subtle vibrations of the waves against its base. She didn't like to think about the Churukh who were sick and starving for both food and vhe, though she'd seen enough of them already. She didn't like to think about Alira and Caeph putting themselves in danger or the Vherahna wearing themselves to extinction in an effort to save the Churukh, though she could see that happening, too.

To take her mind off it all, Amanda leaned against the nearest post and watched the Churukh passing by with horses and carts full of goods. The seaport was the busiest place she'd seen yet in Terra-V. Ships of varying sizes returned to deliver loads of fish and seaweed. A wide, well-worn road traversed the length of the shore and led further east, heading toward Terra-V's largest market town and the castle beyond. All around her, the guttural sounds of the Churukh language created a churning, visceral rhythm like a stereo with cranked up bass.

Although it was still early in the afternoon, Amanda figured it was well past midnight back home. The alien environment and lack of sleep were catching up with her again. Her eyelids drooped and a thin buzzing needled her brain.

As she struggled to stay awake, rocking nausea crept into her body. It was a familiar feeling, one she couldn't quite place, but a sensation she'd experienced not long ago. She was still trying to place the feeling when a wagon loaded with colorful blossoms passed by on the crowded road.

"Honeysuckle."

The word slipped out as Amanda recognized the scent.

"What was that?" Brendan called over.

"Oh, nothing," Amanda sat up, stretching her arms. "It's the weirdest thing. I caught a scent of honeysuckle at the same time I was feeling a little seasick, exactly how I felt during that tea thing this morning. Déjà vu, I guess."

Amanda stopped chuckling when she saw a look of muted anger pass over Rory's face.

"What, I—"

Rory was looking past Amanda. She let out her breath slowly as if bracing for bad news.

Alira hurried to Amanda's side.

"What did you feel?" Her pale face glinted pink and teal as she placed a hand on Amanda's arm. *Blink-blink.* "You sensed something here? A premonition from the tea ceremony?"

Alira was nodding urgently while Caeph narrowed her eyes, her own hope trembling to the surface.

Amanda darted her eyes toward Cameron, whose expression was carefully neutral.

"Not a premonition, no. Just this weird déjà vu... um, this feeling like something had happened before... But it was just the waves and the scent..."

Alira's smile was triumphant.

"This proves it," she announced decisively. "We are on the right path and will continue to the market town."

§

As they rode away from the fishing village, Amanda wasn't entirely sure how they'd ended up on this path. Alira had insisted Amanda's experience was a sign pointing them to follow the flower cart toward the market town at the center of Terra-V. Cameron had insisted it was a sign pointing them back to Sage Village where the tea ceremony had been held. Alira reminded him that the interpretation of signs was her responsibility. Cameron reminded her that the safety of their party was his responsibility.

By the time anyone asked Amanda how she would interpret her experience, her head was swimming. She told them it hadn't meant anything. She said the nausea had been a reaction to the waves against the pier and the scent of honeysuckle had been a coincidence.

"There are no coincidences," Alira had intoned gently. "You are the waking dreamer. You are the one who will lead us to the treasure we have missed without knowing. You will begin our world anew. You say where we should go, and we will follow."

Amanda had examined the faces waiting for her reply. She saw Alira's utter and total belief in her, Caeph's hope for their future, Cameron's expectation of loyalty, and Rory's antipathy. But it was the wary skepticism of the other knights that raised Amanda's self-doubt.

Who was she to be telling these seasoned soldiers where they should go in a dangerous, alien world? *I'm fifteen,* Amanda thought desperately. *Barely fifteen. Who am I to be making these decisions?*

"I want—" Amanda's voice had cracked, and her eyes had blurred. She was suddenly exhausted.

"Sage Village," she'd said, after roughly clearing her throat. "I think we should go back to Sage Village."

"You heard her." Cameron waved a hand in the air, gesturing to round up his team. "Let's head back while it's still light."

He winked at her as he passed by, leading them to the stables. But it was the look of disappointment in Caeph's eyes that haunted Amanda during their ride back.

CHAPTER 15
THE WAKING DREAMER

The view from the balcony overlooked lush fields of pineapple plants. Amanda sat with her back against the stone wall and her knees bent against her chest. Though it had still been light when they returned, Amanda had gone straight to bed. She could have used the proximal door to sleep at home, but she'd told Cameron that she'd rather rest in the guest suite and visit Judy in the morning. When she woke, it was deep night and the other women were asleep in their beds around her. Having no idea of the time, either here or back home, Amanda had crept onto the quiet balcony where she could breathe in the starlight.

Was this a view her dad had seen when he was in Terra-V? Amanda imagined him here, with the Vherahna and the Churukh. How many times had he visited this world when she was a child, or before she was born? Had it changed since he was here last?

She tried to remember his funeral.

There was a hazy image of an antique-filled house where people gathered in dark clothes around a shiny silver vase with a lid. Amanda now knew it was an urn holding his ashes, but at the time she didn't understand how her dad could be inside that little vase. It had felt like a game. A sad game that no one wanted to play, but one they were all playing anyway. She couldn't remember seeing the urn again after that day. Had her mom buried it? Did Aunt Judy have it?

Were his ashes even in there?

Amanda tightened her arms around her bent legs, trying to contain the pain in her chest.

It had been nine years since her dad had died. More than half Amanda's life. Her memories of him were thin and fragile. Feelings more than pictures and words.

What if he hadn't actually died?

Pain burned through Amanda's ribs. She drew in short gasps of air, feeling her neck strain with the effort to control her sobs. It was too much. The pain, the hope, the grief. Amanda told herself it wasn't possible. Her dad would never stay away all this time. He'd never let them think he was dead if he wasn't.

Unless there was something keeping him away?

Amanda shook away the nagging voice. He had died.

For years, she'd dreamed that he was still alive only to wake up and face the painful truth all over again. Once she'd accepted that he was gone, those dreams had stopped. She wouldn't let herself go back to that cycle of false hope and crushing truth. Not anymore.

She inhaled the cool air and exhaled the hurt.

Moonlight shimmered on a decorative pond at the opening of the pineapple garden. Amanda watched the play of light and shade before letting her eyes drift over the shadowy plants. Before coming here, she'd had a vague idea that pineapples grew on trees, like bananas or coconuts. She'd been surprised to see them growing at the center of leafy, tropical plants with spiky blades that reminded her of the snake plant in Judy's living room. While the pineapple plants were green, unlike other Terra-V flora, they were tipped in streaks of deep purple. Amanda suspected that was a contribution from the alien soil.

A night breeze rippled over the plants, sending a shiver through Amanda's tense body.

She thought of the Terra-V in her short story, the purple world her dad had described so vividly. If she'd never come here—never developed psychic travel abilities—that would be all she'd ever known of this magical place. She wouldn't have known there were pineapples growing in this walled garden or horse-shaped creatures covered in sleek feathers. She'd have never learned about the Churukh or the Vherahna's struggle to process enough vhe to keep an entire, dependent species alive.

Maybe that would have been better.

As she sat alone on the balcony, watching two moons in an alien sky, Amanda imagined what her life would be, right now, if she'd never opened that attic door. Would her biggest worry be homework? Would she be like the other girls at school, frantic to find a dress for the Winter Formal? Would she still be bothered by Drew dating Trina? Would Drew *be* dating Trina?

The sound of the balcony door pulled Amanda out of her thoughts. She didn't have to turn her head to know who had come outside. She sensed Caeph's energy as she settled beside her on the stone floor, not touching but within easy reach.

Caeph said nothing. Though she was weaker than she'd been at the beginning of their journey, she still exuded an energy that washed over Amanda like a warm bath. In Caeph's presence, Amanda could feel her back melting into the stone wall and her arms softening their hold around her legs. There was a steadiness in her heart and mind.

"I owe you an apology," Caeph offered gently.

"What? No, you don't." Amanda kept her gaze over the pineapple plants, but she could clearly picture the disappointment in Caeph's eyes as they rode back from the fishing village.

"Yes," Caeph insisted. "When our journey began, my heart ached. We sat on that ridge, overlooking the farmlands, and my body shivered as the sun lowered without the shelter of the tuntum trees. I had never felt so cold, so uncertain, despite my training. It was as if my body could not move. Could not feel. And you were there."

Amanda shifted, reliving the moment, and wanted to downplay the little she'd done.

"You are not Vherahna," Caeph continued, in an awed voice. "You do not channel vhe. Yet you stepped close and offered me what strength you had to give. It was a gift unlike any I've known. It made me strong in the face of my fear. It has helped to sustain me during these long days and uneasy nights.

"Yet, today, when you faced your own fear, I stood apart and did nothing to help you trust your inner voice."

"Caeph, no." Amanda shook her head, turning to face Caeph's serene sincerity.

"You were afraid," Caeph persisted, "and I waited for you to take charge on your own. Because you are the waking dreamer, the one who will lead us. But I was wrong. Being chosen to lead does not take away one's fear."

Amanda sat crossed-legged, elbows on her thighs, and bowed her head to rest on her clasped hands. She didn't want Caeph's apology. Fear hadn't driven her decision. Not in the way Caeph meant. It had been more of an acceptance of her true place in this journey. Cameron and the other travelers had the experience to keep them safe in Terra-V, she didn't. She was there to make Alira happy and play along with the prophecy, not to actually lead.

"I wasn't afraid," Amanda explained carefully. "I was considering the risks, and the experience of people more, uh, well, experienced."

"Because you were afraid," Caeph nodded. "You were afraid to speak your truth."

"No." Amanda sat straighter. The dizzy sensation of everyone watching her on that pier, hanging on her words, was fresh in her body. "I mean, sure, I was a *little* afraid of saying the wrong thing."

"You didn't want to disappoint your elders."

"Not exactly." Amanda paused. "But they have the experience here. And I don't."

Caeph faced Amanda fully, her legs crossed before her, and Amanda unconsciously echoed her pose. As they sat in silence, Caeph's deep blue hair gleamed on either side of her face. Her violet eyes picked up glimmers of blue and rose in her opal skin. *Blink-blink.* Her chin slowly lowered, casting shadows beneath her angular cheeks and making her eyes seem larger. More intent. *Blink-blink.*

Amanda felt a catch in her chest.

"You felt a calling," Caeph stated knowingly. "You felt an urge leading you toward something."

Amanda remembered the scents and sensations that had so eerily echoed her experience during the tea ceremony. That *had* felt like a pull toward something, even if she didn't understand it. Caeph nodded.

"And how did it feel when you didn't follow that call? When we came here instead?"

A sick dread churned in Amanda's stomach. She hadn't gone home to sleep, not because she'd been too tired to make the trip but because she'd felt ashamed. She hadn't wanted to face her aunt's questions.

Amanda's mind told her siding with Cameron was the right choice. Her heart and gut cried in disappointment.

"I didn't want you and Alira to be in more danger. Because of me."

"You were afraid for our safety," Caeph clarified.

"Yes."

Caeph shook her head. "Our safety is not your concern."

"Of course, it is!"

Caeph offered the same bemused smile Amanda had often seen on Alira's face.

"Amanda," she assured calmly, "you cannot cause or prevent our harm."

"But if I lead you to a more dangerous place—"

"You can only lead us where your heart says to go," Caeph interrupted. "Whatever happens next is not in your control."

"But," Amanda tried again, "if I lead you to a place where there's danger…?"

"Then it is the *danger* that may harm us. The harm would not come from you."

Amanda's lips parted as she struggled to form a clear argument. Caeph frowned, wanting to help.

"The Churukh farthest from our home are the most in need," she began.

"Yes," Amanda jumped in, grasping at an important idea. "They're also the most likely to hurt you."

"And the most likely to die without our help."

"But *you* could die trying to help them!" Amanda countered hotly.

"Yes, I could." Caeph's easy agreement surprised Amanda. "Yet if we are each likely to die, our risk is the same. Would you have me let them die to save myself?"

"Yes," Amanda blurted without hesitation.

The idea of Caeph, or Alira, dying was too horrible for Aamanda to imagine.

Caeph tilted her head to one side and waited.

Amanda pictured the Churukh she'd met on their journey. The young, the old, the pleasant, the gruff. She'd met those who worked with calloused hands and aching bodies, as well as those who were too sick to work at all. Some had frightened her with their bitter resentments, and many had impressed her with their gratitude and selflessness.

She remembered Rory telling her that the Churukh were strikingly human and later predicting the Vherahna would sacrifice themselves, giving their vhe—their life force—until they had none left to give.

"If the Churukh die, it's from a lack of resources." Amanda puzzled through the logic of the situation. "But if you, or Alira, died, it would be because some Churukh stole your life. Like, purposefully stole your life!"

"Because they lack resources," Caeph agreed sadly.

"And that's okay?" Amanda was horrified.

Caeph let her eyes drift out of focus, seeing beyond Amanda. "It is a risk worth taking to find a path that will change this dynamic."

"You think that's what we're doing?" Amanda felt her anxiety rising. "You think that's what my feelings—what these *sensations*—are leading us to?"

Caeph smiled enigmatically.

"When the waking dreamer stumbles in, the world begins anew."

§

By first light, Amanda was in the stables, preparing for the long ride ahead. After talking to Caeph, she had gone home to shower and have breakfast with her aunt, then returned for a private meeting with Alira. They'd sat under the stone arches in the library while Amanda carefully described her experience on the pier, and the regret she had felt since then.

"What do you think, Iveryn?" Amanda murmured while smoothing the rose-tipped feathers on the side of his neck. She spoke quietly, hoping Rory wouldn't hear from the stable door. "Did I do the right thing?"

Gently nipping a fresh chunk of pineapple from Amanda's hand, Iveryn tossed his head as if to say nothing but his treat mattered to him at the moment.

"Lotta help you are!" Amanda laughed. Her good humor faded when Cameron walked into the stables.

Between his hunched shoulders, drawn face, and the dim morning light, Cameron seemed like a different person than the mentor who had trained her over the past month. The horses sensed it as well. From her neighboring stall, Cameron's horse skittered her feet and fanned her tail in a brilliant display of purple and gold. The other horses followed suit, a ripple of movement sending brightly colored quills standing on end. Amanda felt the down on Iveryn's body lift beneath her hand. The other horses seemed larger, too, puffed up under their soft coats.

"Whoa, Ynhara," Cameron coaxed, stepping over to rub his horse's muzzle. "It's okay, girl."

He slowed his breathing, seeming to take his own comfort from calming his horse.

"They're sensitive creatures," he added, once the horses had settled. His voice was heavy with insinuation. And maybe accusation.

Amanda agreed about the horses, wondering if Cameron realized it was his dramatic entrance, and not their plans for the day, that had caused their distress.

"Rory, why don't you go see if Alira and Caeph are still meeting with Mhevek? Maybe prod the others along while you're at it."

Rory hesitated by the stable door before nodding curtly and promising to be back soon. Amanda watched her go, wishing Rory would stop acting like her babysitter. They hadn't even left Sage Village and she was already sticking close. Watching her every move. Amanda shook her head. She didn't know what Rory was so worried about in a walled village full of monks. It was hard to believe she'd be skeptical of the gentle Churukh who lived in Sage Village. Though if anyone could be cynical in this walled paradise, it would be Rory.

"So, we're going to the market town," Cameron began as if he were offering new information, "and maybe to the castle beyond."

"I never said we should go there," Amanda told him.

After her meeting with Amanda, Alira had announced she and Caeph were traveling on to the market town with or without English protection. Cameron had spoken with her privately, eventually storming out and shouting that his team should gear up for a long ride.

Cameron ignored Amanda's protest. He lifted down Ynhara's saddle and inspected its surface. There were stable workers who would saddle the horses when it was time to leave, but they hadn't come in from their breakfast yet.

"I mean, she kind of hears what she wants to hear."

Amanda gave Iveryn her last piece of pineapple, trying to remember if it was bad to feed a horse too much fruit before reminding herself Iveryn wasn't *really* a horse.

Cameron studied Ynhara's saddle more closely.

"You know, you don't have to come with us."

Amanda looked up sharply.

"Alira and Caeph are determined to go on, and my team will be there to keep them safe." Cameron straightened and shadows fell across his face. "Maybe you've done enough."

Amanda flinched but stood her ground. What was the point of her being here, she thought, if she wasn't supposed to speak up when she had a feeling about which way to go? Wasn't that why the High Council had decided to send her on this journey? Was she supposed to ignore all that just to make Cameron's job easier?

"Why did you bring me here?" Amanda shot back. "You don't believe in the prophecy. Or that I belong here."

"I didn't say that."

"But you *don't* believe in the prophecy, do you?"

"Do you?" Cameron sounded genuinely interested in her answer.

"Well, I—" Amanda was ready to say that she did believe but the words stuck in her throat. "I don't know. But I know I feel *something*. Like, something from that tea ceremony is coming back to me and, I don't know, pulling me toward something."

Cameron walked around the saddle, sat on the bench beside it, and rested his forearms on his knees. Amanda stood taller, trying to use silence and confidence as effectively as Alira would. If she showed she was strong, that she was proud of her actions, maybe he would let her stay. Without conscious thought her eyelids fluttered in a fair imitation of the Vherahna. *Blink-blink.*

"Relax," Cameron sighed and looked down at his fingers. "I'm not sending you back."

"Oh." Amanda sat on the wooden bench opposite him.

"I do think you belong here." Cameron spoke to the floor and Amanda appreciated having a moment to contain herself. "And the prophecy… Well, that's something we'll have to come back to later."

"Cameron." Amanda bit her lip and glanced around the quiet stable. "My dad…?"

Cameron looked up and the shine in his blue eyes startled Amanda.

"Gabe would be so proud of you."

"You, uh," Amanda cleared her throat. "You knew him?"

"Yes." Cameron's shoulders drooped forward with a long exhale, "I knew him very well."

"Here? In Terra-V?" Amanda felt her ribs tighten.

"Yes, when we were here."

Cameron stared toward the ground, lost in a thought, then shook his head and sat up, bracing his hands on his thighs. Amanda watched his mood shift, seeing her chance slipping away.

"This isn't the time for that talk, but when we get back home. Okay?"

"Uh, yeah." Amanda shook off her list of questions, trying to remember what they were saying before.

"Now. I'm not going to make you go back home yet. If you're sure that's what you want?" Amanda quickly agreed. "But we need a new rule about these sensations, or visions, or whatever it is you're feeling.

"From now on, no more blurting out whatever feeling comes up. You quietly tell me, and I'll tell Alira when we're in a safe place. Got it?"

"Yeah, okay."

Amanda jumped to her feet, following Cameron as he paced toward Ynhara and Iveryn. The horses perked up, then settled into a doze once they saw there was no sign of their treat bag. Cameron pivoted and walked toward the rack of waiting saddles. Amanda followed, picking up his restless energy.

"Another thing," he continued, turning to make sure Amanda was listening. "We get into a hostile situation—any danger at all—and you're done. It's through the house to New York. No arguing. No questioning. Deal?"

"Deal."

The horses shuffled in their stalls. In the distance, Amanda could hear the voices of approaching Churukh, the stable workers arriving to prepare their horses. There wasn't much time before they'd be back on the road.

"Cameron?" A knot twisted Amanda's stomach. "Did I let you down? By telling Alira what I felt?"

"No," he answered without hesitation, meeting her eyes squarely. "You were brought on this journey for a reason and you spoke up when you felt it was important."

"But you wanted me to steer the Vherahna home."

Cameron looked away. When he turned back, his brow was furrowed intently.

"Look, Amanda. There's a delicate balance when it comes to weighing instinct against experience. It's a tough judgment, and I shouldn't have let you get caught in the middle like you were at the pier. There are things at play here— Amanda, I'm figuring this one out, too.

"But I shouldn't have made you think you had to hide your feelings from me. I don't want you to hide whatever you're feeling just because you think it will upset me, okay? From now on, let's just talk about this stuff together and figure it out together. Okay?"

"Yeah, okay," Amanda agreed, but her thoughts had gone elsewhere. "Uh, Cameron. There's something I have to do before we go."

§

Drew met Amanda in Judy's apartment minutes after Amanda arrived.

"You're okay!" He smiled with relief as Amanda answered the door. "I've been waiting by my phone, but I didn't expect you back until—"

"I don't have much time," Amanda cut him off with a raised hand. Judy waved a grim hello from the kitchen table, before Amanda led Drew to the privacy of her makeshift bedroom.

"You're going back?" Drew asked as soon as the door was closed.

"Look, we're friends," Amanda told him, ignoring his question. "We've been friends a long time, right?"

"Uh, yeah." Drew studied Amanda's face, before tucking his hands in his pockets. "Why would—"

"I want us to stay friends."

Amanda had her hands on her hips. She still wore her travel tunic with her small knife belted at her waist. She'd left her bow and quiver in Terra-V but stood with the authority of a fighter. Drew's mouth hovered around a half-smile and his eyes squinted in uncertainty.

"I want that, too."

"Good," Amanda nodded briskly. "But you have a girl-friend now, and—"

"But that doesn't—"

"You have a girlfriend now," Amanda spoke over him, though her voice cracked with her first sign of emotion. "And I don't know what that means. For us."

Drew blinked. He shook his head slowly before stepping closer. His fingers twisted in a loose clasp.

"You don't want me to date Trina?"

"No. Or yes." Amanda threw up her arms and let them drop by her sides. "I mean, I'm totally fine with you having a girlfriend. Trina or whoever. But I don't want us to stop being friends because of it."

"Amanda." Drew ran one hand over his mouth and rocked his head from side to side. "We *are* friends. That's not going to stop because I have a girlfriend. It wouldn't stop if you had a boyfriend, right?"

"I don't want a boyfriend!" Amanda snapped, before seeing the worry in Drew's face.

"I mean… well, I don't, but if I did have one, we'd still be friends." She tossed her head, feeling tears crowding in and briefly wondering when she'd become this person who cried all the time. "I just don't understand why anything has to change!"

"Because we're growing up?"

Drew sounded both confident in his answer and at a loss as to what that meant.

"Look." He grabbed Amanda's hand as if expecting her to run away. "Is this about me dating Trina… or is it about that stuff Trey said about us? Under the bleachers?"

243

Amanda pulled back and turned her face to one side, but she made herself leave her hand in his. She'd thought about those stupid rumors, night after night before she'd left for Terra-V and day after day during her monotonous hours in the saddle.

"Why do people have to think that about us?" Amanda felt her face burn. "Or think anything about us? Why do they suddenly think we're— I mean, just because you're a boy and I'm a—"

Amanda bit her lower lip, holding back the mixed-up feelings that turned her stomach to jelly.

"I don't know." Drew shook Amanda's hand, trying to make a joke. "Maybe because we're both such hotties?"

She laughed, despite her frustration, and shook her head at his wink.

"See, it's not soooo bad. Whatever they think, right?"

Amanda stopped laughing.

"Not for you," she told him honestly. "Or for Trina. To them, you're the guy who all the girls like. Trina is the girl you picked. And I'm…"

She turned away again but looked back when Drew prodded her to go on.

"I'm the girl you just wanted to make-out with," she answered bitterly. "I'm the trashy one who hooked up with you under the bleachers and is currently trying to break up you and Trina. So, yeah, that's me now. Amanda: the boyfriend-stealing slut."

Drew let go of her hand, genuinely surprised and concerned.

"Amanda, that's not what—"

"No," Amanda agreed. She smoothed her braids, knowing she had to get back. "But it's what Trey thinks, and what a bunch of them think."

Drew's face darkened. He sat on the edge of Amanda's airbed, ran his hands over his head, then seemed to think better of where he'd sat, and quickly stood up.

"Look, forget it." Amanda checked the time on the portable clock next to her bed. It was nearly one in the afternoon, but she had no idea how long she'd been home. "It's not your problem."

"Hell yes, it is!" Drew flexed his fingers in anger. "Look, Amanda, I'm sorry. I didn't think— I mean, I know how some people think, but that's not cool. You're my friend, and I'm not cool with people saying things like that.

"I mean, not that there's anything wrong with a girl meeting a guy to make-out or whatever... I mean, if she wants to, not that she *has* to... or... Hell, I don't know what I'm saying!"

Amanda laughed, touched by his anger and by how seriously he was taking her feelings, even if that had left him nervous and babbling. It felt good to say her thoughts out loud and have him understand why she was upset.

"I'll talk to Trey. And I'll be more aware of speaking up to stop stupid talk like this. Okay? Is that good?"

"Yeah." Amanda checked the clock again, frustrated by how fast the minutes were passing. "We're good."

"Good." Drew let out a sigh of relief.

Amanda said she had to get back to Terra-V.

Drew said he was proud of her and wanted to hear everything when she got home.

They were both glad they'd talked.

"And Amanda." Drew stopped her at the door. "You're not a boyfriend-stealing slut."

"Uh, thanks," Amanda laughed awkwardly.

"I mean it," he smiled. "You're a psychic traveler. The waking dreamer even. That's like a superhero."

Amanda blushed, but she didn't disagree.

CHAPTER 16
A FOREST OF STONE

The horses entered the town with their feathers ruffled and their crests at high alert. Amanda could feel the tension in the air, though there were no acts of aggression toward their party. If anything, there was admiration as they passed into the busy market town. The teeming streets parted easily when the Churukh caught sight of the Vherahna riding within the circle of English knights. Awed murmurs rippled out from the main thoroughfare and Amanda saw curious Churukh approaching from narrow side streets.

Iveryn's reins felt warm in Amanda's clenched fists. Her mouth twitched at the Churukh around them, unsure whether to smile graciously like the Vherahna or keep her expression neutral like Cameron and his team. Her eyes lifted to take in their surroundings.

The market town was an eclectic mix of wood and brick buildings. Some reminded Amanda of the well-designed construction that filled Sage Village, but many looked like they'd been slapped together to fill in any available space. The castle was situated on higher ground south of the market area. Amanda saw glimpses of its high walls and stone turrets in the distance.

Near their entrance to town, Amanda was surprised to find an outpost of psychic travelers complete with guest quarters and stables to board their horses. Cameron had clearly messaged ahead. The outpost knights were ready for their arrival with a simple meal and clean rooms for them to clean up after their long ride.

While it was nice to be in a safe place, the travelers stationed at the castle outpost were overly curious about meeting Amanda. They asked simple questions about the journey, then watched her closely, looking for signs of her potential abilities. Amanda ignored their attention and asked about the care of their horses. She was relieved Iveryn would have a safe place to rest but also reluctant to leave him to the stable hands.

"He'll be fine," Sam, the outpost sergeant, promised. "Country horses are always a bit skittish in the city, but we'll calm them in no time."

Amanda fed Iveryn the last of the pineapple in her sack, smoothed the fine feathers above his nose, and told him that he was a good horse.

She didn't know how long they would be here, but Amanda's time was running short. It was Friday evening back home. They had just one day left before she was due to return. Remembering her promise to Cameron, Amanda hoped she wouldn't have to leave Terra-V without seeing Iveryn again.

It was still light, though late in the day, when they moved into the market square. Three knights from the outpost had joined their group, putting Amanda, Alira, and Caeph within a ring of ten soldiers, each with weapons at the ready.

Amanda thought that was a bit much until she saw how the Churukh swarmed the Vherahna, shouting for their healing transfer of vhe. She self-consciously unslung her longbow and took a single arrow from her quiver. She hadn't needed the weapon yet, though she'd practiced with it during some of their breaks and gotten tips from Davis, who carried a bow of his own.

The knights had their hands full guarding Alira and Caeph. The Vherahna stepped freely among the Churukh. They extended their arms to lay hands on any who came near and wound their way to those with the palest eyes. Their humming song reverberated through the masses, bringing more Churukh to join the growing crowd.

The Vherahna also attracted the attention of some armor-clad Churukh who carried weapons and shields. They were short and stocky like the other Churukh, but they looked broader and more muscled under their protective metal. Their bright green eyes flashed toward Cameron before they leaned together in conversation.

"They're the castle guard," Cameron explained, with a hint of derision.

"They don't look happy," Amanda noted, resisting the urge to crowd close and wishing she had chainmail over her tactical suit.

The bow and arrow felt clumsy in her hands.

She searched for the Vherahna, seeing their deep blue hair and pale skin gleaming among a sea of gray skin and brown tunics. Five knights stayed close to Alira and Caeph, maintaining a protective semi-circle between them and the crowding Churukh. Davis and one of the knights from the outpost had found higher ground on piles of wooden boxes at either edge of the crowd. They bows were drawn but lowered, watching for trouble.

Cameron stayed with Amanda, along with Rory and Terrance, another outpost traveler. She felt both grateful and guilty for their protection. But when she asked if it would be better to have all the knights help with the Vherahna, Cameron told her to leave security to him.

Amanda clutched her bow and arrow in both hands, doubting her ability to use them in this crowd. After a few minutes of fidgeting, she awkwardly slid the arrow into her quiver and thread the bow over one shoulder, where it was easier to pull free but wasn't occupying her hands.

"Is there something I should be, uh, doing here?" Amanda asked nervously.

"You tell me." Cameron raised an eyebrow before grinning to soften his response. "Is the prophecy leading you to anything?"

Amanda shrugged, gazed around the square, then focused on Rory standing only a few feet away. Her lips were compressed to a paper-thin line and her right hand clenched the hilt of her sword. A small blade flashed in her other hand.

Amanda watched the intensity of Rory's eyes moving across the crowd, trying to ignore the way Terrance's eyes burned into her just as intently. He was gawking, just like the travelers who had stared during her first arrival at the PTS building in Chicago. *Will this ever stop?* She wondered. *Will I ever be just another traveler?*

Turning her back on him, Amanda studied the market. Many sellers stood behind covered tables and craned their necks toward the Vherahna. Some had abandoned their stalls to push into the crowd, not caring that less scrupulous shoppers were pilfering their wares.

The sellers closest to Amanda called to the knights in the guttural grunts and rumbles of the Churukh language. One Churukh man in particular caught Amanda's eye. He was older and frailer than the others, with a wrinkled face and a pronounced stoop. Despite his haggard appearance, he beckoned to Amanda with a friendly smile and a faint glint in his dull, clouded eyes.

Amanda smiled instinctively, before remembering her surroundings. She quickly switched back to her cautious, neutral expression, but it was too late. The seller's grin stretched wider and he waved more emphatically, saying something short and sharp in Churukh.

"You've made a friend?" Cameron chuckled, then gestured for her to lead the way to his booth.

Between his gruff snips of foreign words, the man pointed at Amanda saying, *"You! You!"*

"He's welcoming you to the market," Cameron explained, once they were close enough to clearly hear his excited words above the humming of the crowd.

"He's calling you *pretty girl*," Rory added grimly, still scanning the area.

"She *is* a pretty girl," Terrance agreed, earning a look of scorn from both Amanda and Rory.

Cameron said something to the man in Churukh.

Amanda browsed his booth. There were paintings pinned to the wooden beams and rolled in crates on the rough table. Small, clay sculptures sat between the crates. They were crudely shaped like flowers and small animals. Another shallow crate held a collection of even smaller statues carved from purple stones. It took less than a minute for Amanda to find one that was clearly meant to be a horse with its tail on full display. It had a rough texture to show a downy coat and simple gouges to represent the eyes and mouth. Cameron told Amanda there were other artisans with much better horse sculptures, but something about this gleaming, purple horse had captured her heart.

After a burst of staccato grunts and yaps from the seller, Cameron shook his head, then nodded and smiled.

"He wants you to have it," Cameron told Amanda, indicating the horse. "No charge."

"Oh, I can't," Amanda protested but stopped Cameron from repeating that in Churukh. Instead saying, "Tell him I said, thank you and I love it."

She slipped the tiny statue into her tunic's concealed pocket. *Iveryn.* She named the statue after her horse, happy to have a memento of him. But when she turned back to the seller, the smile faded from her face.

"What is it?"

"Nothing," Amanda waved Cameron's question away. Her eyes were locked on a small drawing pinned to a back-corner beam and half-covered by other paintings.

"It's just… something about that picture, down there, under the red-and-blue one."

Through a protracted exchange, Cameron pointed out the ink drawing, then bickered with the seller who waved his hands, shook his head, and tried to redirect them to three other paintings. Eventually, the seller shrugged and passed the picture to Cameron, still making dismissive *ptuh ptuh* sounds over it.

"He says he has better paintings," Cameron translated briefly, eyeing the paper in his hands critically. "Gotta say, I think he's right."

The coarse paper was heavily creased and ragged around the edges. It showed a series of dark, jagged spikes clustered ominously to the right of an otherwise blank page. On closer inspection, a faint line seemed to indicate a low horizon with faded splotches scattered below. The entire piece was washed in a somber gray that only made the jagged spikes gloomier.

"That the stone forest?" Terrance asked with a glance over Cameron's shoulder. "Out by the ruins?"

"The stone forest?"

Amanda felt a nervous fizzing building inside.

"It's nothing," Cameron shrugged. "Just some big rock structures out by those ruins I told you about. Remember? The place with one of the proximal doors?

"We've been through them. There's nothing left out there. Just jagged rocks."

He said something to the seller in Churukh and was about to hand the small drawing back.

"That's what I saw."

Amanda spoke softly, her inner gaze still lingering on the shape of the dark spikes.

"During the tea ceremony," she clarified. "I saw a cluster of jagged spikes. *That* cluster of jagged spikes. Exactly."

Cameron pulled the picture closer, away from the seller's waiting hands.

"This? But it's nothing."

"*Noth-ing*," the seller repeated with an odd accent, nodding proudly at his recognition of an English word, then reaching insistently for the painting.

Cameron held fast. After another brusque exchange in Churukh, he offered the picture for Rory and Terrance to examine more carefully. The seller had said something that made the travelers look at the painting with more interest. Cameron asked another question and raised an eyebrow at the seller's lengthy response.

He watched intently as the other travelers studied the picture. Finally asking, "What do you think?"

Rory frowned and said she hadn't spent enough time there to know for sure.

Terrance slowly nodded his head and said he thought the old man might be right.

"Though it's hard to believe," he added in an awed voice. "You think it's possible?"

Amanda watched helplessly as the seller launched into another torrent of the guttural sounds that meant nothing to her. Cameron shook his head, repeating the same sounds three times before moving on to what sounded like a series of additional questions.

"What's he saying?"

Ignoring her, Cameron pulled a shiny piece of metal from his pocket. He handed it to the seller, who smiled and bowed in gratitude.

"He says this isn't the stone forest by the ruins, but one closer to this end of the rocky desert," Terrance explained. "Maybe an hour or so from the castle by horse."

Cameron and Terrance shared a grave look as Cameron folded the drawing and tucked it inside his tunic. As usual, Rory kept her focus on their perimeter, though Amanda felt sure she was well aware of what was happening and why they were upset by the seller's words.

Cameron made a sweeping hand gesture, gathering the knights who were guarding the Vherahna.

"I don't understand," Amanda told Terrance.

"All of our maps show only one stone forest in the rocky desert." Terrance ushered Amanda behind Cameron as he explained. "And we've only explored it from the ruins because coming at it from this side would mean crossing land ceded to the Churukh royals in our treaty."

They moved rapidly, parting the crowded streets as they tried to rendezvous with the rest of their party. There were even more Churukh gathered now. The newcomers were eager to approach Alira and Caeph, and those who had received their vhe were reluctant to move away.

Amanda considered Terrance's explanation and what it implied.

"So, if there are two stone forests, instead of one," Amanda tried to puzzle through an idea that she only half understood. "Then there's one you've never explored? Does that matter?"

They stopped walking, waiting for the Vherahna and their guards to close the remaining distance between them. Davis and the other archer held their stations, watching warily. The energy of the crowd had shifted. Those who had not yet gotten close to the Vherahna seemed to sense their chance slipping away. The Churukh began to press closer, jostling for position and calling out in what Amanda assumed were pleas for the Vherahna to stay.

"There's more," Terrance went on. "There have always been rumors of a hidden fortress where the Churukh royals keep their most valuable treasures. Only the royals insist the fortress isn't real. The locals say it's a haunted place in the ruins where no one dares to go.

"We've never found anything out there, so just figured it was a ghost story. A second stone forest though, in a whole area we didn't know existed? *That* might be big enough to conceal a small fortress."

"Hey!" Rory snapped. "Can we save the history lesson for later?" She was using her shield to fend off the crush of Churukh who had become frantic in their need to be near Alira and Caeph.

Cameron raised his voice and lifted his arms, calling to the Churukh in their own language.

"He's telling him that the Vherahna need a rest to recharge their vhe, but they'll be back in the square in the morning," Terrance translated. He and Rory were side by side, creating a close barrier behind Amanda.

The Churukh stood in place with uncertainty. They grumbled among themselves but had stopped pushing forward.

Alira and Caeph were soon back beside Amanda. The knights surrounded them, facing outward to keep the remaining crowd at a distance. Cameron signaled for Davis and the other archer to rejoin their group, preparing to go back to the outpost for the night.

"Has something happened?" Alira asked in English, a language that the Churukh within earshot would not likely understand.

"Maybe," Cameron glanced at Amanda. "We'll discuss it back at the outpost."

Alira restrained him with a hopeful hand on his arm. Beside her, Caeph's face glowed through her obvious exhaustion.

"The prophecy?" Alira asked him urgently.

Cameron patted her hand.

"Maybe," he smiled. "Your waking dreamer led us to something. Now, let's get to a safe place so we can figure out how valuable it might be."

Alira beamed at Amanda, then took hold of her hands and bowed her head. When Amanda returned the gesture, Alira leaned in, letting their foreheads meet. Amanda closed her eyes, feeling a warmth spread through her body. *Was this it? Was it over?* Amanda felt joy at Alira's touch, but it didn't feel like their journey was complete.

"All right, there's time for that later!" Cameron laughed lightly, but the happy sound was lost in a sudden scramble of dispersing Churukh.

Amanda opened her eyes in time to see more than a dozen of the castle guard riding in from all sides. They were surrounded. The knights drew their weapons, facing off against the armed Churukh, but Cameron lifted his arms, telling them to hold their places.

"Damn," he muttered quietly, then turned to Amanda. "Be ready."

Rory had gotten separated from Amanda. She quickly sidled closer, shield up as she switched places with Davis, then Terrance, to position herself by Amanda's side.

While she was moving, the horses directly in front of them parted to let three Churukh step forward. They wore the same armor as those on the horses, but their shoulders were swathed in green capes. The Churukh in the center also had a spray of green and black horse quills fanned around his collar.

"Time to go." Cameron nodded to Rory, who grasped Amanda's arm urgently.

Amanda remembered her promise. It was time to go through the house to New York, but her heart hammered in her ears and the scene unfolding before her remained stubbornly solid. *Antique living room. Fancy inlaid-wood door.* Amanda tried to imagine herself in the house, standing in the posh living room and facing the mahogany door that led to New York, but the world around her was too vivid, too gripping.

"She will stay." The Churukh with the feathered collar surprised Amanda by speaking English. He scanned Amanda slowly, smiling at her wide eyes and shaking breath, before turning his attention back to Cameron.

"Gherut." Cameron stepped ahead of the others, his shield arm ready, despite his casual stance. "Here to invite us to the castle?"

"You will come to the castle," Gherut agreed, in English that was fluent even if it did not flow easily.

"We accept your invitation." Alira tried to step forward, but the nearest knights blocked her way as they kept their shields held before her.

"You will *all* come to the castle now."

Amanda!

Rory's voice echoed through Amanda's head. The house began to take hazy shape around her.

"Go!" Cameron hissed back at her, his eyes flashing.

Amanda nodded rapidly, concentrating on Rory's voice, picturing the living room with its elegant sofas and fancy piano. It was calm there. Quiet and safe. *Go to the living room. Be in the living room.*

"She will stay." Gherut's assured voice pulled Amanda's attention back to the stand-off. He went on, keeping his eyes fixed on Cameron. "She cannot leave fast enough. Not anymore."

Amanda!

Rory screamed in her head. Amanda saw her standing beside one of the living room's built-in bookcases. Her hand rested on the door handle to New York. She was ready to pull them through to safety the moment Amanda let go of Terra-V and moved her mind fully into the house. She was nearly there, the house was becoming solid, beginning to replace the sight of Gherut and his castle guard... Until his last words floated through her mind.

"Not anymore?" The question tumbled out as Amanda's vision sharpened on Gherut and the market square around him.

"Amanda!" Cameron barked at her, swiveling his head to catch her full attention. "Go! Now!"

A slow smile spread across Gherut's face.

"Your English magic takes time," he told Cameron, "A short time, but some time. She can be fast enough to go before a strike of a sword. Maybe. You can be fast enough to block an arrow with that shield…"

Amanda!

Rory's voice was desperate but too distant to break through the hold Gherut had taken over Amanda's attention. Cameron swiftly moved toward her, lifting his shield.

Amanda felt rooted in place.

Gherut gave a tiny nod. The Churukh on either side of him pivoted slightly, swinging *something* out from under their capes.

"Can any of you be faster than this?" Gherut asked.

Amanda's throat went dry. Dizzy nausea shook her ribs.

The caped Churukh each held a semi-automatic rifle pointed directly at her.

Chapter 17

Sovereignty

Once they were taken to the castle throne room, Amanda's fear was tempered by her curiosity. It felt like she had stepped onto a movie set.

The castle was constructed of gray-brown bricks, complete with high walls, portcullises, turrets, an inner courtyard, and a towering keep. Yet each of these elements featured touches that infused the entire structure with the other-worldly feel of Terra-V. The crenellations at the tops of the walls and towers were designed with gracefully sweeping arcs, creating a sense of motion reminiscent of the spiraling tuntum trees in the Vherahna forest. The tower roofs were similarly topped with twisting spires covered in various shades of purple tiles.

Inside, the great hall boasted freestanding frames of stained glass that lined the stone walls and stretched effortlessly toward the elevated ceiling. Tapering columns of polished opal separated each glass panel, offering a muted glow in the daylight that filtered through the high windows near the rim of the gently domed ceiling.

As the fading sun hit the columns, Amanda couldn't help but see the similarity between the gleaming stone and the shimmering complexions of the Vherahna beside her. In fact, Amanda noticed that many features of the castle reflected the delicate, willowy lines of the Vherahna. Yet they also blended with ease into the solid, ash and earth grounding of its basic structure.

At the front of the hall, on a raised dais, two ornately carved thrones flanked a narrow panel of stained glass. A male and female Churukh sat in each of the thrones.

Unlike the home-spun clad townsfolk Amanda had seen in the market square, these Churukh wore finely woven, colored robes that draped with a satin sheen. Jewelry made of metal and precious gems sparkled at their wrists and throats while swirling crowns graced their heads. Their eyes were so bright, so brimming with vhe, that they seemed to glow in the shadowy hall.

Amanda, Cameron, Alira, and Caeph stood before the royals. The other knights had been taken into a separate room, guarded by one of the Churukh who carried a gun. Gherut and the other caped Churukh stood to the side of the hall.

Though the guard still cradled the rifle in his arms, Amanda's initial terror had lessened. She didn't know if the Vherahna's presence had a calming effect or if she were in denial, but she was reasonably sure that the Churukh had no intention of shooting her.

Not that she was ready to test that theory.

After taking in her surroundings, Amanda saw that the king was assessing Alria and Caeph carefully. She then startled to realize that the queen's piercing green eyes were scrutinizing her.

"This is a surprise." The king addressed them in a cool, almost genial tone, speaking as if they had not been brought there at gunpoint. "We were not told of your plan to visit our domain, Alira."

"We had not known where our journey would lead," Alira responded diplomatically.

"I see." The king turned his attention to Cameron. "Did you think we would not welcome a visit from the Vherahna?"

"We were only passing through," Cameron shrugged, "and didn't want to take your time."

"And now you have," the king frowned. "I expect you to know better, Cameron. Secrecy breeds distrust."

"With all respect, King Otmurkh, couldn't I say the same about you concealing your new weapons?"

Amanda tensed, but the royals only laughed.

"These weapons are not between us and your English. They are a separate matter."

Cameron took a half-step forward, shaking his head. Before he could speak, the guard lifted his gun, and Gherut barked an order to stay back. With a knowing look toward the king, Cameron resumed his place in line and held up his palms to show he meant no harm. His own sword was still in its sheath, and he made no move to use it.

"They do seem to concern us now," Cameron pointed out mildly.

Amanda watched the guard relax his aim, then tried to steady her choppy breath.

He will not shoot us. He will not shoot us.

Whatever the king said in response was lost on Amanda, as he'd switched back to his native language. She watched helplessly as Cameron and Alira took turns answering the king, speaking in Churukh as well. At one point the king addressed Caeph, who bowed in greeting before offering her own response, also in the rough syllables of Churukh.

Reduced to deciphering their body language, Amanda puzzled over expressions and gestures. Tone of voice meant very little, as even the kindest messages sounded harsh in Churukh. She was studying Caeph's face, which seemed to show emotion most easily, when the familiar sound of English cut through her thoughts.

"I want to know more about the small English." The queen spoke for the first time, directing her words to the room at large, but keeping her attention fixed on Amanda. "So much smaller than any English we've seen before. With no armor and no understanding of our tongue. Why bring her along? What is her special skill?"

Amanda swallowed, unsure of what to say, when Cameron broke in with a dismissive wave.

"She's not important. She was brought on the whim of the Vherahna, as a companion and no more."

He shifted his weight, slightly turning his back toward Amanda, as though only interested in the Vherahna on his other side.

"Now that Alira and Caeph have had a chance to see more of the world for themselves, it's time I take everyone back home to the forest. Until Mhevek hosts our next summit at Sage Village, where I'm sure we'll meet again."

The queen pursed her lips and smiled tightly. The glint in her eye chilled Amanda to the bone.

"Back to the forest? Which forest would that be? The Vherahna forest of twisted trees or our forest of stone?"

She lifted one hand in a signal of beckoning. Two guards entered, roughly pushing the old seller along until he stood between Amanda and the thrones. Returning to Churukh, the queen questioned the seller as he quivered in fear. With everyone focused on the seller, Amanda wondered if this was her opportunity to escape. She chanced a look toward the guard with the gun and saw that he was the only one in the room still intently watching her every move. He sneered when he caught her eye and she quickly looked away.

"*Noth-ing.*" The seller pulled out his word of English, gesturing toward Cameron, who reluctantly responded with a few words of Churukh. The seller's exaggerated nod suggested Cameron had backed up his defense, and Amanda was relieved—until one of the castle guards struck the old seller across his mid-back, hitting hard enough to knock him to his hands and knees on the stone floor.

Amanda gasped. Cameron extended an arm to hold Alira and Caeph back.

The queen again displayed her unctuous smile, with lips pursed and only one corner of her mouth curving upward. Her opposite eyebrow arched as if to balance the malevolence across her face.

"We have not asked you about this matter," the king told Cameron coldly. "Kindly wait until we do."

He spoke harshly to the seller, who was struggling to get to his feet. With a bowed head, the old Churukh uttered a submissive response. Amanda did not know what he said, but she felt Cameron straighten up beside her. One of the guards left the seller's side to demand something with an open palm. Cameron sized up the guard before fishing the tattered drawing from his tunic and handing it over.

The king unfolded the worn paper and let his gaze rove across the picture. His face showed no expression as he let the drawing flutter to the floor.

The queen appeared amused.

"You did not need to take so much trouble," she told Cameron archly. "We'll be happy to bring you there."

§

As the open cart jounced over the rocky desert, Amanda missed Iveryn's loping grace. She and Cameron sat on one side of the cart. The Vherahna sat on the other. Gherut sat with the driver in the raised seat behind the horses, and the guard with the rifle rode backward on a lower perch, watching them all intently.

Cameron and Amanda had been warned to stay alert and keep talking, as the Churukh knew blank silence would be a sign of the travelers disappearing. Amanda suspected Cameron would be able to appear alert and talkative while simultaneously escaping through the house, but she didn't have that kind of control yet. As she'd proven when she wasn't able to leave the market square.

"It was the stress of the situation," Cameron told her as they bounced along the packed sand and dry dirt. "Usually, the instinct to flee makes it easier to jump through the house, but sometimes the opposite happens. Something was holding you here."

"I tried to leave." Amanda remembered Rory's voice calling her from the house and felt sick with worry.

"I know." Cameron patted her leg. "It's not your fault. I meant that something in your subconscious mind was holding you here. I should have anticipated that."

They sat quietly, each wanting to take the blame from the other, until the guard's grunt startled them back to attention. Cameron spoke shortly in Churukh before returning to English.

"How are you holding up?"

His question was directed at Alira and Caeph, who were slumped together. Caeph lifted her head from Alira's shoulder long enough to say that she was fine.

"We are weak," Alira conceded, "but we are drawing strength from each other to pull what vhe we can from the elements around us."

Cameron nodded, leaving them to their meditation.

Ahead of their cart, Amanda could see the closed carriage that led the way. They hadn't seen who rode in that carriage, but its ornate carvings and bright flags suggested at least one of the royals was inside. Amanda felt sure it was the Queen.

"The others are okay." Cameron repeated his earlier reassurances with more confidence.

"You've heard from them?" Amanda asked cautiously, unsure if their guard understood her words. From his high seat, Gherut continued talking to the driver.

"Yes." Cameron lowered his voice for Gherut's benefit but didn't seem to care what the guard might overhear.

"I don't have details, but our team escaped the castle guard and notified the outpost. PTS sent the two strike teams on standby, and they're assembling reinforcements. Those rifles have changed our situation here."

"How could they have guns?" Amanda chanced a look at the guard's weapon. She knew very little about guns, but it looked like something she'd seen military soldiers carry in modern war movies.

"I have a pretty good idea," Cameron answered darkly but did not elaborate. Instead, he went back to speculating on PTS' next moves.

"The strike teams are in Terra-V now. The others will follow soon, but it will take hours for them to get here from the nearest proximal doors—which are back in Sage Village and the Vherahna Forest. Some might try to approach from the ruins, but we don't know how far that is from this uncharted area. Likely too far to be useful."

Amanda almost asked how there could be an uncharted area like this, when the travelers had been here for nearly 100 years. But then she realized Cameron was probably asking himself the same question.

"We're going to be okay," she reassured him, more to show that she could be brave. Or at least act braver than she felt.

Cameron tightened his jaw, and Amanda saw his fist lightly clench as well.

"There's a team waiting for you in New York." He looked straight ahead, across the empty desert terrain.

"I can't leave Alira and Caeph here, but I can create a distraction for you to go back." He faced Amanda, searching her eyes. "Can you do that?"

"I—" Amanda coughed as the cart kicked up a cloud of fine dust. "But what if…?" Her lungs ached and eyes burned, but she choked out her fear. "They could shoot you!"

"They won't," Cameron insisted.

"They could!" Amanda felt the same shaky terror from the market square rising up in her chest.

"They wouldn't dare," Cameron blustered with a raffish smile. "Besides, I have Alira here to take care of me."

Amanda frowned, seeing Alira and Caeph huddled together. Their eyes were closed. Their faces were chalky, without their usual iridescence, and their hair had lost some of its deep shine. Even their bodies seemed smaller, frailer against the dark wood of the rough cart.

"I can't," Amanda admitted honestly. "I mean, even if I— It's like the house doesn't exist anymore. Even if I try to see it, it's just not there."

She explained how this had happened before, after the first time she'd seen Cameron in the attic. She told him how she'd only gotten back to the house during a meditation at school, and then with Drew's help in the park.

"Maybe if you stop thinking about the house," Cameron suggested slowly, as if thinking through the problem as he spoke. "Try picturing your reasons for going home. Your Aunt Judy, your mom, this Drew person."

Amanda pictured Judy in her apartment and Drew in his room, both waiting for her safe return. She felt a slight pull, like a tugging on her mind, as an image of the house began to take shape. The piano. The cluster of fancy furniture. Amanda imagined what would happen if her mom came home and she was still gone. Or if she never came back.

And the house disappeared.

If she were shot while trying to leave... If something else happened to her... If her mom had to go through that again... If her mom lost her daughter, the same way she'd lost her husband—without answers—Amanda knew it would destroy her. She shouldn't have come on this trip. Shouldn't have put herself in this position. Not without telling her mom. Not without being better prepared. Better trained. She'd been selfish. Stupid and childish.

Amanda felt her chest heaving as she gasped for air.

The Churukh guard barked unknown words.

Cameron shook her arm.

Warmth spread over her body, slowing her racing heart.

Amanda opened her eyes and saw Caeph kneeling before her. Her hands rested on Amanda's legs, while Alira channeled her energy through Caeph's shoulders.

Amanda caught hold of her breath and gently lifted Caeph's hands away.

"Don't," she told her. "You need your strength. I'm okay. It's okay."

Cameron settled beside Amanda, putting a protective arm around her shoulder.

"I'm sorry," Cameron whispered, sounding more worried than Amanda had ever heard him.

Gherut had twisted in his seat, yelling back and forth with the guard, but they stopped when Amanda quieted.

He shouted something to Cameron, who replied in terse Churukh.

Everyone calmed as the cart continued to bounce over the rough ground. Amanda's tears dried on her cheeks.

"Cameron?" She spoke in a hoarse whisper, looking out from under his shielding arms.

"Shh, it's okay." Cameron rocked her gently, like a child. "I won't push. We'll find another way to keep you safe. It will be okay."

"Yeah, but Cameron." Amanda pulled herself upright, loosening his hold. "Look."

They'd crested a ridge that opened onto a flat expanse of rocky desert. In the distance, stone monoliths loomed. They clustered tightly, almost appearing to be one solid, mountain wall, except for the play of dark shadows that suggested narrow paths winding through the labyrinth.

The stone forest, Amanda said to herself. They were nearly there.

§

Though their destination was in sight, it was still a long way off. As they crossed the desert, the stone towers grew and the sky darkened. The view began to eerily match the blue-washed drawing they had found in the market. Amanda shrank into the cart and Cameron's jaw twitched in agitation. Yet Alira and Caeph sat taller. With each passing moment, they appeared to be perking up. Their eyes flashed purple and their skin gleamed in the fading light. They spoke in the vibrating song of their own language, drawing Cameron's attention.

"Do you not hear it?" Alira inquired when Cameron asked what they were sensing.

Amanda listened, hearing nothing but her own pounding heartbeat.

"Hear what?"

They passed through the first layer of spikes, weaving their way around the wide, stone bases into a twilight where the last glimmers of day were swallowed by shadows. Amanda's hand rested on the small knife at her waist. It was reassuring to feel the cold steel under her palm.

After several minutes, the towering stones began to thin. They could see beams of light threading between the wider spaces and hear a faint, but familiar sound echoing off the smooth rock. *Tuntum. Tuntum.*

"It can't be," Cameron breathed in wonder.

Seeing the serene glow pass over the Vherahna, Amanda knew the sound was true.

The cart rounded the last line of rock and came upon a wide clearing amid the forest of stone. A tall, narrow fortress filled the open space. It was a crude, cement brick structure without the graceful touches of the royal castle. Solid walls enclosed a square ring of squat buildings connected by narrow hallways. At their center, a stone-paved courtyard gave way to a wide circle of purple grass. Within that circle, three small, thin tuntum trees were making their slow, humming descent.

They stopped at the edge of the stone courtyard, staring in awe at the delicate trees. While it would take three or four people, with arms extended, to ring the base of any tuntum tree in the Vherahna Forest, Amanda could get her own arms around one of these frail trees. Their twin trunks teetered unsteadily as they lowered, and their branches were half bare. The leaves that did grow drooped weakly from their boughs, and the luminescent flowers that normally flourished on tuntum trees were only scattered buds that flickered dimly.

"How…?"

Amanda blinked in the rapidly darkening light.

Two members of the castle guard moved around the courtyard, lighting torches mounted on tall metal spikes. Alira and Caeph stood with their arms linked, pain etching their stone-like faces. They were so still Amanda had the impression that time had stopped.

"It's not possible," Cameron insisted, despite seeing the trees with his own eyes. "There are legends of the tuntum trees once filling this desert, but our scientists tried to enrich the soil and could never get the cuttings to take root. The project was abandoned ages ago."

"You were not worthy."

An icy voice preceded the queen's entrance from the shadows. She was flanked by castle guards and had a deep purple cape draped over her silken blue gown. The impressive crown she had worn in the throne room had been replaced by a silver circlet.

Cameron and Amanda pivoted to face her, while Alira and Caeph continued to peer at the trio of thin trees. The queen grinned at their speechless wonder and her eyes flashed with delight.

"Go on," she encouraged, in a tone just shy of a taunt. "Feel their twisted magic for yourselves."

Cameron's eyes shifted rapidly as if considering every possibility of the situation. Amanda wasn't sure if he was planning his next move or still puzzling over how the Churukh had gotten the tuntum trees to grow so far from the Vherahna Forest. If PTS scientists couldn't accomplish that with all their resources, it was hard to believe the Churukh had found a solution.

Then she saw a look of dread on Cameron's face.

"They are proof of our sovereignty," the queen gloated. "Only the royal line is both worthy of our own supply of vhe and able to maintain it."

"Maintain it…?" Cameron sounded horrified, though Amanda couldn't see why. Having their own tuntum trees growing in a secret fortress was a huge surprise, but…

Her line of thought faded away as she remembered the tuntum trees alone were not enough to provide the royals with vhe.

Amanda swiveled toward Alira and Caeph who were carefully easing their way toward the trees. Alira spread her arms wide, palms upward. Caeph trailed a few steps behind, her own palms open and her shoulders quaking. The trees swayed, nearly settled into tight coils. The air was still. The pale moonlight was warmed by the torch flames. Amanda shifted her attention between the cautiously inching Vherahna and the queen who rocked on her heels in anticipation.

Cameron stood taller, squaring his shoulders. Amanda followed the line of his gaze, her stomach clenching in fear. There was movement in the distance. Amanda squinted, afraid to see.

From the shadowed edges of the courtyard, figures were timidly emerging. Figures with long limbs and dusty white skin.

The Vherahna within the fortress walls were slim and weak with gaunt features and dull hair. They trembled on unsteady feet and darted wary eyes toward the outsiders. Amanda's heart ached to see their fearfulness after witnessing the strength and vibrant joy of the Vherahna in their own forest home.

A low sound, raw and mournful, reverberated across the courtyard. Alira had stopped walking. Her vibrational tone swelled into a haunting melody, amplifying as it echoed off the surrounding stone and cement walls. Caeph took Alira's hand.

Their voices linked.

Their refrain grew in sonorous waves.

Step by step, the captive Vherahna crept forward. They linked arms, leaning on each other. Amanda counted nine Vherahna of varying sizes and sexes. When they reached Alira and Caeph, the lost tribe dropped to their knees, crowding near. Alira and Caeph crouched in the midst of them, pulling them close, laying their hands on one after another. Soon the captive Vherahna joined the wordless keening. Powerful swells of energy washed over Amanda, bringing an exquisite mix of sorrow and hope.

Dizzy with emotion, Amanda turned to see the queen basking in the vhe-infused energy. Her eyes were closed in ecstasy, her arms open to better receive the vitalizing force. Her castle guards were similarly enraptured, their attention relaxed. Amanda was sickened by the queen's enjoyment of this heartbreaking reunion. Without a conscious plan, her hand wrapped around her small knife, quickly prying it from its leather sheath.

Amanda's focus narrowed on the loathsome queen, but before she could cover much ground, an unknown man deliberately stepped between them.

"Watch your trainee, Cameron," the stranger goaded, "before she does something stupid."

The queen sneered at the interruption.

Amanda stopped in her tracks.

Cameron stepped partially in front of Amanda.

The two men regarded each other warily, maintaining a healthy distance.

"Lucas," Cameron greeted coolly, despite the disgust lingering in his expression. "I wondered when you would show up."

CHAPTER 18
LUCAS FLYNN

Lucas Flynn wore black cargo pants, a black long-sleeve shirt, and combat boots. A thigh holster held a sleek, narrow handgun. His dark hair was long and messy on top but shaved close along the sides of his head, and a thin beard wrapped around his jaw and upper lip. His expression was bemused. His stance was challenging.

His modern look seemed out-of-context to Amanda after her time in Terra-V.

Though she'd stopped walking when he stepped in her path, Amanda kept her hand on her small knife. She didn't have a conscious plan, but the image of the captive, malnourished Vherahna still burned in her chest. The queen sneered behind Lucas' protection, taunting Amanda. Gherut snapped an order that made the Churukh guard lift his rifle menacingly. Amanda eyed him, fighting her urge to hurt the one who had hurt these defenseless creatures before finally lifting her hands in surrender.

Cameron positioned himself between Amanda and the guard.

"There's no need for that," he reassured the Churukh before turning back to Lucas.

"So, you're an arms dealer now? Are you sure you picked the winning side here?"

Lucas grinned.

"Well," he sighed and spread his hands wide. "You did tarnish my name with the Vherahna."

"You don't need me to tarnish your name."

Amanda puzzled over Cameron's casual approach. *Who was Lucas? What was happening?* She wanted to shake Cameron for answers but remembered her earlier promise. He would tell her what she needed to know when she needed to know it. She had to trust him.

It was the hardest promise she'd ever tried to keep.

Lucas laughed good-naturedly and Amanda felt its brittle undertone.

Several yards away, the Vherahna still huddled together. Their keening had stopped. Caeph remained at their center, while Alira stood in front of them. There was fire in Alira's eyes and her skin flashed in the torchlight. Her restrained power took Amanda's breath away. Even Queen Enghrid shrank at the sight of her. Amanda waited for Alira to charge the queen, but she held her position, protecting her new kin from any who dared to come near.

"I only gave them the two," Lucas told Cameron, indicating the rifle.

"Oh, if it was only two!" Cameron threw his arms in the air with exaggerated sarcasm.

Lucas suppressed a laugh as he approached the guard and reached for the rifle. There was a tense moment as the guard resisted, but a bark from Gherut settled the matter. Once he had the gun, Lucas walked back toward Cameron, still maintaining a wide distance. He held the weapon out for a visual inspection, tossed it deftly, and took aim at an empty area across the courtyard.

"These weapons wouldn't have hurt you," he assured Cameron before swinging the muzzle toward the queen and squeezing the trigger.

Chaos ensued. Gherut and the other guards leaped in front of the queen, knocking her to the ground in the process. Cameron spun to a crouch, shielding Amanda against his chest with his back to Lucas. The Vherahna scrambled to the tuntum trees, cowering beneath the shelter of their thin branches.

It took several seconds for Amanda to realize nothing had happened. There was no sound of gunfire. There was no smell of gun smoke. Cameron checked that Amanda was okay before turning to survey the scene.

Lucas' mocking laughter broke the silence.

"Dammit, Lucas!" Cameron thundered. "What is wrong with you?"

Lucas let the rifle dangle from one hand.

"No bullets!" He called back, still laughing.

Back on her feet, the queen launched an angry tirade in Churukh. Lucas responded, settling her down before turning back to Cameron with a sober expression.

"Cameron," he cajoled. "You don't really think I'd risk them shooting our little protégé?"

For the first time since his arrival, Lucas focused his attention directly on Amanda.

"We haven't met yet," he told her charmingly. "I'm Lucas Flynn. Yes, that Lucas Flynn." He saw Amanda's confusion and was taken aback. "You mean you haven't heard of me? Wow. Now that is surprising!

"Cameron," Lucas shook his head sadly. "You bring the girl here—to a foreign, hostile world—and don't even warn her about me?"

Cameron shrugged as if Lucas had been the least of his concerns. Yet, as Amanda thought back over the knights who had shadowed her throughout the journey—and Rory's constant vigilance of their surroundings—she began to wonder...

"Shame," Lucas tsked softly. "I'd expect it of PTS, but you, Cameron? To use the poor girl as bait like that? And not even tell her?"

"She was never bait!" Cameron fired back.

"No?" Lucas raised his eyebrows. "Okay. If you say so. You brought her here, knowing I wouldn't miss a chance to see her for myself, but she was never bait."

Amanda's heart raced. She stared at Cameron's back, reminding herself that she trusted him.

"Now, before we go any further," Lucas turned to Amanda, "we do have an important piece of business."

"You have no business with her." Cameron spoke harshly, dropping his pretense of friendship.

Lucas held Amanda's gaze.

"Oh, but I do," he assured. "Amanda, you need to know that I wouldn't *dream* of hurting you. I give you my word that *I* will tell you nothing but the truth and always let you make up your own mind. Do you believe me?"

"She doesn't need to hear your twisted version of the truth."

Cameron moved between Lucas and Amanda, breaking their eye contact. Lucas stepped to one side, then the other, and Cameron mirrored his every stop. Amanda found herself shifting to look around Cameron, too curious to remain hidden. Lucas winked at her.

"Still," Lucas shrugged off Cameron's words. "Amanda is not going anywhere. Are you, Amanda?"

"I—" Amanda suddenly realized that she could leave Terra-V now. If she wanted to. There was no longer a gun on her. Cameron was blocking her from immediate danger. She could safely fade into the house and step through the door to New York. Judy, or someone from PTS, would help her get home.

But she didn't leave.

"No, she wants to stay and hear what I have to say," Lucas went on knowingly. "And…"

Amanda felt herself leaning forward, intrigued by Lucas. Whoever he was.

"She doesn't want anything to happen to you," Lucas told Cameron stoically. "Or to her Vherahna friends. Isn't that right, Amanda?"

His question knocked Amanda off balance.

"You see, Amanda." Lucas now spoke directly to her, using the same steady, friendly tone. "Actions have consequences. I'm not here to hurt you. Or anyone else. I *only* want to talk, but if—"

"Don't listen to him," Cameron cut in, turning so he could shift his attention between Lucas and Amanda. "Go home, Amanda. Now."

"Not so fast," Lucas interjected quickly. "As I was saying, I only want to talk. And it's in both of our interests for you to hear me out. As long as you stay, I *promise* not to harm Cameron or your Vherahna friends. But if you leave now... Well, I would have no incentive to keep your friends from harm, now would I?"

"Don't threaten her." Cameron inched forward. Lucas warily inched back.

"Threaten her?" Lucas acted surprised. "I'm not threatening her. I'm teaching her that travelers must be aware of what they leave behind.

"It's harder to just pop away when people you care about are in danger, isn't it?" He sympathized with Amanda, shaking his head before brightening with a smile. "Life is much easier without those ties. But we'll talk more about that later."

Amanda swallowed, noticing how dry her throat had become. Would Lucas really hurt Cameron if she left now? Amanda felt sick with worry. Would he hurt Alira? Or Caeph?

"Okay, good!" Lucas clapped his hands, smiling as if Amanda had agreed to stay. "Now that we've settled that..." he fixed his attention on Cameron. "Where is it?"

Cameron smiled slyly. Amanda struggled to keep up.

"I don't know what you're talking about." Cameron inched forward, again causing Lucas to inch away. Neither made any move toward their weapons.

Watching them maintain such a careful distance, Amanda thought of the longbow still slung over her back. An arrow would easily reach Lucas. If she were able to unsling the weapon, pull out an arrow, and aim the bow before Lucas realized what she was doing. Unfortunately, Amanda knew she wasn't that skilled.

"Oh, come on," Lucas scoffed. "I know about the serum. What are you calling it now? Still Psylo4C? Or are you up to Psylo4D? You've been trying to track me down since it passed trials. You really expect me to believe you wouldn't have it with you when you're dangling our young friend for me to come running?"

"Search me." Cameron held up his hands. "You won't find it."

Lucas glanced at Amanda assessingly. She could feel the confusion written across her face and Lucas seemed to recognize it as well. He dismissed her and sent Gherut to pat Cameron down.

"You see, Amanda." Lucas watched the search, only glancing her way occasionally. "PTS has a way of dealing with those who don't fall in line. They've had paralytic drugs for some time, the kind that dull the senses and keep a mind from psychic travel, but that wasn't enough for them. Now they've developed a hypnagogic drug. One that puts a mind in a trance-like state—a highly suggestable conscious state—where a traveler can still be led through the mindspace. Maybe even a state where his mind—his *viewpoint*—could be altered."

"That sounds like science fiction," Cameron called as Gherut patted down his chainmail-clad legs.

"Doesn't all of this?" Lucas shrugged.

Gherut stood up then, signaling that he hadn't found anything.

"You used to believe me." Cameron sounded mildly irritated as he adjusted his chainmail and straightened his tunic.

"When I didn't know better," Lucas answered in a softer voice, sounding sincere for the first time.

Amanda's mind raced as she took in every word.

"Amanda," Lucas called over dully. "I'd like to speak to Cameron alone now. Can I trust you to stay here with Alira and the others? Good girl."

Cameron faced Amanda. His eyes seemed to be telling her… something? Amanda could see the intensity in his look but had no idea what he wanted her to do.

"I'm not leaving her with them." Cameron nodded toward Queen Enghrid and the Churukh.

"Neither am I," Lucas agreed with a sigh. His heart seemed to have gone out of his performance. "Gherut and the queen are coming with us. The others will guard from outside the courtyard. Where we can see them."

He spoke to the castle guard in Churukh, repeating his orders.

The queen glared at Amanda smugly before sweeping ahead of them into the fortress enclosure. Lucas told Amanda they would be in the next room and wouldn't be gone long.

"It's okay," Cameron reassured Amanda, adding an encouraging wink.

And then they were gone.

Amanda stood in the flickering torchlight. She felt the cool air on her skin. She sensed the Vherahna and tuntum trees behind her. As the courtyard stretched around her, Amanda's mind went blank. She tried to process what had happened but there was too much. An echoing hum trembled through the night air, bringing Amanda back to the moment at hand. She wished she knew what she was supposed to do now.

She wished she knew what Cameron's wink had meant.

§

Under the tuntum trees, the captive Vherahna shrank from Amanda's approach. Caeph calmed them, while Alira moved to the edge of the purple grass. She stopped Amanda from stepping off the courtyard's stone floor, then reached for both of Amanda's hands and said it was best to allow a safe perimeter for the others.

"They are weak," she told Amanda plainly.

"How are they even…? How are the trees…?" Amanda couldn't finish a thought.

Alira invited her to sit on the ground at the edge of the grass circle. The stones were cold through Amanda's pants, and she could sense a faint barrier emanating from the thin trees. Amanda had never quite understood the border around the Vherahna Forest, even after feeling it for herself. From what she'd learned, the tuntum trees created an invisible forcefield that would only allow passage for those the Vherahna wanted to let in. It seemed the tuntum trees here were too frail to keep the Churukh—or anyone else—from crossing onto the grass.

"The trees and people here are both fragile," Alira explained. "They each need the other to thrive, yet neither has had enough energy to grow well. The thieves have bled too much vhe, too rapidly. They have sacrificed the health of both Vherahna and trees to infuse their own excessive vitality."

Amanda nodded, having gathered that much herself.

"We will bring them home with us," Alira vowed with her eyes flashing. "When the English come, the thieves will be made to let us return to our forest. But these trees…"

She trailed off in a perplexed way that disturbed Amanda beyond her worries about Cameron and what she should be doing to help him. Alira had never faltered in front of Amanda before.

Amanda looked at the tuntum trees at the center of the grass circle. They were small but probably too large to be moved. The thought of abandoning the trees—with no Vherahna to nurture them—appeared to distress Alira as much as if she were asked to leave her own child behind. Amanda's heart hurt at the sight of Alira's pain.

"My people will be here soon. If there's a way to save the trees, they will find it."

Amanda patted Alira's hand, hoping she was not making false promises.

A gleam of unshed tears filled Alira's eyes. She lifted her arms to cross her hands delicately over her heart. The familiar double-blink of her eyes matched the rhythm of the trees as the settled into their final coiled resting place. *Tuntum. Blink-blink. Tuntum. Blink-blink.* Her gaze drifted down. Her eyes closed. Amanda watched her chest rise and fall with a slow, deep breath. When she looked up, there was a calm serenity in her eyes.

"You are the waking dreamer," Alira declared with whispered awe. "You have led us to a greater gift than I had ever imagined. I thank you on behalf of my people. Of *all* my people."

Glancing over Alira's shoulder at the group of cowering Vherahna, Amanda felt her own tears well. She didn't know if she believed in the prophecy, but she was grateful for where it had led.

Even if she and Cameron were now in danger.

Thinking of Lucas and Cameron—and whatever was happening in the next room—Amanda slipped her longbow off her back. She reached into her quiver, determined to be ready when they returned, but Alira stopped her from nocking the arrow.

"More English will be here soon," Alira reminded. "We are in no immediate danger."

"I'm not so sure about that," Amanda muttered, remembering Lucas' implied threat if he didn't get what he wanted. Then she recalled something else he'd said.

"Alira," she began urgently, "what do you know about this Lucas Flynn?"

"Lucas Flynn," Alira sighed his name. "We no longer associate with him."

"Okay…? But why not? He said Cameron told you things about him. Bad things. So, what do you know?"

Alira looked down at her hands, which now rested lightly in her lap, and silently considered the question. Her blue hair fell forward, reflecting the fiery torchlight from their right. Just when Amanda was about to prod her for an answer, Alira lifted her face.

"It would be better if I leave English matters to the English."

Amanda clamped her lips shut to keep from harshly pointing out that they were in trouble and knowing more about Lucas could be important for the safety of them all. She knew better than to push Alira on a point once her decision had been made. If Alira did not want to tell her, she would not tell her. *Just like Aunt Judy.* Amanda frowned, then brightened.

There was someone else to ask.

"I need to contact my aunt," Amanda told Alira, trying to sound confident. "It will take some... concentration. Is that something you can help me with?"

Her stomach was in knots at the idea of messaging her aunt, but Amanda knew it was her best option. Cameron and the Vherahna would be in danger if she simply left. But she could send a message through the house without leaving Terra-V. Maybe that was what Cameron had been trying to tell her with his cryptic wink.

Between racing thoughts, Amanda estimated it was early Saturday morning back home. If she slipped into the house while trying to send a message, her origin point would be reset. She would have to go through the house to New York and let PTS transport her home. Hopefully before her mom returned on Sunday.

If she didn't try to send the message, they were still at least six hours from a proximal door that could take her directly back to her aunt's apartment. Either way, any more complications could mean she wouldn't be home before her mom returned—

Amanda stopped that thought.

"I can help you concentrate," Alira bowed her head, gathering her strength. The movement stirred a momentary guilt in Amanda. Alira's energy was low from the trip and she had given much of her remaining vhe to the captive Vherahna.

"Thank you," Amanda told her gravely.

They sat cross-legged in the flickering light. Amanda sat on the cold stone floor. Alira settled into the purple grass. Amanda's bow and arrow waited beside her.

With a deep breath, Amanda looked into Alira's purple eyes. Alira gently lifted Amanda's hands and turned them so her palms rested on her own knees. She then covered Amanda's hands with her own. When she did, a jolt of energy fizzed up Amanda's arms. It wasn't the calming comfort of the healing touch she'd experienced before. This energy came in a steady buzzing. It was slightly uncomfortable, but oddly hypnotic.

Focusing on the tremor in her arms and the cold seeping into her legs, Amanda set her awareness on her physical surroundings. *I am here. I am in the courtyard. I am in Terra-V. I am with Alira.*

After several breaths, the area around her stood out in sharp relief. The shadows were deeper. The torchlight crackled with a trembling glow. The stone floor and walls were solid, rough, and immoveable. Alira's serene face took on the appearance of marble, though her eyes danced with the intensity of her concentration.

Over this tangible reality, Amanda drew a hazy image of the house into her mind. Now that she'd stopped trying to find the door to New York, her thoughts naturally went to the shadowy coolness of the attic alcove. Six silver-blue doors hovered in her mind's eye. She saw the aged wood floor and the faded gray walls. She smelled the dust and felt the chill in the air. Yet the attic remained a hazy picture, like an overlay transposed on the reality where she stared into Alira's steady gaze.

Aunt Judy. Amanda called out mentally, imagining her aunt was there in the attic and would step from the shadows at any moment. Yet she remained alone.

Aunt Judy! She tried again, putting her heart and soul into calling for help.

The attic doors came into sharper focus. The courtyard faded away. Until Amanda felt the pressure of Alira's hands deepening on the backs of her own. Her attention went back to Alira's eyes, looking for the flecks of cobalt that added depth to her violet irises.

An ache built in the left side of her head as Amanda tried to hold both places—the attic and the courtyard—in equal measure. Her breath sped up. A high-pitched whine cut through her ears.

Aunt Judy! The attic sharpened as the courtyard faded. *Look at Alira's eyes.*

The courtyard sharpened as the attic faded. Amanda's lungs pricked and burned.

Judy stood in the attic.

Amanda could see her, but the image was transparent. Judy wore pajamas and squinted without her glasses. Her mouth was moving rapidly, but Amanda could not hear her words.

As she strained to listen, a pressure on Amanda's hands pulled her back to Alira's glittering eyes. For a moment, she saw the women as one, with Aunt Judy's mouth and Alira's eyes. Then, they separated, one on top of the other. Each face shifted in and out of focus as Amanda's stomach clenched and the ache in her head became a pounding throb.

I'm in the attic. I'm in the courtyard. Aunt Judy! Send help! There's someone here... someone who... I'm in the courtyard. I'm in the attic. Alira! Help me hold on! There's something happening...

Amanda knew she could let go. She could slip into the attic and talk to Aunt Judy while Alira watched over her physical body. Losing the origin point didn't matter anymore.

But something stopped her.

Amanda's mind refused to enter the attic completely. It refused to move back to the courtyard completely. As the pain in her head grew, Amanda was trapped.

She was in the attic.

She was in the courtyard.

Fear overtook her. *I want to go home!* She thought of her mom, of Drew, and even of Trina and Chad. But the pictures of Alira, Caeph, and Cameron crowded in as well. Even Lucas leered from some distant place deeper in her mind. *I want to go home!*

Her breath shortened until she was hyperventilating. *I'm in the attic.* Sharp gasps racked her chest. *I'm in the courtyard.*

Amanda felt the world spin as she floated in a swirl of darkness and sensed the most important people in her life flickering around her.

Until her mind split with a thunderous *Crack!*

§

"*A* manda? Amanda?" She heard voices and felt the hard stones under her back. When her eyes parted, Amanda saw she was back in the conference room at her PTS hearing. Aunt Judy was crouched beside her, offering something that tried to clear her mind. *A vial of Vhelox?* Director Alvarsson was on her other side, holding her hand and stroking her arm.

"So, it's true then!" A man with short dark hair and a trim beard loomed into her vision.

Lucas Flynn.

Amanda blinked. She was in the courtyard in Terra-V. Alira was by her side, emitting a familiar hum. Cameron was on her other side, holding her hand. The torchlight hurt her eyes. Her stomach churned. Darkness threatened from her peripheral vision. But when she lifted her head, trying to prop herself up on her elbows, Amanda trembled in disbelief.

CHAPTER 19
CHANGES

"Are you awake?"

Amanda blinked at the smooth white ceiling. The bed was soft beneath her. The air was quiet around her. The room felt close and comforting. When she angled her head, Amanda saw her aunt sitting on a large cushion with her back against the wall. She was home.

"I think so." Amanda's voice was gritty with sleep. She cleared her throat and when she tried to sit up her head was slightly dizzy.

"Slowly." Judy helped Amanda prop herself up with pillows, then brought her a glass of water with a thin metal straw. "There are some PTS doctors in the other room who are eager to check you out again, now that you're awake, but they can wait while we talk."

"Doctors?"

Amanda looked at the portable clock sitting next to her airbed. It was one in the afternoon. "What day is it?"

"Saturday." Judy pulled her cushion closer to the bed and sat down again. "You came home from Terra-V at about four in the morning, and you've been asleep since then."

"Oh." Amanda took that in. She remembered being in Terra-V. She remembered being in the courtyard. She remembered— "Wait, did I, uh...?"

"Create a proximal door that connects an alien world to an attic alcove in a Victorian house that only exists in a shared mindspace? Yep."

Judy smiled, her eyes dancing.

"Been practicing that one?" Amanda laughed, then winced at the dull ache in her head.

"Maybe a little," Judy chuckled. "I had some time while you were asleep."

Amanda nodded.

The drawn shades muted the sunlight, but she could tell it was afternoon even without the clock.

Amanda was wearing a long, soft sleep t-shirt. She vaguely remembered her aunt helping her out of the tactical suit and clothes she'd worn in Terra-V, but her hair was still in messy braids, and she felt the grit and grime of her adventure clinging to her skin. Her stomach grumbled as she took another long drink of water.

"Did you use any of that time to cook some food?"

"You're hungry?" Judy shifted, preparing to stand up. "That's a good sign."

"Is it?"

"Huh." Judy paused, thought about it, and then laughed. The blue streaks in her dark hair picked up the faint sunlight. "I don't know actually. But it seems like it would be."

"Wait!" Amanda gestured for her aunt to sit back down. "Before food, I need some... uh..."

"Answers?" Judy settled back in her seat with a serious expression.

"Do you have any?" Amanda rubbed her eyes and straightened up. "Answers, I mean."

"Depends on the questions."

"Fair enough." Amanda expected Aunt Judy to say something like that. Her head was starting to feel better. The ache was fading, and her thoughts were clearing. It felt like the clouds in her head were drifting away and revealing a field of questions that grew larger by the moment.

The room was still as Judy waited for Amanda's first question.

"So... I *am* an architect, then?"

"Yes," Judy nodded. "You are an architect."

What does that mean? How did I make that door? Do I have to make more now? What if I can't? How do I learn to be an architect when I'm the only one? Are there books? Are there instructions?

Amanda pushed the crowding questions away. There were too many. They buzzed and pressed and tumbled over each other. Breathing slowing, Amanda told herself there was time for that later. There were other things—other people—to ask about.

Cameron! Amanda bolted upright, suddenly alert. *Alira. Caeph. Rory.*

"Cameron? Rory?"

Judy moved to Amanda's bedside, soothing her with soft shushing and gentle hands. The airbed shifted beneath her added weight, knocking one of Amanda's pillows onto the floor with a soft *thump*.

"They're fine," Judy reassured. "They're all fine. Alira, Caeph, the travelers, and the other Vherahna, too."

She explained that Rory and the other knights from their group had overtaken their guards at the castle and escaped, following Amanda and the others to the hidden fortress.

"They arrived soon after you created that door, and they helped Cameron secure the fortress. Along with an additional strike team that was able to use your new door to attack the Churukh from inside the courtyard.

"There was fighting at the castle, too, but I think that's pretty well settled now. Once we came in with modern weapons, it didn't take long to overwhelm the Churukh royals and their castle guard. The political fallout may take some time to untangle, but our tactical teams are all okay. Some minor injuries but, from what I've heard, nothing that won't heal."

Amanda pushed aside the picture of Churukh soldiers armed with swords and arrows being overwhelmed by guns and grenades and whatever else the PTS teams had used to sweep in and take control. She tried not to think about the unarmed Churukh who were likely caught in the crossfire or hurt while running from the fighting.

She'd caused that, she thought sadly. If they hadn't gone to the market... But then they wouldn't have found the captive Vherahna either.

"And the Vherahna? The, uh, *new* Vherahna? They're okay, too?"

"Well, yes." Judy was more hesitant. "They will need time and care, but Alira—"

"Lucas!" Amanda's mind had flashed from the scared, weak Vherahna to the brash man who seemed to have had something to do with their captivity. "What happened to Lucas?"

Judy frowned and tried to quiet Amanda's anxious questions, but an insistent knock called her to the bedroom door. Amanda heard murmuring and remembered the PTS doctors waiting in the living room.

After a short exchange, Judy closed the door and returned to Amanda's bedside.

"We don't have much time," she told Amanda gently. "The doctors want to check you out and bring you to a nearby clinic for some additional tests—just to be safe—and you'll still need to eat and clean up, before your—"

"Lucas," Amanda insisted, cutting her off mid-sentence. "What happened to Lucas?"

"He was the first through your door," Judy answered reluctantly. "He slipped through as soon as it was created, while Cameron and Alira were helping you. He was gone before anyone knew what was happening."

Amanda nodded, unsurprised.

She'd already put together that Lucas had been evading PTS for some time. It made sense that he would disappear before reinforcements had a chance to arrive.

"But who is he?" Amanda tried to remember what he and Cameron had said in the courtyard, but her thoughts were still crowded and fuzzy. "Why was he working with the royals?"

"Lucas is…" Judy trailed off, then glanced at the door. "Lucas Flynn is a long story."

"What's the short version?"

Amanda hugged her knees to her chest, watching her aunt's expressions shift as she weighed the possible answers. After a minute of thought, she said it would be better to discuss Lucas when they had more time and tried to distract Amanda with offers of food, but Amanda was tired of waiting for answers.

"Just give me something now," Amanda insisted, recalling snippets of Lucas' words. "Is he dangerous? Did Cameron really bring me to Terra-V just so he could catch Lucas?"

"No!" Judy responded quickly without clarifying which question she was answering. She looked away sharply, then faced Amanda with a sigh.

"I didn't know Lucas personally—not the way Cameron did—but he was considered a prodigy when his abilities developed. Like you, he was able to go through a door without any training or any understanding of psychic travel. That happens sometimes, though not very often.

"Usually, new travelers have such a driving need for answers—and for guidance—that they subconsciously open themselves to being seen by more experienced travelers in the house."

"Is that how Cameron saw me?" Amanda broke in eagerly. "That first night in the attic? Before I went through the door?"

"Ye-es," Judy drew the word out, the way she did when the answer was more complicated than she wanted to explain. "Though he wasn't actually the first to see you, even if he was the first traveler *you* saw."

Judy held up a hand to stop Amanda's questions. "Yes, you do have to be open to seeing each other in the house, but new travelers don't have much control over their abilities yet, so they're often glimpsed for a few days—or in some cases weeks or months—before we make actual contact. It's another way counselors know to be on alert for meeting someone new.

"See, whenever a new traveler is discovered, a PTS counselor—like me—is brought in to ease their transition, but there are also some travelers in PTS counseling whose primary responsibility is to watch for newcomers in the house. It's usually a job for counselors in training. Anyway, they send out a sort of psychic invitation that usually makes it easier for new travelers to see them. It's kind of hard to explain…"

"I think I understand." Amanda felt odd knowing that other travelers had caught sight of her in the house without her knowledge. She remembered when Judy had said she suspected Amanda was in the house and had shown Cameron her picture before coming to visit.

"But Lucas wasn't seen by anyone?"

"No," Judy frowned sadly. "No one saw him in the house—at least not enough to make contact—and then he was one of the few who made it through a house door on his own. When that's happened before, the new traveler usually runs into an experienced traveler pretty quickly—either in the other place or when they return to the house—but that didn't happen with Lucas."

"Lucas was…?" Amanda felt a knot in her stomach as she suspected where the story was headed.

"Lucas didn't know to look for a proximal door," Judy confirmed. "He was so surprised by the world he found himself in that he went straight back to the house—mentally—which reset his origin point. So, when he tried to wake up from the house…"

"He was still in the alien world," Amanda finished with a shudder. "He was stranded there."

"Yes."

Amanda nodded sadly, now understanding her aunt's earlier insistence on not traveling alone and why she had lectured Amanda on not losing her origin point.

"Lucas didn't understand what was happening. Instead of reaching out for help, he jumped through house doors, one after another, and ran from any travelers who spotted him. He was travel sick and scared but managed to evade PTS for—"

Judy stopped herself, changing the course of her story. "He was only twenty-two, but he'd already led a life where he'd had to rely on himself more than anyone should."

"How long before PTS found him?"

Judy stood up, saying they'd left the doctors waiting long enough, but Amanda needed to know.

"Aunt Judy, please. How long before they found him and explained everything?"

"Almost nine months."

Amanda felt the answer in the depths of her chest. *Nine months?* She thought of the travel sickness she was still learning to manage—with medication—and the initial terror of thinking she was losing her mind. And she'd been able to come home. She couldn't imagine hopping through strange worlds and figuring out how to survive on her own for nearly nine months.

"But once he was found, Lucas was given intensive counseling and care." Judy sounded hopefuly, or maybe defensive. "Cameron took him on as a sort of personal apprentice and they were very close for several years."

Amanda considered how Lucas and Cameron had spoken to each other, as if they had once been friends. What had changed? What could possibly make Lucas want to turn his back on PTS and be alone again?

She remembered what Lucas said when he accused Cameron of using her as bait to trap him. *I'd expect it of PTS, but not of you.*

"All of that time on his own damaged Lucas more than we'd realized," Judy concluded, before unpacking some fresh clothes from Amanda's bag.

"He's developed some disturbed ideas, and he's been encouraging others to join him. It's sad, but PTS will catch him and sort that out eventually.

"He wouldn't have hurt you though," Judy turned suddenly, remembering what Amanda had said earlier.

"Cameron wouldn't have put you in danger."

"Yeah, I know," Amanda agreed slowly, though it was a lot to take in.

She was about to drop the subject when she remembered something else that Lucas had said.

"Aunt Judy, uh, what's a hypa— hypogrog— or, uh, that drug Lucas asked Cameron about?"

"Hypnagogic," Judy answered automatically, then frowned. "Hypnagogic just refers to that state a person is in when they're half-awake and half-asleep. Like if you start to wake in the morning but are still sort of caught in a dream. Lucas asked about that?"

"Yeah, he said it was some new drug PTS created."

Amanda considered what else he'd said, adding, "He also said PTS uses another kind of drug to keep people from being able to use psychic travel. Some kind of paralyzing drug? Is that true?"

Judy sighed and set Amanda's clean clothes on the edge of her bed.

"Psychic travel can be complicated. Some of the more difficult situations require special medical intervention. Just like any other human can have conditions that need to be controlled. Now, we really don't have time to talk about this anymore. Not today."

"Yeah, but—"

Amanda couldn't shake an image of travelers locked up in jail cells with orderlies holding them down for daily injections that would keep them from escaping.

"Amanda," Judy spoke more firmly. "We need to get you some food and a shower, and let the doctors do their tests before your mom comes home tonight."

"Tonight?" Amanda looked up in surprise. Her mom and Chad were supposed to come home on Sunday afternoon.

"Yes," Judy smiled impishly, "It sounds like things didn't go very well with Chad's family. Your mom is flying home tonight. Without Chad."

"Oh." Amanda startled, forgetting all about Lucas and psychic travel. She repeated the words to herself, feeling confused but hopeful. *Without Chad. Without Chad.* She didn't know what that meant, but her mom was coming home early. *Without Chad.*

A smile slowly spread across her face.

§

By the time Patty Jones returned from her disappointing Thanksgiving weekend, all signs of travel had been erased from her sister-in-law's apartment. Amanda's tactical suit and weapons had been returned to PTS, the doctors had removed themselves—and their portable equipment—from the premises, and the small bruise from Amanda's blood tests was covered by long sleeves.

The only item that remained from her trip was a tiny horse-like statue carved from purple stone, and it was tucked away safely in Amanda's overnight bag.

The trip to the local clinic had been relatively simple. Amanda had been asked to lie still in an MRI machine. Doctors then stuck small wires to her head for an EEG test. Finally, she'd had to perform a bunch of silly tasks like touch her finger to her nose, stick her tongue out in different directions, and stand on one foot with her eyes closed.

They were strange exams, but nothing hurt, except for the blood test and that was over quickly. Amanda suspected there would be more tests and questions in her future, but for now the doctors were satisfied. Her lingering headache had faded, and she felt much better after eating lunch and drinking a lot of water.

Amanda had lasagna heating in the oven and was making a salad when Judy brought Patty home from the airport. After dropping her bags in their own apartment, Patty didn't mind that they were having dinner in Judy's penthouse. She was pleased to see how Amanda had set the table with flowers and candles.

"I missed you so much!" Patty hugged her daughter tightly.

Amanda held on just as tight, feeling a swell of emotion at the sound, feel, and smell of her mom. She held on so long that Patty glanced at Judy questioningly before swaying Amanda side-to-side and softly stroking her hair.

With her eyes closed, Amanda didn't see Judy shrug and smile back. She didn't know that Judy had anticipated some emotion and had prepared Patty by saying Amanda was having some teen drama with Trina over something at school. She'd suggested Patty not bring it up directly but be gentle with Amanda for a few days.

When they settled around the table, Amanda asked her mom about meeting Chad's family.

"Was it just awful?" She cut into her lasagna and didn't see her mom take a large sip of wine. "Were they as bad as Chad? Worse?"

"Amanda," Judy used a warning tone that made Amanda look up in surprise. For a moment, the look on her mom's face made Amanda think she might burst into tears, or start yelling, but Patty surprised them all when she burst into laughter.

"Yes!" She rolled her eyes toward the ceiling and shook her head. "It was awful! They were so… Well, it doesn't really matter what they were. But they weren't people I wanted to spend a weekend with, let alone have as a permanent part of our lives."

Judy set down her fork and placed her palm over Patty's free hand. Their eyes met in a way that told Amanda her mom had already explained exactly what was so bad about Chad's family on their way home from the airport. She didn't mind though. Amanda didn't care about the details as much as she wanted to know what it meant for their future.

"So, they were like Chad then?" Amanda broke the silence with a light, casual tone and was surprised to see the annoyance on both her mom's and aunt's faces.

"What? Isn't that why he stayed with them? Or… is he still coming back?"

"Amanda," her aunt warned again, but this time Patty lifted her hand to stop Judy from saying more. She sighed and studied the lasagna she'd barely touched.

"It's not definite yet, but… Well, yes, I think it's over with Chad."

Amanda squeezed her lips shut to keep from smiling, and Judy kicked her foot under the table.

"Oh, um, I'm sorry?"

Amanda had tried to sound sympathetic, but her mom raised an eyebrow cynically.

"Thanks."

Patty lowered her eyes and picked at her salad with her fork. Amanda knew there was more she wanted to say, but her mom could be so maddeningly slow at picking her words. Just when Amanda was about to start talking again, her aunt's voice echoed through her mind.

Amanda. The word came with an image of a formal living room with tufted chairs and plush rugs. *Go easy on your mom. There were things she liked about Chad, even if you didn't see them, and this is hard on her. Don't make it harder.*

Amanda shook the voice away and shot her aunt an irritated look. But she knew Judy was right.

"No, really." Amanda forced herself to see the sadness in her mom's face and tried to think of something nice to say. "I mean, I'm not going to pretend he was my favorite person in the world, but I know he made you happy and stuff, and I don't want you to be lonely or anything."

Patty wiped the corners of her eyes and ran her hands over her hair.

"You know, I did feel less lonely with Chad," she admitted slowly. "And it was nice to have another adult around, helping with the bills and parenting stuff."

Amanda bit her tongue, but she didn't have to say anything for Patty to rethink that statement on her own.

"Though we didn't really agree on much when it came to that sort of thing," she added thoughtfully. "Actually, we didn't agree on a lot of things. So, I don't know. Maybe those aren't the best reasons to stay with someone."

"Patty," Judy spoke before Amanda could reply. "I'm sorry I haven't been here more. To help you out, since Gabe…"

The table was quiet. Amanda pictured her dad. She remembered the whisper of his bedtime stories, then remembered what Cameron had said about him. He had more to tell her. He'd said they would talk when they were home from Terra-V. But would they? Her heart skipped as she wondered if she'd missed her chance.

When she tuned back into the conversation, Amanda gathered that she'd missed something important while thinking about Cameron and her dad.

"I couldn't," her mom was saying, though it was a weak refusal. "What happens when you have to move on? I couldn't afford this on my own. Besides, your company is renting it for you, not for your extended family."

"That's not a problem," Judy insisted. "They wouldn't mind at all, and they've promised I'll be here for the next four years at least. That's long enough to get Amanda through high school. And who knows what will happen then."

Patty started to object, but Judy rushed on. "And I can help you find a better job. I know people who have a lot of connections around here."

"Judy, I—"

"Just think about it, okay?" Judy smiled warmly. "It would mean a lot to me, to live with family."

Amanda held her breath, unsure about this suggestion. Moving in with Judy might help her mom get by without Chad's help, but how would they hide Amanda's psychic travel if they were living in the same apartment? Did Judy think it was time to tell her mom what was really going on? Would PTS allow that?

"Okay," Patty smiled, and a weight seemed to drop from her shoulders. "I'm not saying yes, but I'll think about it. What do you think, Amanda?"

"Oh, um." Amanda looked rapidly between her mom and aunt. "Yeah, maybe?"

"No pressure!" Judy laughed into the heavy silence. "Just something to think about!"

"I do appreciate the offer," Patty assured her, before taking a bite of lasagna. "Amanda, this is really good! Thank you so much for making dinner. And for setting such a beautiful table! You really are growing up so fast!"

"Uh, huh." Amanda tried to smile.

Chad was moving out. Her mom and aunt were getting along. She was getting what she wanted.

She should be happy, she thought, but instead everything suddenly felt uncertain.

Change is weird, Amanda decided.

And her life was definitely changing.

CHAPTER 20
A NEW WORLD

Amanda studied her reflection in the bathroom mirror. She felt different after her time in Terra-V and was surprised that no one at school had noticed. Wasn't there something brighter in her eyes now? Weren't her expressions wiser, more mature? She dried her hands and assessed her reflection one more time before accepting that she basically looked the same.

Something had changed between Amanda and Trina though. As she continued to dry her hands with the same damp paper towel, Amanda turned over the conversation she'd had with Trina and Drew during lunch.

Despite a few odd looks from other tables, hanging out had felt mostly okay. Amanda couldn't tell Trina about her time in Terra-V, of course, but she could talk about her mom breaking up with Chad and her aunt's offer for them to live together. It had felt good to talk about it. And to be finding a new normal with Trina and Drew.

During English, Trina and Amanda had sat together again, and Mr. Hewlett had noticed, graciously looking the other way when he saw them trading notes.

Amanda knew Drew was the reason she and Trina were friends again. He'd had talked to Trina about their friendship while Amanda was in Terra-V, and she was feeling better about the situation.

Trina didn't care that Amanda was Drew's friend, as long as she was his girlfriend. Amanda didn't care that Trina was Drew's girlfriend, as long as she was his friend.

Maybe they would be okay, Amanda hoped, as she threw the paper towel in the trash and picked up her hall pass from the edge of the sink.

She smiled to herself on her walk back to class, until she turned a corner and saw Trey lounging against the lockers near her Geometry classroom. She stopped walking and scanned the empty hallway, turning the flimsy hall pass between her fingers. Trey wasn't in her Geometry class, but Amanda thought he had a class across the hall. Had he seen her leave for the bathroom and come out to wait for her? The thought made Amanda's skin itch.

Trey pushed himself upright and stalked her way. Her throat went dry as Amanda hoped for someone else—for anyone else—to show up in the hall with them.

"Hey." Trey's voice was low and husky. His eyes were unnervingly intense. "Ditching math?"

"No, I, uh." Amanda waved the hall pass, then let her hand drop back by her side.

The hall was very quiet with the heavy classroom doors shut. The mechanical tick of a large clock echoed from its mount high in the center of the hallway. The class period was barely half over. They were alone. Amanda glanced toward her Geometry class, but she would have to pass Trey to get to it.

"So." Trey inched closer. Amanda inched back.

"I have to get back to class," Amanda told him.

"Do you?"

"Yes."

"Hold on." Trey stepped close to block Amanda from passing. "I have a question first."

Amanda waited, feeling sizzling sensations in her cheeks and butterflies flapping against her ribs. She eyed the door behind Trey and reminded herself that there were people behind that door, and behind all the doors around them. They weren't really alone.

Trey leaned down, lowering his head closer as Amanda pulled back.

"When are we going out?"

He grinned, and Amanda blinked.

"Going out? Us?"

She was so surprised, she didn't notice his arm move until his fingertips trailed he line of her jaw. On instinct, Amanda swatted his hand and jerked away.

Trey laughed, again closing the distance she'd put between them.

"Yeah, us."

He reached for her arms and Amanda spun away, the hall pass slipping from her fingers. She looked at it on the floor between them. If she claimed she lost it, would Ms. Randall send her right back out to look for it?

"Oh, come on, Amanda." Trey stepped over the hall pass and kept approaching as Amanda backed away. "Don't play me like that."

"I'm not playing like anything." Amanda held her ground, determined to show that she was serious.

"When are we going out then?"

"Uh, we aren't." She tried to sound confident, but everything about Trey made her uncomfortable.

Trey laughed, looked away, then swooped forward, rushing Amanda back against the row of lockers. His arms were on either side of her, pinning her in place.

His breath was hot as he leaned in to say, "What's wrong? You aren't shy around Drew. You scared of me?"

Without thought, Amanda clasped her hands together and brought them down hard over Trey's right elbow. His arm buckled and he lurched forward, leaving a gap for Amanda to slip away from the lockers, just as she'd broken free from Cameron's hold in Terra-V.

She had no reason to kick Trey to the ground though. Her move was so unexpected, he stumbled into the lockers and hit his forehead with a resounding clang.

"What's going on here?"

A shout echoed down the hallway as one of the assistant principals came storming toward them. Trey was holding his head. Amanda was standing in a fighting stance in the center of the hall. She dropped her fists self-consciously when Mr. Sawyer looked her way.

"He—"

"She knocked me into a locker!" Trey yelled over Amanda's explanation, adding, "Crazy b—"

312

"Hey! None of that language," Mr. Sawyer snapped at Trey before turning to Amanda. "Are you okay?"

"Is *she* okay?" Trey interrupted, pointing to the red mark on his forehead. "I just asked her out and she went all psycho on me!"

"What is going on out here?"

Ms. Randall stepped into the hallway and quickly shut her classroom door behind her. She scanned the scene, seeing Trey's growing bruise, Amanda's pale face, and the hall pass forgotten on the hallway floor.

"Amanda?"

Mr. Sawyer waved Trey's sputtering to silence while everyone waited to hear Amanda's side of the story.

"He—" Amanda choked, suddenly afraid of what they would say. Had she overreacted? In a small voice she said, "He pinned me against the lockers."

"We were just fooling around!" Trey jumped in.

The teachers ignored him.

Trey stood behind them mouthing, *Be cool,* with wide pleading eyes. In an instant, Amanda imagined what would happen next. If she told the truth, the rumors would start again. This time everyone would say she was a psycho who knocked Trey into a locker just for asking her out. If she covered for him, maybe he'd be grateful enough to not mess with her again.

But then Amanda remembered the fear she felt when he'd loomed over her.

"Amanda." Ms. Randall's voice was kind but firm. "Did *you* think it was just fooling around?"

Amanda avoided Trey as she shook her head.

"No," she answered quickly. "I just wanted to go back to class and he wouldn't let me."

"Okay." Mr. Sawyer clapped his hands together. "Trey, time to call your parents. Again."

"Oh, come on! You're gonna believe—"

"Save it." Mr. Sawyer cut him off. "I saw what happened when I came around the corner. Amanda, we will have to call your parents, too. It's policy when there's a physical altercation."

Amanda nodded, but Ms. Randall held her back.

"Steve, why don't you take Trey to the office, and I'll send Amanda along in a minute? I want a quick word with her first."

Mr. Sawyer glanced between them then agreed with a sigh of relief, glad Ms. Randall was saving him from an uncomfortable talk. Trey flashed Amanda a look of disgust, then launched into a series of complaints as they walked to the office.

Once they were gone, Ms. Randall peered through her classroom door, then walked toward the center of the hallway. Amanda picked up the discarded hall pass and tried to remember what she'd been thinking on her walk back from the bathroom.

"Are you okay?"

"Yeah," Amanda shrugged, wanting to show that she could take care of herself.

"It's okay if you're not," Ms. Randall suggested. "It's okay to be a little shaken or upset when someone tries to intimidate or harass you."

"Yeah, I know, but it's cool."

Amanda wasn't sure why she was downplaying what happened. It was kind of embarrassing. She wanted to tell Ms. Randall that she'd been through worse, and even had a gun pointed at her just two days ago! If she could handle that, she could handle a jerk like Trey. But she couldn't tell anyone about that.

"Right," Ms. Randall glanced back at the classroom door. "Your aunt told me you were tough, and I know you're holding up well given some challenging circumstances. But high school is its own kind of challenge and I'm here to help. If you want to talk."

"Thanks, but I—" Amanda stopped short. "Wait. My aunt? You mean, you're a— Are you a…?"

They stood together silently sizing each other up.

Ms. Randall offered a wry half-smile as she watched Amanda figure it out.

"Judy thought it might be useful, in case you needed help with school, or anything else."

Amanda frowned. At the beginning of the year, Ms. Randall had said she was new to the school. But would PTS really send someone to watch her at school? Was that how they knew about the short story she'd written?

"But you've been here since school started. Since before Aunt Judy knew that I…" Amanda trailed off.

"Yes," Ms. Randall smiled again. "But we'd had reports of a young girl being seen in the house since early summer, and your aunt thought… just in case."

She winked, leaving Amanda feeling even more unsettled.

"You're here to keep an eye on me?"

"Well, no," Ms. Randall frowned. "Not exactly. There are a lot of us who work regular jobs in places where we can watch out for people who might have our abilities, people who are family members for instance. I normally teach math in college, where these things are more likely to happen, but your aunt put in a request...

"I'm here to help you, Amanda, if you need it."

"Uh, okay," Amanda agreed, unsure how she felt. On one hand, it was nice that Aunt Judy wanted her to have support at school. On the other, it was creepy to know Ms. Randall had been sent there just for her.

Amanda remembered the new desk clerk at her apartment building and wondered who else PTS had inserted into her life.

§

That night, Amanda stood in the attic alcove looking at the seventh gray-blue door. *Her door.* It was identical to the other six doors. It had the same shape and style. It was made from the same aged wood, and it had a matching oval doorknob.

The door didn't look new. It looked as if it had been in that alcove as long as the attic had been in existence. Amanda thought of Edmund Robinson. Had he planned the design of these doors? She wondered how her mind had managed to copy them so perfectly when it had instinctively made her own door.

"It's pretty amazing."

Amanda continued to study the door as Cameron stepped beside her.

"Did you know this would happen?"

Cameron laughed at her question.

"Absolutely not!" He shook his head and crossed his arms over his chest. "You surprised us all with that one."

Amanda glanced his way. Cameron wore jeans and a sweater. It was a different sweater than the one he'd worn to Judy's apartment at the start of their mission, but it was a similar style.

"But you did think I might be the next architect?" she asked hesitantly.

"Yeah," he admitted. "I thought it was possible. But I didn't expect to find out like that. And not so soon. It took Edmund a few years of traveling before his other skills started to show up."

"Right." Amanda thought about that. "But if he built the house…?"

"That's a complicated question," Cameron answered before Amanda could finish speaking.

"Let's start with a different question then."

Amanda's palms felt sweaty, even in the house where she knew her body was only an illusion.

"Okay." Cameron looked a little nervous himself. "Is it about Lucas Flynn?"

"No." Amanda saw his shoulders relax. She quickly added, "Well, sort of. I mean, Aunt Judy already told me about him. At least, some things about him. But I have a question for you. When you came to my hearing, it sounded like there was someone you were looking for. Someone you thought you might find—or find out about—in Terra-V. You were talking about Lucas, weren't you?"

Cameron pressed his lips together and nodded slowly as if he'd been expecting this.

"Yes, but, Amanda, what he said to you, about me using you to—"

"No, not that." Amanda cut off his explanation. "I don't think you— I mean, we're okay, about that. I know you wouldn't have brought me there if you thought it was too dangerous for me."

"Okay, then…?"

Amanda cleared her throat. Her face felt hot and for a moment the attic blurred around her.

"I thought you might have been talking about my dad."

Her voice was small and tight, but Cameron heard her. His eyes widened and his lips parted in surprise. She glanced up in time to see the realization spread across his face.

"Amanda." His voice was so gentle that she knew what he was going to say. "Your dad—"

"He's dead." Amanda saved him from saying it. "I know that. I really do. But when you said someone was last seen in Terra-V. And you knew him there. And I only saw an urn. And this tiny part of me just thought…"

She didn't have to finish her explanation.

Cameron ran his hand over his mouth and chin, then faced her directly.

"Amanda, I was there when your dad died. Well, not there at that moment, but shortly after. I brought him back to PTS myself. I wanted to be the one to tell your mom, but they thought it was better to send a counselor to talk to her. And to Judy. Though I did go to his funeral."

"You were there?"

"Do you remember that day?" Cameron nodded with understanding when Amanda shook her head no. "You were very young. I watched you there and I knew that if you turned out to be a traveler, someday, I would watch out for you. Just the way he would have, if he were here.

"He was a good friend," Cameron added somberly. "He meant a lot to me."

Amanda nodded, feeling tears rise and then fade without falling. She had one more question.

"Did you have that drug with you? In Terra-V? That drug Lucas thought you had?"

Cameron crossed his arms over his chest again, but he looked Amanda in the eye with the same openness he'd had when he'd asked her to trust him in Sage Village.

"Yes," he answered plainly. "And I'd have used it on him if I'd had the chance."

Amanda appreciated his honesty, after her aunt's earlier evasion.

"But they searched you." Amanda had been thinking about it ever since she'd gotten back. "If you didn't have the drug on you…?"

"You had it," Cameron grinned. "Your quiver had a false bottom."

"What?" Amanda thought of the leather quiver of arrows she'd carried throughout Terra-V. She hadn't noticed any hidden compartment, but then she hadn't looked for one either.

"It wouldn't have hurt him," Cameron explained. "But it would have let us get him back to PTS safely, and that's important for reasons you don't understand yet.

"It was also our best way to keep you safe if he showed up and things went differently. That's why I hid the syringe with you. Rory and the other knights knew it was there, and one of us was with you at all times."

"Huh." Amanda frowned, not entirely understanding why the drug was necessary or why they'd need to bring Lucas to PTS if he didn't want to be there. Though Judy had said Lucas had been spreading his ideas to others. Was he a threat to PTS and the other travelers? He had given the Churukh guns, even if they weren't loaded.

"Amanda." Cameron broke into her thoughts. "Do you still trust me?"

She looked at him critically. He could have lied to her about the drug, she thought, but he didn't. Even if there were things she didn't understand yet, he was telling her what he could. And he'd been friends with her dad. Close friends, if she could believe what he'd told her.

"Yes," Amanda answered cautiously, "until you give me a reason not to trust you."

"That's fair," Cameron responded easily. "And I'll do my very best to never let you down."

They stood together, looking at the door Amanda had created. She was beginning to feel overwhelmed by all of the ways her life was changing. She wished her dad was here to tell her what to do and who to trust.

"There you are!" Judy appeared beside them.

Amanda realized that she'd sensed her aunt moments before she arrived but hadn't actually seen her walk into the alcove. She'd simply shown up, though that seemed perfectly normal in the house.

Cameron gave Amanda one last, gentle smile before switching to his more casual attitude.

"How was the meeting? Alvarsson still breathing?"

"He's hanging in," Judy laughed, then turned to Amanda. "Though you have them all scrambling to figure out what to do next!"

"Me?" Amanda felt both embarrassed and pleased to be at the center of everyone's attention.

"You'd think with all the years they've been waiting they'd have a plan in place for when the next architect showed up," Judy continued. "Turns out they have about twelve plans, and none of them with international agreement. This is going to be an interesting experience!"

Amanda studied her door. She had so many questions about how she'd made it appear and what she was supposed to do next, but no one seemed to have the answers.

"The house is Victorian," Amanda began slowly, thinking as she spoke. "And Edmund lived in Victorian times. Does that mean he remodeled the house? When he was adding new doors?"

"He didn't remodel it," Judy answered, "and he didn't just add doors."

Amanda turned to her questioningly and saw Judy and Cameron exchange a look she didn't understand.

"He built the birdhouse," Judy clarified. "It's officially called The Robinson House, but travelers in the field tend to nickname things, and that's the one that's stuck."

"Oh." Amanda cared more about how it was built that what it was called. "But if there were architects before him...?"

"I think you should show her," Cameron told Judy with a sly smile.

"Do you want to come with us?" Judy offered, but Cameron declined.

"I have to check in with the High Council and then head back to Terra-V. Amanda, can I tell Alira you'll come to visit them soon?"

"Yeah," Amanda answered absently, still focused on what Judy had to show her. "I'd like that."

"Will do!" Cameron gave a quick nod and turned for the stairs. "See you soon."

He was gone before his hand touched the railing.

"Ready?" Judy winked at Amanda. "Come on."

In a blink, they were no longer in the attic.

They were standing in the main foyer beside the ornately carved front door. Amanda's heart leaped as Judy reached for the large brass door handle.

If every door in the house led to another place, Amanda thought the front door must lead to somewhere extra special. Yet when Judy opened the door, all it revealed was a porch that seemed to perfectly fit the Victorian house.

Amanda followed her aunt outside. She looked back into the foyer, reassuring herself they hadn't physically traveled anywhere. They were outside the house but still in the mindspace.

"We're still…?"

"Yes," Judy grinned. "Let's look around."

Judy stepped off the porch and onto the flower-lined walkway. Amanda followed, her eyes widening with every step they took.

The Victorian yard merged with a wide-open world of rolling hills, desert patches, tropical oases, exotic jungles, and every climate Amanda could imagine.

On each section of land, Amanda saw houses in a chaotic array of styles. The neighboring lot had a plain brick and stone house with small windows and a simple wooden door. The house across a narrow street stood out as a Tudor design with white plaster walls and crossed wooden beams. Other houses reminded Amanda of structures she'd seen in her World History textbook.

There appeared to be buildings from China and India, as well as clusters of primitive wood homes with thatched roofs. Many buildings were too far away to see the details, but it looked as if a history of world architecture had been gathered together in the strangest neighborhood Amanda had ever seen.

"These are all… houses?" Amanda didn't know what to call them. "They were all built by architects? Different architects?"

"Yes."

"They all have doors in them? To different places?"

"Yes."

"We can go into them to get to other places? Like we do with this house?"

"Yes."

Judy watched Amanda closely. Her face was carefully cheerful, but Amanda recognized the hint of worry behind that expression. Amanda stood on the stone walkway and scanned the impossible world around her.

It was a lot to take in.

"And that means," Amanda swallowed hard, "I'll build my own house?"

"Someday," Judy agreed. "Not any time soon, but in the future. When you're ready."

"Uh huh," Amanda nodded.

She turned in a slow half-circle, looking at the mind-space beyond the house she knew.

It was so much bigger than she had suspected.

There was so much more for her to learn.

She turned back to her aunt and felt a smile of wonder spreading across her face.

Judy smiled in return, nodding her encouragement. She didn't have to say that she'd be with her or that Amanda wouldn't be alone. Amanda already knew that.

Dazzled, Amanda let it all sink in.

"What do you think?" Aunt Judy asked after several moments of silence.

When Amanda answered, there was both determination and concern in her voice.

"We're going to have to tell my mom."

"Huh," Judy cocked her head to one side, then nodded. "I think you're right."

"Yeah," Amanda agreed, then pushed the thought away. "But not today."

"Not today," Judy echoed with a laugh.

They went back into the house, closed the heavy front door, and settled in by the fireside.

They had a lot of planning to do.

The Story Continues...

A manda Jones' adventures with *The Psychic Traveler Society* will continue. As she travels to new realms and meets new people, will her special skills put her in special danger?

Visit SusanQuilty.com for series updates.

Discussion Questions
Spoilers ahead

1.   Before Amanda discovers the truth about her psychic travel abilities, Drew suggests the house in her daydreams may represent her mind, with its doors leading to her memories. What do you think about his theory? Do you have any recurring dreams or daydreams? If so, what do you think they might mean?

2.   Amanda's psychic travel abilities are life-changing, but she tells the High Council that learning about them was a relief. In her place, how might you react to your new abilities? How might you feel about discovering a secret society of psychic travelers living among us?

3.   Director Alvarsson does not want Amanda to use her psychic travel abilities until she is an adult. Do you think adults often underestimate kids' abilities? Do you think it can be good when adults try to keep kids from growing up too quickly?

4. How does Trey's rumor affect Amanda's friendships with Drew and Trina? Why do you think Trina was so upset? Do you think Drew should have done more to set the story straight? Do you think they resolved it well in the end?

5. In Terra-V, Alira tells Amanda, *"You are not being asked to assess the risk of our journey or interpret our prophecy. You are only being asked to choose a direction."* Caeph later says Amanda does not have control over the Churukh's actions. Do you think the Vherahna set healthy boundaries by accepting what a person can and cannot control? How might that affect the way they work as a team?

6. The Vherahna and the tuntum trees have a mutual symbiotic relationship where they draw strength from each other. In our world, bees have a similar relationship with flowering plants. Can you think of any other symbiotic relationships in nature?

7. When Lucas Flynn shows up, he's surprised that Amanda has never heard of him. Do you think Cameron should have warned Amanda about him? Why do you think Lucas was working with the Churukh king and queen?

8. In the end, Amanda shows clear signs of being a psychic architect. How might the High Council and other psychic travelers react to that development?

9. Amanda is navigating both high school and her place in the Psychic Traveler Society. How might those worlds collide? Do you have any predictions on what will happen next for Amanda?

Acknowledgments

For me, *Healers and Thieves* began with a daydream about twisting trees that would spiral up toward the morning sun and wind back to the earth in the dusk of twilight. I didn't know what to do with those trees. They lingered in the back of my mind, and I wrote about them (privately) from time to time. I imagined people living in the shelter of those trees and the healing magic they might offer. I imagined a girl stumbling into that forest and being mistaken for someone else. Eventually, I came up with a way to get her there.

For years, Amanda, Drew, Aunt Judy, and the rest lived in a notebook of scribbles and sketches. I'd occasionally pull that book out, adding new elements, imagining adventures, and working out the mechanics of psychic travel. I'm beyond thrilled to finally introduce this fantasy world to all of you, and I'm deeply grateful to everyone who helped me along the way.

Special thanks to my early readers who have been with me since my first novel: Wendy McMullan, Jen Pool, Angel Fischer, and James Beaver. As always, your feedback and encouragement have been incredibly valuable! This story required extensive world building and that led to countless, complicated conversations about the ins and outs of psychic travel. I'm truly grateful for my family's patient listening—and challenging questions. Thank you to my sons, Brian Dunne and Michael Cherry, and to my loving, supportive husband, Peter Quilty. I'd be lost without you.

Thank you to the owners and staff at Comic Logic Books & Artwork. It's local stores like yours that encourage indie creators and build true community. I'd love to list all the friends who have shown up for me in so many ways, but I'm too afraid of leaving anyone out. I appreciate every one of you! You make my book signings a joy and your messages have often pushed me past moments of self-doubt. (Shout out to my self-proclaimed #1 fans—you know who you are and you're *all* #1 to me!)

To everyone who's read *Healers and Thieves*, thank you for taking this first journey into *The Psychic Traveler Society*. I hope you've enjoyed it and will continue to follow Amanda's adventures. Without your support, these stories would still be living in the scribbles of a tattered notebook and it's much more fun to set them free!

ABOUT THE AUTHOR

Susan Quilty has previously published two novels: *The Insistence of Memory* (2017) and *To the Left of Death* (2018). Before sharing her fiction with the world, Susan spent nearly 10 years working as a freelance writer. *Healers and Thieves* is her first young adult novel.

You can learn more about Susan and her upcoming projects by following her on social media or visiting her website: SusanQuilty.com.

Freely Written: A Podcast

Are you ready for a story break?

Join author Susan Quilty as she uses simple prompts to free write her way into strange, silly, or poignant tales. Weekly episodes offer new stories, while bonus episodes share behind-the-scenes commentary. Episodes are short, about 10 minutes each, and suggestions for future writing prompts are always welcome!

Find **Freely Written** on your favorite podcast app.